FOR YOUR EYES ONLY

Jenny put down her book and said, "You're worried, Antony."

He came back with something of a jerk to the present and picked up the untidy sheaf of papers on which he had made his notes. He came across to the fire and scattered the pieces of paper over it. "It's nothing," he said. "A long day, and damn' all to show for it . . ." He saw the disbelief in her eyes, and added quickly, "Did Uncle Nick tell you I'd been to see John?"

Jenny spoke carefully, her eyes on his face. "He said, 'I'm afraid you may have to resign yourself to the fact that your husband is getting mixed up with that gang of thugs in Whitehall again.' " Her anxiety faded as she saw his frown give way to laughter. "And I'd rather know," she added.

"Of course. But there's nothing . . ." Her gaze was steady and disconcerting, and he looked down at the fire. "I *couldn't* refuse," he said, after a moment, and there was something like desperation in his voice.

THE THIRD ENCOUNTER

Sara Woods

AVON
PUBLISHERS OF BARD, CAMELOT, DISCUS AND FLARE BOOKS

AVON BOOKS
A division of
The Hearst Corporation
1790 Broadway
New York, New York 10019

First Avon Printing, March 1986

AVON TRADEMARK REG. U. S. PAT. OFF. AND IN
OTHER COUNTRIES, MARCA REGISTRADA, HECHO EN
U.S.A.

Printed in the U.S.A.

K–R   10   9   8   7   6   5   4   3   2   1

PROLOGUE

NOVEMBER, 1943

IN A SMALL studio in the building occupied by Radiodiffusion Français in Paris, a young Englishman was reading the news. This was the home bulletin, German inspired, but he read fluently; and it was a fact that, though he had been broadcasting now for nearly three months, none of his colleagues—nor any of the Gestapo who seemed everywhere in that unhappy city—had any suspicion of his nationality.

As he read his attention wandered a little; once the script was prepared it was better to give it no more thought, to forget, if possible, where the hidden meaning lay. It was unlikely that the code could be broken, but emphasis laid in the wrong place might start someone thinking, and even that would be most undesirable. So far he had been lucky; the advantages gained by his present employment far outweighed the slight inconvenience of being considered a collaborator by his neighbors—in fact, he inclined to regard this last as an insurance against suspicion. And now there was barely a week to go. He had lived close to fear for too long to feel any elation; besides, there were many risks still to be run. All the same . . .

From the corner of his eye he noted a small stir in the room beyond the soundproof glass panel. That would be the arrival of the German Kommandant, new to Paris, who was to inspect the studios, so he had heard, that evening.

1

Herr Ohlendorff, they had called him, in a tone that left no doubt as to his importance. The Englishman turned a page in his script and glanced across in faint curiosity—to find himself looking straight into the eyes of the one man who could recognize him, the one man he knew without doubt he had cause to fear. No chance of being unnoticed, though the encounter was so unexpected; even as he looked he saw recognition light in his enemy's eyes. Ohlendorff? That must be the name of the father of whom he had boasted at their last meeting; in England he had borne another name, and though it was true that his mother had been English the young man who had been broadcasting wondered now that he could ever have accepted him as a compatriot. Ohlendorff was a tall man, with thick, fair hair, frosty blue eyes, and a determined chin. The change lay in the set of his mouth, the rigidity of his bearing—and the difference they made was unbelievable. Also, he was in uniform, and appeared—as the Englishman already knew him to be—typical of Germany at her most inhuman.

These were not conscious thoughts, and they passed in a flash. He looked down at the script again, and heard with faint surprise his own voice, as even as ever, still announcing calmly the truths and lies and half-truths that were recorded there. He had to fight against panic as he realized his position; time and to spare for that later, as he knew only too well. Just now there was still a chance of saving something from his own personal shipwreck. He went on speaking, without change of tone.

"Ecoutez bien, chers auditeurs! One must still wait during one week. After that—" his mind was racing, and the pause almost imperceptible—"after that, the decision is yours." That ought to cover it; no time to worry, anyway. "I have been recognized, and I shall not be able . . ."

His voice trailed off as he realized that the microphone into which he was speaking was already dead. He stood a moment, folding the sheets of his script with unnatural care. His mind was free now: there was nothing more he could do. He thought, with habitual self-mockery, "The rest is silence," and knew a sudden thrill of fear as he realized the horrid aptness of the quotation. Silence, indeed, God willing. And now the coming week, that a moment ago had seemed so small an obstacle to surmount, loomed ahead of him—terrifying, and endless as the Arctic night.

Behind the glass panel someone was moving to open the door. He was suddenly very weary, and it needed a conscious effort for him to straighten his back and start across the room. The door swung open, and beyond was a bewilderment of sound; it formed a background for the figure of Ohlendorff, who ignored everything but the approach of the Englishman. He was smiling slightly, as he waited.

The young man who had been broadcasting did not see the smile; the few steps across the room seemed to take an age to accomplish. He wanted to think—what to do, what to say?—but for the moment everything in him was concentrated on reaching the German. When he did so he raised his eyes at last and prayed silently that they would not betray him: for he was afraid.

Ohlendorff saw a dark young man, with clear gray eyes and an untroubled air. For a moment his hatred blinded him; he was conscious only of an insane desire to smash, to destroy that look of confidence. None of this appeared in his face. There were more artistic ways of achieving his ends, and meanwhile there was need of information. His smile broadened a little.

"Guten Abend, Herr Maitland," he said.

CHAPTER·ONE

It was an old-fashioned upright telephone, and its voice was strident. Antony Maitland, who had been staring in something suspiciously like a coma at the document on his desk for at least ten minutes, came to himself with a start and stretched out an unwilling hand. Two more minutes, he thought resentfully, and he might have got it; now the thread was gone, and most likely he would never come so near again to understanding the mind (undoubtedly, the most tortuous mind) of the chap who framed that contract.

"Maitland," he snapped at the telephone; and the telephone replied apologetically,

"It's a Dr. Martin, sir. He *says* it's urgent." The emphasis implied that Hill was accepting no responsibility, and Antony grinned a little to himself, the edge of his impatience blunted.

"Of course. Put him on." Though what the good doctor could have to say that was "urgent" was anybody's guess. Perhaps one of his inventions—which, indeed, were only too apt to run riot over the lives of his friends; or perhaps it was Gerry again, though surely . . .

"You're through, Doctor," said Hill's voice in his ear, and he heard the subdued click that meant the clerk had cut himself off from the conversation. But instead of old Dr. Martin's genial roar there was only silence.

Somehow, an uneasy silence. Which is ridiculous, said Antony sharply to himself; but his "Hello, Doctor" had a tentative sound, and he didn't really expect an answer. He jiggled the receiver with renewed impatience.

"What the devil are you playing at, Hill? You've cut us off."

"You're still through, Mr. Maitland." The voice sounded injured. "He must have rung off," Hill added brightly, after a moment. "Shall I ring him back for you?"

"No, don't bother." Antony replaced the receiver, and gazed at it reflectively. A patient, he thought, arriving unexpectedly. The doorbell, and his housekeeper out for the afternoon. What did it matter, anyway? The old boy would ring back when he was ready, and meanwhile, most probably, wouldn't welcome an interruption. He looked down again at the contract he was studying: an ingenious mass of clauses and sub-clauses, woven together with a subtlety that suggested nothing so much as diabolic inspiration. When the phone rang he had been on the edge of something important. . . . Perhaps, after all . . . He picked up his pen, and after a moment began to write steadily.

It was two hours later, and turned six o'clock, when he again thought of the doctor. The opinion was finished: page after page of clear and steady reasoning. Altogether, he congratulated himself, not a bad bit of work. He got up a little stiffly, listened a moment, and then went across to push open the door that led to his uncle's room. It was quiet and unoccupied, and the fire was dying. Sir Nicholas must have gone straight home from court, unless they were sitting late. The clerks had gone by this time, so the phone would be switched through. He fumbled for a pocketbook and found the note Dr. Martin had written for him— "Streatham . . ." half across the page, and the number an all-but-illegible scrawl. Now that he was no longer preoccupied he was aware of a sudden sense of urgency. It wasn't often, after all, that the doctor interrupted his working hours; he couldn't, in fact, recollect that he had ever telephoned him in chambers before. And there had been something odd—or hadn't there?—about that uncompleted telephone call.

His own call was answered promptly: a man's voice gave the number, cautiously. And again, as he replied, Antony was conscious that he was uneasy.

"Is Dr. Martin there? I'd like to speak to him."

"I'm afraid the doctor isn't here just now." Definitely, the voice was cautious. And where had he heard it before? Not the doctor himself, certainly not Gerry; that left only the housekeeper, so far as he knew. He said, "Oh!" rather blankly.

"Are you a patient, sir? Can I take a message?"

"No, I . . ." A comfortable, north-country voice, that he hadn't heard for nearly three years. "I know who you are . . . you're Sykes!" (And that didn't explain a thing, for what was a detective inspector from Scotland Yard doing in the Streatham surgery where Dr. Martin was doing locum for a colleague?)

"Yes, I . . . who is that speaking?" The voice had quickened, and the inquiry came sharply.

"Maitland here. What's going on? What are you doing there?"

"Are you a friend of the doctor's, sir?"

"I've known him all my life. Sykes, you must tell me. . . ." He was aware as he spoke of a sudden, cold desolation. If the police were in possession it could only mean . . .

"I'm sorry, Mr. Maitland, Dr. Martin is dead." He paused, and Antony thought afterward that perhaps during that brief respite the other man was searching vainly for words to clothe a fact that was unpleasant at best—that he, himself, found almost intolerable. "He was strangled," Sykes said, at last.

Antony sat very still. In spite of the coldness of the day and the dying fire, he found that his palm was sticky with sweat where he gripped the receiver. He said, in a voice that didn't sound like his own, "At four o'clock?"

"That I can't tell you," said Sykes. And waited.

"He telephoned me here—in chambers. He told the clerk it was urgent. But when I got on the line there was nobody there, so I thought—of course—that he'd been called away. I suppose it could have been then."

"Well . . . perhaps." Antony became aware that he did not have the detective's undivided attention. There was someone speaking in the background, and a sense of urgency was conveyed, though the words were indistinguishable; then Sykes's voice, unruffled as ever. "Yes . . . yes, I'll tell him." He spoke again, directly to the telephone. "Mr. Martin sir, would be glad if you could come out here immediately."

"I'll come," said Antony. "It's Dr. Forbes's house, isn't it? I have the address somewhere."

"That's right, Mr. Maitland. But I'll ask you to come straight to the station, if you will, at Streatham Hill. We were just on the point of leaving here."

"But, Gerry . . ." The phone went dead, and he realized that Sykes did not, just then, wish for questions. He replaced the receiver, waited a moment, and then picked it up again and dialed his own number.

The Divisional Inspector's office at Streatham Hill police station was both cold and stuffy when Antony was shown in at a little after seven o'clock. It had already the subtly raffish look of rooms which have had, in the space of a single day, more than their normal period of use; there was a tray with dirty crockery on top of the filing cabinet, and the papers on the desk were pushed into a wild disorder. At least three ash trays had their quota of cigarette stubs, and there seemed to be ashes everywhere. Antony wrinkled his nose a little at the stale smell of smoke, but the two men who turned to greet him seemed unconscious of any defects in the atmosphere.

Inspector Sykes was a squarish, fresh-faced man who, from his habit of wearing tweeds, contrived to look like a prosperous farmer on market day; though never a farmer, perhaps, was blessed with his outstanding serenity of manner. His companion, the local man whom he introduced as Inspector Foster, had a steely eye and an unbending manner, and flashed a pair of horn-rimmed glasses worthy of the Efficient Baxter himself.

"It's good of you to come, Mr. Maitland." Sykes spoke with his usual placidity and ignored the newcomer's inquiring look around the room. Inspector Foster pushed a chair forward with a gesture that was obviously intended as an invitation. Antony ignored them both, and said abruptly, "I came to see Gerry Martin. Where is he?"

"Well, now," said Sykes, with a sidelong glance at the

local man. "There'll be time enough for that, Mr. Maitland, when we've had a few words together."

"Where is he?"

"Why, here, Mr. Maitland. I'm sorry to tell you, he's under arrest." Sykes, making a virtue of necessity, was telling no more than he must; but Inspector Foster, speaking for the first time since Antony had come in, snapped suddenly, "He has been charged with the murder of his cousin."

There was a pause. Antony's expression grew blank as he considered this information. His first reaction—"But he wouldn't do a thing like that"—was a phrase by which he had often been irritated when he had heard it from others in the course of his profession. He said at last, evenly, "That was quick work, Inspector," and Sykes shrugged a little as he replied.

"We can't go against the evidence, Mr. Maitland." (And, after all, there was nothing strange in being called in to get Gerry Martin out of a mess of his own making. But strangling—?)

He spoke his thought aloud. "How did he die?"

"As I told you, Mr. Maitland, he was strangled. We haven't found what did it, but it seems as if someone came up behind him with a silk stocking—"

"Nylon," said Foster. "Nowadays."

"Well, nylon then. There's nothing to it if you're quick, or so I'm told," he added, and if his words were blunt, his air was faintly deprecating.

Antony said, as he had said earlier, "Was it at four o'clock?"

"Earlier than that, Mr. Maitland."

"But I told you—" He broke off as Sykes asked quietly, "You didn't speak to Dr. Martin yourself, Mr. Maitland? Would your clerk know his voice?"

"No, he wouldn't." Antony hooked the chair which Foster had offered toward him with his foot, and sat down without taking his eyes from Sykes's face. "You'd better tell me, Inspector."

"You know the household, I take it."

"I knew he was doing locum for a Dr. Forbes, who is ill, I think."

"Dr. Martin was retired?"

"Yes. He used to practice in Tilham, where I grew up. After I lived in London I used to stay with him sometimes. He was a nice old boy, you know." He stopped, frowning, but went on after a moment, without being prompted, "Mrs. Martin died a few years back; he retired soon after that, said he needed a change. But he was always ready to help out, so he seemed to be nearly as busy as ever."

"How long had he been at Streatham?"

"Just about a month. He had lunch with me in town when he arrived, and he gave me his telephone number. Then he came up last week to have dinner with us. He expected to be there at least another month, and was planning a night out—a show of some kind—a surprise for Jenny."

"He had three tickets for *La Belle* in his wallet," said Sykes in an expressionless voice. Antony's lips tightened. He was well aware that the detective spoke with some reason . . . to alienate his sympathy, perhaps, from the man who was under arrest. But first, he'd have to be convinced. He said, "That makes sense, he was always fond of musicals," and returned Sykes's look with one of exaggerated innocence.

"But he told you about his household," Inspector Foster prompted.

"There was just a housekeeper . . . Dr. Forbes's housekeeper. A queer name, I remember, something like—"

"Goodbody," said Sykes.

"Yes, well . . . Gerry was staying there, too."

"Doesn't Mr. Martin normally live with his uncle?"

"No, but he stays with him frequently. And—not his uncle, Inspector, his cousin."

"My mistake. There's such a disparity in their ages—"

"This is beside the point, Inspector. You were going to tell me—"

"Was I, Mr. Maitland?"

"Oh, I think so. As Mr. Martin's legal adviser—he hasn't asked for a solicitor, I take it?"

"No."

"And he hasn't," added Foster, acidly, "made any sort of statement."

"Very proper." Antony's tone was approving. He got up and looked from one to the other of his companions without any great evidence of amiability. "Are you going to tell me, or shall I see my client right away?"

"All relevant information will, of course, be given to Mr. Martin's solicitor." Sykes spoke formally, but Antony was conscious of a measure of amusement behind the words and found it irritating. "But I see no reason," the detective went on, "why you shouldn't see Mr. Martin. Do you agree, Mr. Foster?"

Gerry Martin joined him in a sort of waiting room, even colder than the office, and redolent of horsehair and dust. He was rather short, and slight of figure, with expressive brown eyes and nervous hands. His greeting inclined to the querulous, and Antony brushed his remarks aside without overmuch display of sympathy.

"You'd better tell me the setup, Gerry."

"They've arrested me," said Gerry. Hands and eyes combined to express his incredulity.

"I know that. Tell me what happened." He sounded impatient, and added before the other man could speak, "And don't, for goodness' sake, pretend to yourself that it isn't serious."

Gerry Martin sat down, and looked up reproachfully at his friend. "Cousin Henry is dead," he remarked sorrowfully.

"I know that, too. And you're in a mess."

"Well, then!" Gerry suddenly became practical, and abandoned his injured pose. "We had a row yesterday. Did they tell you that?"

"They did not. What was it about?"

Gerry looked up at him for a moment, and then spread his hands and contemplated them earnestly. "There was a girl," he said. Antony took a quick turn down the little, bare room, and returning to stand by the table said through his teeth, "Of course there was a girl! Who was she?"

"Well . . ." said Gerry. He looked up again—a swift, appraising glance, only too familiar to his companion. "Not a *nice* girl," he admitted.

"No," said Antony.

"Well, it was really none of Henry's business," Gerry was indignant again, "but he chose to take a high moral tone, and by the time we'd finished I was just about fed up. So I walked out on him."

"What were you doing in Streatham, anyway?"

The other shrugged. "You know me better than that," he said. "Would I be likely to pass up the chance of a couple of months' free board and lodging, when Cousin Henry was established within striking distance of town?"

"I suppose not," Antony conceded. "What are you working at now?" he inquired.

"Well, just at the moment—" Gerry spread his hands.

"I see." Antony sounded grim. "You're a fool, Gerry," he added.

"Dear old boy, have I ever denied it? But there was I, enjoying for the moment a most pleasurable freedom from bills, and there was Henry, cutting up rough about poor little Daisy. And what business was it of his, after all?"

Antony realized that he was genuinely aggrieved by what had happened. He said impatiently, "Dammit, Gerry, if he was supporting you—"

"Well, I don't see that gave him the right to run my whole life."

"He may have felt he had a right to say how his money should be spent," said Antony. (And what was the use of arguing with Gerry? His genuine inability to see things from any point of view but his own was almost disarming on occasions less serious than this.) "What happened then?"

"I went up to town. Daisy lives in Victoria," said Gerry promptly. "I didn't get up specially early this morning, but when I did I got to thinking things over, and I couldn't but see it was awkward, Henry being like that. So after lunch I came out here to see him."

"What time was that?"

"Oh, about—about three o'clock, I suppose. I was with him for half an hour or so." He stopped, and added with sudden, uncharacteristic earnestness, "That was queer, Antony. He didn't seem interested any more."

"What do you mean?"

"Well, I don't mean he exactly gave me his blessing, but he didn't seem to care very much."

"Were you coming back to stay with him?"

"We didn't get as far as that. He—he maintained his position, but he did it without conviction, you know. I was pretty sure he'd come round before very long." He looked a little anxiously at his companion, and added defensively, "I know it doesn't sound very likely. But it's true all the same."

Antony declined to be drawn. "You left him at about three-thirty, then?" he asked.

"Yes. It couldn't have been long after, because I went to have tea at a place in the High Street, and I looked at my watch *after* I was served, and it was a quarter to four."

"And then—?"

"Well, then I went back to town. We were going out to dinner, but the police came round before Daisy had finished getting ready. I saw Henry scribbling the address on his blotter; that must have been where they got it. They asked me to come with them—to help their inquiries, they said—and out we came in a taxi. But I didn't care for their questions much, so I thought I'd better not say anything. I suppose they think I did it with one of Daisy's stockings," he added fretfully.

"Very likely," Antony agreed.

"So when I heard Sykes was talking to you I thought you might as well come along." He looked consideringly at his companion. "That ought to make it all right, oughtn't it? I mean, if he talked to you at four o'clock, I have an alibi."

"Unfortunately, he only spoke to Hill. I'm afraid that won't help, Gerry. If we tried to use it as a defense, they would maintain you made the call yourself, to try and establish your innocence. And if they've any kind of evidence he died earlier than four o'clock, it would even be prejudicial. Because you know very well of my friendship with Dr. Martin, but how many other people do?"

"A good many, I should think."

"Yes, but people who were in Streatham this afternoon—people who had a motive."

"Well, I don't see . . . honestly, Antony, I don't see why anyone should want to kill him. I mean, a burglar wouldn't be likely to be out in midafternoon, and if he were . . . I say, it *is* pretty beastly, isn't it?''

"I find it so." And as for the lack of motive it was, he realized, one of the most telling points which would, eventually, be made against Gerry Martin. "I suppose the doctor has left you his money?" he said abruptly.

"Well, I should hope so," said Jerry, with a frankness which could at once horrify and disarm. "I mean . . . you're going to find me a solicitor, aren't you? And how am I to pay him, otherwise?"

Antony got up. "Then we must hope for the b-best," he said, and he was shaken by anger as he spoke, so that the other looked at him curiously.

"I say, old boy, you're not getting any ideas into your head, are you? I mean . . . I *liked* him, you know. I wouldn't have done anything to hurt him."

"I suppose not." He was suddenly weary of the conversation, conscious only of an overwhelming desire to escape from the situation, from all that had happened since he picked up the telephone that afternoon. He forced himself to speak quietly. "Have you anybody in mind? To act for you, I mean."

"No. The legal profession isn't much in my line, really."

"Then I'll phone Geoffrey Horton. Be honest with him, Gerry. He won't be able to help you unless you are." He looked at his companion steadily for a moment, and then added more gently, "He's a good chap, you'll like him."

"Well, I dare say." Gerry sounded doubtful. "But . . . you'll be in on it, won't you? You and Sir Nicholas?"

"If you want us," said Antony, and for once in his life found the suggestion of a brief unwelcome, so that he could add nothing to the bald acceptance. He went to the door and pulled it open; there was a policeman in the corridor outside, and as he turned back for a moment he caught the look of panic that flared in Gerry's eyes. He went away with his farewells unspoken.

Sir Nicholas Harding—although a bachelor, and in possession of a good set of chambers in the Inner Temple— lived, as his father and grandfather had done before him, in one of the tall houses on the north side of Kempenfeldt

Square. On that cold evening in January when his nephew heard of Dr. Martin's death, he was sitting in his study (his favorite room when he wasn't entertaining), and his niece, Jenny Maitland, was keeping him company.

Jenny had joined the household on her marriage during the war, and since Antony's demobilization the two young people had occupied an apartment which was more or less self-contained at the top of the house—a temporary arrangement which, as things had turned out, none of them had ever wished to change.

Antony got home about eleven o'clock and, having noted as he crossed the square that there were no lights upstairs, went straight to the study. He saw as he went in (as he had seen so often before) Sir Nicholas, stretched out at ease before the blazing fire, raise a hand in languid greeting; and Jenny, curled up with a book on her lap and her back to the door, turn with a quick smile of welcome so that, as she moved, the lamplight tangled strands of gold in her brown hair. Because of the contrast with the place he had just left, the comfortable, familiar scene was for a moment vivid and unexpected, so that he looked at it blankly before he crossed the room and bent to kiss his wife. She cried out as he did so, "Darling, you're cold!" and he smiled at her, though still a little absently, and moved nearer the fire and stretched a hand to the blaze.

Sir Nicholas, whose face was in the shadow beyond the circle of lamplight, waved a hand invitingly toward the tray on the side table, and asked quietly, "The news you gave us earlier proved correct, I suppose?"

"Dr. Martin is dead. Yes, sir, I'm afraid so."

"Murdered?" insisted his uncle.

"Yes," said Antony again. And looked into the fire, and told them what had happened. "That's all I know," he concluded. "The police were being cagey, but we'll get it all from Geoffrey Horton, in time."

"I'm so sorry about the doctor," said Jenny. "But to say Gerry did it—"

"I didn't believe it," said Antony, "the first time Dr. Martin told me he'd been helping himself to the petty cash. That was within three months of his being articled to that firm of Chartered Accountants."

"He should have known better than to attempt a fraud on them," Sir Nicholas put in dryly.

"I didn't believe it," Antony repeated. "If Gerry hadn't told me himself . . . but he didn't even pretend to be ashamed of what had happened." He looked at his uncle and added uncertainly, "I suppose it could be part of the same kink . . . that he can't see anyone's point of view but his own."

"It seems a reasonable assumption," said Sir Nicholas.

Antony made an abrupt movement, and sat down rather heavily in his usual chair on the right of the hearth. After a moment he put up a hand to cover his eyes.

"The whole business makes me sick," he said violently.

Jenny got up, and made for the door. Her husband raised his head as she moved. "Good lord, I'm not hungry," he protested.

"Well . . ." said Jenny. "I'll bring you some soup, and then we'll see," she temporized.

As the door shut behind her, Sir Nicholas sat up. "Well, Antony?"

"Well, sir?"

"You're bothered about something . . . something that goes beyond Gerry Martin's predicament. You'd better tell me. And don't," he added, "give me any nonsense about Dr. Martin. His death is a grief to you, I know; but neither sufficiently deep nor personal to account for your attitude."

Antony lay back in his chair, and stretched out his legs. "How well you express yourself," he said admiringly.

Sir Nicholas got up, to stand with his back to the fire: a handsome man, tall and fair-haired, with an unconscious air of authority. He said, "You haven't answered my question." And the mildness of his tone made his nephew look up quickly.

"I can answer in your own phrase. Something *is* bothering me, but neither deeply, nor personally."

"That is not," said Sir Nicholas, "the impression you convey." He paused, and added with disarming casualness—an echo of his own courtroom manner, "You don't really believe Gerry Martin is guilty, do you?"

The younger man was silent for a moment, and when he spoke the note of strain was again evident in his voice.

"Should I shock you, sir, if I said . . . I wish I did not think so?"

"Well . . . hardly."

"I don't mean it, anyway. It's only . . . if I could be sure, one way or the other—"

"I don't know what all this is about," said Sir Nicholas, with sudden impatience, "but I won't have Jenny worried!"

Antony got up in his turn, and now he looked at Sir Nicholas steadily. He was as tall as his uncle, a dark young man with untidy hair and a thin, intelligent face. In his City clothes he achieved, painfully, a certain elegance that was foreign to him; he was no lover of formality, his taste being for the casual. He said, picking his words, "If you remember, during the war Jenny hated my job, but she never interfered."

Sir Nicholas frowned. "I remember," he said, shortly.

"I can't explain." Antony sounded impatient. "It's so vague, there's nothing to tell really—just something the doctor once said that makes me wonder—"

"For heaven's sake, boy, say what you mean, and don't dither."

Antony grinned. "There's probably nothing to it. I'll have a word with John Welwyn—tomorrow, if he's free. Ten to one that'll be the end of it. In any case, it'll be out of my hands."

"So that's it! All right, Antony, you'll do what seems best, of course. I hope you'll succeed in laying your ghost."

"I expect I shall, sir." He sat down again, and eyed his uncle hopefully. "I could do with that drink now, Uncle Nick, if the offer's still open. And you can tell me how you got on today."

Jenny, returning with a tray, found them deep in legal shop.

CHAPTER TWO

ANTONY MAITLAND could have made, had he so desired, two claims to distinction from the majority of his fellows. He had a wickedly accurate gift of mimicry; and a facility in foreign languages that was as much a part of his nature as is the absorbent quality of a sponge. The second of these attributes had been greatly strengthened by his father— not of set intent, but because he himself loved to travel and saw no reason why his son should not accompany him whenever that was possible. As a result Antony, long before he left school, had an exact and colloquial knowledge of German, French and Spanish, together with a working acquaintance with Dutch, and a smattering of Portuguese and Italian. And it had been this accomplishment, largely, that decided his wartime career.

He was musing on that period of his life when he left home the following evening. He had been two months past his eighteenth birthday at the time war was declared, and had decided (as so many of his contemporaries had decided) that his duty was obvious. But his intention of volunteering was anticipated by a certain Colonel Wright, who paused for long enough in a long and complicated anathema of the Public School system to telephone Sir Nicholas and inquire testily whether young Maitland was the genius at languages his father had always made out. Sir Nicholas replied guardedly, and reported the conversation when Antony came in, adding, "I've heard of Wright, he's something fairly important in Military Intelligence."

That had been the beginning. Afterward Antony wondered exactly how it had all come about. He couldn't
remember that anyone had ever asked his opinion, though
he supposed he could have backed out if he had wanted to.
Colonel Wright had eyed him fiercely, and said "Hum" in
what he felt to be a sinister way. He had then handed him
over to a pink-faced captain with a laconic introduction
and the added comment, "Too young, of course, but the
best we can do. Speaks everything." The captain had been
more explicit; he was an old hand, and though Antony had
never seen him again—for he was killed in a back street in
Reading while the war was still young—Antony remembered him with gratitude as the one sane person he had met
that bewildering day, in a world gone suddenly mad. It
was some time, naturally, before the work became—
interesting. Later, of course—but that was a different matter, and no need to dwell on it now.

He was bound, not for the familiar office in Whitehall,
but for John Welwyn's flat in Westminster. Major Welwyn
had been his superior officer for more than four of his
seven years in the army, and because of the nature of their
work they knew each other very well indeed. The Major
was now in his early forties: a slight, fair man, who hid a
forceful personality beneath a surface, studied normality.
He received his visitor without comment, provided him
with a drink, and apologized half-heartedly for not having
been available earlier.

"That's all right; but I hope I haven't driven Bobbie out
into the cold."

"She's away for the week end. I was working." He
gestured toward the desk, and Antony eyed the spread of
papers with disapproval.

"Mon pauvre petit Jean! I always knew you couldn't get
on without me."

Welywn pulled a face. "The paper work never gets any
less, certainly."

"I wouldn't mind betting some of those things are
leftovers since my day."

"Very probably. You can't expect us to replace anyone
so valuable all at once."

"How's the Colonel?"

"His blood pressure declines each year, and his doctors now consider the danger of apoplexy much reduced." Welwyn's tone was solemn, and Antony grinned.

"You pain me. I always thought I was good for him—he'll probably be a mass of complexes now, through not expressing himself freely."

"Oh, we manage to keep him amused. How are you, Antony?"

"Busy. Too busy."

"And Jenny?"

"Blooming." He sipped his drink, and gazed at the fire. Welwyn began to fill his pipe, and eyed his visitor quizzically.

"It isn't often I see you during the term," he said.

"No, I—I'd better come to the point, I expect. I want some information."

John Welwyn sat suddenly very still. He said, after a moment, "Official secrets, Antony. Have you forgotten all you ever learned?"

"Well, call it advice, if you'd rather. I'd better explain."

"It might be as well. I make no promises, however."

"As you please. As a matter of fact, if you can tell me I'm making a fool of myself I'll be vastly relieved."

"I'll do my best to oblige you, of course. Go on."

"Did you see the papers this morning? The murder in Streatham?"

"The doctor who was strangled? Martin, was it?"

"That's right. Dr. Henry Martin. He used to practice in Tilham, and I've known him as long as I remember. I won't bore you with the details, they aren't pertinent. He was doing locum in Streatham, and somebody killed him there." He paused and went on, watching the effect of his words on his companion. "Do you remember, just before we went to France in 1943 Wright asked me if I knew anybody familiar with the Compiègne district who might have reliable contacts there?" Welwyn considered and shook his head. "Well, anyway, he did, and it was Dr. Martin's name I gave him."

"That's a long time ago, Antony."

"It is, indeed. Later, after we were home again, I asked him once whether he'd been able to help Wright. He was a matter-of-fact old boy, you know, and I remember particularly because it was the only time I ever remember seeing him really perturbed. He said, 'I gave him the information he needed.' Then he sat and looked at me, or through me, for a long time without speaking—only, somehow, it wasn't the sort of silence you could break—and then he said, 'Whose was the responsibility? I knew the risks, but so did they. So did they. And nobody could have guessed—' He broke off there. I don't think he knew he had spoken aloud. And after a moment he began to talk about something quite different. And that was all—I never felt like asking him what it was about. In fact, I'd forgotten it, until yesterday.''

Welwyn was eyeing him intently. ''Is there any more of this—this rigmarole?''

''That's the lot.''

''It seems a trifle vague. What, precisely, is the point you wish to make?''

''Dammit, I know it's vague,'' said Antony, crossly. Ever since he had begun to speak he had been conscious of a growing sense of unreality. He went on slowly, trying to recapture the urgency he had felt the day before. ''Look at it this way: Dr. Martin was an extremely ordinary person. Well, he had his eccentricities, but they weren't the sort of thing to lead to murder.''

''What sort of thing?'' said Welwyn. His tone was light, but his eyes were watchful.

''He had a positive mania for inventing useless gadgets. They were always going to make him famous, and at least I expect they kept the Patent Office amused. But what I was trying to say is this: I know only two unusual things about him . . . unusual in a—in a sinister way, I mean. One, the scrap of conversation I've just related; the other, the manner of his death. Is it straining credulity too far to imagine one might explain the other?''

''As far as I'm concerned, yes, it is,'' said Welwyn bluntly. ''Anyway, if I remember rightly, they've made an arrest already.''

Antony got up, and moved restlessly across the room and back to stand on the hearthrug. Not five minutes since, the matter had been clear in his mind; now there was only a sense of futility. The police had arrested Gerry Martin and—of course!—that was the end of it. He looked down at the fire and thought, with a flicker of amusement, that it was like John to have forgotten it needed mending. He wondered whether it was worth trying to explain. . . .

"That's the answer you wanted, isn't it?" said Welwyn, abruptly.

"I suppose so." Antony spoke without turning his head. "Only you see, John, you've no idea how—how unmurderable old Dr. Martin was. And though I've no proof Gerry didn't do it, if I happen to be right—"

"Well?"

"It isn't exactly a pretty thought." He remained a moment longer, looking down at the fire, and then shrugged his shoulders and turned to look at his friend. "All right, John, I'll try to heed the voice of reason. Sorry to have wasted your time."

Welwyn said absently, "Always glad to see you," and his tone made Antony glance at him with more attention. Then, apparently reaching some decision, "I'll talk to Wright, and I may ring you tomorrow. Will you be at home?"

"Yes, I expect so. Though we'll probably be in chambers for an hour or so in the afternoon; we've got a conference."

"Right, you'll hear from me." His decision made, the other wasted no more words on the matter.

"Then I'll leave you to your overtime." Antony was puzzled, but questions, he knew, would get him nowhere; nor did he feel inclined to prolong the interview. He took his departure without much delay.

When his visitor had gone John Welwyn sat down again at the desk and picked up his pen. But it was some time before he turned again to his work.

Antony made his way home in a reflective frame of mind. It had been strange to come up against a warning not to trespass on ground that had once been so familiar, but only what he might have expected. Put into words, his fears had been revealed for the nebulae they were. Now Gerry Martin's troubles could be dealt with like any other case; the personal aspect couldn't be ignored, of course, but just for the moment it might at least be shelved.

It was past nine-thirty when he turned into Kempenfeldt Square. The night was clear and frosty, but at that hour few people were about. Across the square a car door slammed, and a man set out to cross, skirting the dusty patch of garden in the center. Then at the corner he paused, standing in the deeper shadow cast by the bare branches of the sycamore that grew there. Something about the tall figure standing there renewed Antony's feeling of disquiet. He told himself impatiently that it was foolish; in that light he could not see the stranger clearly, let alone make out whether he was, in fact, being watched. This was what came of letting memory run riot over the past. Now imagination had taken over, and here he was, peopling the square with his own private ghosts. If there was one thing more certain than another . . . he turned a resolute shoulder toward the man in the shadow, mounted the steps to the front door, and heard, with a moment of self-derision, footsteps walking away, doubtless on some errand as innocent as his own. He swore softly to himself and fumbled for his latchkey.

CHAPTER THREE

SUNDAY AFTERNOON found Sir Nicholas and his nephew in chambers with the fire well stoked up and a comfortable confusion of books and papers. They were joined by Geoffrey Horton, a young solicitor who had red hair and a normally cheerful disposition. On this occasion he appeared subdued, and eyed Sir Nicholas warily as though unsure of his welcome.

Antony said bracingly, "You're finding your client a problem, I gather. Don't worry . . . you can't tell us anything we don't know about him."

"Well . . ." Geoffrey's smile was tentative. He put down his brief case on the desk and began to rummage in it. "I don't mind saying, he's a new one on me."

"For which you should be grateful." Sir Nicholas had picked up a pencil, and was sketching busily, his glasses on the tip of his nose. He looked up briefly, and grinned at the newcomer. "Stop fidgeting, Geoffrey. You can't have so much to tell us that you need notes."

"No, I haven't." Horton was still suddenly, then he snapped the brief case shut again, and looked from one to the other of his companions with an air of resolution. "I don't know much, and what I do know . . . I don't like."

"Sit down and tell us."

Geoffrey obeyed, choosing a chair near the fire. "The facts," he said, "are these: the housekeeper, Mrs. Goodbody, was out in the afternoon from about two-thirty. She went shopping and didn't get back until four-fifteen.

23

She went in, of course, through the house—not by the surgery door. She had left the doctor's tea ready for him to make—he liked it early. So when she saw he hadn't had it she went to ask him if she should make it then. He was in the surgery, dead.''

"I don't get the time element," Antony complained. "Sykes was already there when I phoned, and—"

"Sykes was in Streatham on another matter," said Horton.

"Irrelevant," said Sir Nicholas, intent upon the string of ducks which were beginning to form a procession across his pad. Antony shrugged and resumed his prowling.

Geoffrey continued, still addressing himself to the fire, "The first thing the police heard when they started asking questions was about the row young Gerry had with the doctor. And one of the neighbors had seen him going in that afternoon. She didn't see him leave, but he says himself he was there for about half an hour." He paused and looked inquiringly at Sir Nicholas, who declined the opportunity for comment and in his turn looked at his nephew.

"If you're thinking of the doctor's phone call at four o'clock," Antony said abruptly, "that's no good to us. I didn't speak to him, Hill didn't know his voice, and I'm bound to admit it's just the sort of damn-fool thing Gerry might have thought up. . . ."

"Oh, well!" The solicitor was resigned. "The rest of his story amounts to no more than he told us on Friday evening. He went in by the surgery door at *about* three o'clock; he stayed *about* half an hour; their talk was more amicable than might have been expected; he left his cousin alive and well. And he knew—of course—that he was the doctor's heir. And that's not the worst. The police searched the girl's flat—well, of course they did. And they found one odd stocking rolled up among her other pairs."

"Hell and damnation!" said Antony. And was aware, even as he sickened at the possibility of Gerry's guilt, of a faint, unacknowledged emotion that could only be relief. He felt his uncle's eyes on him, but before the silence had time to lengthen the telephone rang. Sir Nicholas looked at it rather as if he had unexpectedly come across a snake in his path, picked up the receiver, and spoke gently. A moment later he looked up at his nephew.

"It's John Welwyn, Antony. He'd like to see you right away." His tone was mild still, and only faintly reproachful.

Antony was standing with his back to the window. Horton saw him stiffen, and wondered idly why the message should perturb him. But he could not see the other man's expression, and Antony's voice was even enough when he spoke.

"Is he at home?"

"At the office," said Sir Nicholas. And added, as he replaced the receiver a few moments later, "You'd better take a taxi."

Antony came back to the desk and stood for a moment, staring down at the scatter of papers, and apparently giving the procession of ducks rather more attention than their artistic merit warranted. He was conscious of a wish to prolong the moment, to hold on to the familiar things which this meeting represented. A new case, and the discussion not very profitable at this stage; boring, perhaps . . . or perhaps worrying . . . but there was safety in the very commonplace nature of the occasion. And outside the afternoon was gray, and cold, and unfriendly, and if John Welwyn had something to say to him . . .

Sir Nicholas removed his spectacles, and said gently, "May I remind you, Antony . . ." And the younger man came to himself with a start and took his leave.

Antony found John Welwyn sitting with his chair tilted back, gazing at the ceiling. After a moment he transferred his glance to his visitor. Antony fidgeted. "Your story last night was rubbish," said Welwyn at last. "Still—"

"You know something to confirm it?"

"In some measure. But I don't want—"

"Spare me the lecture. After living so long with Uncle Nick, I never take anything for granted."

Welwyn smiled. "I'm glad to hear it," and Antony looked at him with sudden suspicion.

"What have you got up your sleeve, John?"

"The answer to your query. And a little gratuitous information besides. You should be grateful."

"I'll reserve judgment. Carry on."

"Well, I've been talking to Wright. You must understand, Antony, this is strictly official."

"I don't much like the sound of that. And I don't know what you mean."

"I mean we want your help, if you're willing to give it to us. On an official basis."

"Well, at least," said Antony with some relief, "you can't call me up again."

Welwyn smiled. "No, but we can call you in as a legal consultant. Wright thought that one up. He thinks it will look quite well in the books."

"Good lord!" Antony was appalled.

"At least, you can listen. And I don't suppose you've forgotten how to keep your mouth shut."

"If I do either, it's Without Prejudice. And if you want that explained, John, I'm going home this instant."

"Keep calm. I take your point. And now will you sit down and listen?"

"Well . . . all right." He still sounded doubtful, and Welwyn commenced his story without allowing him opportunity for further comment. "The Colonel remembered Dr. Martin, who proved so informative about the Compiègne district (which somebody-or-other was interested in just then) that they started sending the chaps destined for that area down to Tilham for briefing. In addition, he gave Wright the name of a family called Bonnard. He'd stayed with them many times and was sure they'd be well disposed. That proved correct: it was an ordinary enough matter of sheltering agents, passing on messages, you know the kind of thing. The Bonnard family were Monsieur and Madame, three grown sons, and one daughter of about seventeen. They were farmers, and prosperous for that district. For about a year they formed a most efficient link in the underground chain. Then, out of the blue, they were arrested. You know what that meant: the old people died fairly quickly, the sons over a period of months. As for the daughter, nobody ever heard what became of her. Most likely she, too, is dead."

"I don't understand. That's a beastly story, John, if common enough. But it explains—"

"There's a little more yet. At first the cause of their arrest was not known, then reports began to come in. Did you ever hear of a chap called Teddy Morris?"

"No . . . no, I don't think I ever heard the name."

"I never met him, though I remember hearing him mentioned. He was trained as a commando, then transferred to us and sent on special duties, much as we were. He was parachuted into France, with instructions to make contact with the Bonnard family, and through them with the local Resistance. For about a month everything was quite normal, then one day he walked into Gestapo headquarters, gave them details of the whole organization—that included, of course, the Bonnards—and became, so far as we can ascertain, the complete collaborator:" He saw Antony's expression and laughed without mirth. "Yes, a filthy business, and never the faintest clue why he should do such a thing."

"What happened to him afterward?"

"We heard of him from time to time. He was in Germany. I expect quite a few of our chaps were tripped up through his information. Then they used him for interrogating prisoners—the old sharing-a-cell trick, too, I expect. And that 'friends of Germany' business, he was mixed up in that. When the war ended he just disappeared. They never found any trace of him."

"So the odds are about even, whether he's dead too. Changing his identity would have been easy enough—he must have had plenty of opportunity."

"It's all surmise, of course."

"Of course! But you haven't told me yet how this ties in with the doctor."

"First, a little more guesswork. I told you he'd talked to most of the fellows who were going to Compiègne. He certainly saw Morris at that time."

"Very likely. But I still don't see—"

"Patience, Antony. We now come to the heart of the matter. On Friday afternoon Dr. Martin telephoned to us here, asking for an appointment with Colonel Wright. The switchboard took the call at five minutes to four.'' Having exploded his bomb, Welwyn sat back and gazed at his companion with satisfaction.

That brought Antony to his feet. After a moment, ''I don't believe it,'' he said flatly.

''True, all the same. They made him an appointment for yesterday. Apparently Wright waited for him, not having read the papers, because the first thing he said when I mentioned the matter was 'That explains it—if the feller was dead, stands to reason he couldn't keep his appointment.' You know his way.''

Antony walked to the window, and back again to the desk. ''Did he give a reason—?''

''Just asked when it would be convenient for him to see Wright. No comment, nothing.''

''What a muddle.'' Antony frowned, trying to concentrate. ''He certainly knew what had happened to the Bonnards; if he was still in touch with our chaps I expect they told him Morris was responsible; he'd have recognized Morris, if he saw him again.'' He made a violent, vague gesture. ''But we don't know anything.''

''There's ingratitude! Remember, you started this.''

''I must have been mad,'' said Antony, with conviction.

''Very possibly. There is now, however, the question of following up—''

Antony looked at him sharply. ''No,'' he said, flatly. ''No, no, no!''

Welwyn sat back and eyed his younger companion reflectively. ''Tell me, when you came here yesterday—what did you expect?''

''Oh, lord, I don't know.'' He moved a few paces from the desk and then returned and stood fidgeting with the contents of the *out* basket. ''I was bothered . . . I thought I should—''

''But you asked for information!'' Welwyn regarded him quizzically.

''Dammit, John, I was curious. Besides . . . there's Gerry. We're acting for him, you know.''

''Well, then!'' His tone was bland.

''It isn't quite so simple.'' It was useless, he knew, to

pretend his curiosity was satisfied by what he had just heard. But, after all . . . "After all, it's the middle of term, and our list's very full."

"But, as you said . . . there's your client's point of view. You can't ignore anything that may help him."

"I can't, of course, but that's quite a different matter. . . . I mean, you said you wanted my help officially."

"Yes, but I'm not asking you to give up your normal activities." Welwyn leaned forward, suddenly very much in earnest. "I'm asking you to hold a watching brief for us. You're engaged in this case already—that should make it simple."

"Well . . ." said Antony. "Simple!" He stood a moment, glowering. Then he laughed, rather wryly, and cleared himself a space so that he could sit on the corner of the desk. "I should have known you were up to something," he said.

"We can't take it up officially, you must see that."

"I see you don't intend to. But . . . why rope me in?"

"You won't be content with the obvious explanation—that you're conveniently placed to ask questions?"

"I will not." Antony sounded disgusted. "It's quite obvious if Morris is here and killed Dr. Martin, you can identify him through the police, without any help from me. And do *my* job for me by clearing Gerry into the bargain."

"All right, if you will have it." Welwyn paused, and looked hard at his companion. "There's a leak . . . a bad one."

"Where?"

"My good ass, if I knew would I be sitting here talking?"

"That depends. Well, if you don't know where, do you know what?"

"Secret stuff on aircraft. Well, not just that, on projects by aircraft firms."

"Firms?"

"Oh, yes. At least half a dozen are involved. And you see what that means?"

Antony said slowly, "One of two things: either there's some one person in touch with these firms, and with access to their information, or there are six independent traitors. Either way postulates one kingpin, because the six men would hardly all be in direct communication with abroad. And the one man, I suppose, is the one you're interested in.''

"Exactly. So now you see—"

"Well, not quite. Do you think Morris could be the man?"

"We've reached a stage where we can't afford to miss any possibilities. And you must admit that if Morris (a known collaborator) is alive and in England the further possibility exists that he is in touch with some such organization as I have described."

"I suppose so. It's all beautifully vague, isn't it? Where's the information going?"

"To the highest bidder," said Welwyn, laconically.

"Then, what makes you think there's a Nazi tie-up? I mean, isn't it far more likely—"

"Admitted. But I don't believe that's what is happening. You'll know better than to believe we've attended the funeral of the Nazi party, and for some time now signs of life have been only too evident."

"There have been occasional small paragraphs in the papers," Antony agreed thoughtfully. "They said so little, it was a safe bet there was more they could have said." He looked up and smiled. "But—I'm sorry, John—I still think the police—"

"May the Lord give me patience," said Welwyn, suddenly exasperated. "I said we've been checking up. Well, even if I didn't, you must have known it. You know what this work is well enough. If it's *possible* that your grandmother is an enemy agent you check up on her, no matter whether it is likely, or even probable."

Antony grinned. "And whose grandmother have you been checking up on this time?"

"Well, first, we're checking the firms concerned, and their subcontractors, and we're checking a firm of accountants that happens to audit at least four of them, and we're even checking the Ministry people. Besides which, we are checking our own fellows, with special reference to the section that deals with security clearances; and, of course, the police, because they sometimes get tied up in that work, too."

"Yes, that's all very fine, but you haven't explained—"

"Then let me finish. Do you know what we found, Antony, after weeks of patient work? We found one solitary, insignificant police sergeant, stationed in the suburbs somewhere, who had been a member of the Blackshirt movement before the war (he joined the Force after a spell in one of the services); and who admitted, on questioning, that he had been in the habit of carrying messages between two vaguely described gentlemen, neither of whom he thought he would be able to identify. At this point, Wright went mad."

"I'm beginning to see—"

"He's gone security mad. . . . It's a wonder he doesn't have the calendar taken down from his office wall in case it gives the enemy some vital information."

Antony laughed. "I should be honored, I suppose."

"Well, whatever else you've been doing since you left us, you haven't been peddling information to the enemy," said Welwyn bluntly.

"So you want me to try to get, *sub rosa,* all the information which is probably already adorning the police files. I don't think I'm very likely to succeed, do you?"

"Leaving that aside for the moment . . . are you going to help us?"

"I should think it very doubtful. I'll try, if you like."

"That's all I ask."

"Does the general interdict extend to Uncle Nick, I wonder? It's a little awkward—"

"Don't worry about that. Wright knows Sir Nicholas."

"Well, come to that, I dare say he knows the police on this case."

"Who are they?"

"Detective Inspector Sykes is one. He'll most likely be working under Superintendent Briggs. I don't care for Briggs myself, but I imagine he's safe enough."

"Well, you know, the whole essence of police work is that it's communal. Everything is pooled, just the opposite of our way of doing things. . . . That's what gets Wright really, and I must say, I see his point."

"Oh, so do I." He added, in a troubled tone, "I don't like this business, John. I don't like it at all."

"I don't see what you're worried about. You said yourself it's vague; it's very unlikely there's anything in this particular angle."

Antony shrugged. "All right. I'll go away and make myself unpopular by asking the right people the wrong questions. *So* easy to fit into the proof of evidence for a murder trial . . . 'By the way, are you living under a false name, and were you a traitor during the war?' "

"At least," said Welwyn, with sudden heat, "you can find out if the doctor had contact with anybody who *could* have been Morris."

"So I can. How bright of you, John." He got up, and stood looking down at his friend. "I did mention—didn't I?—that I am not enamored of the program you have outlined for me."

"A lot I care for that," said Welwyn bluntly.

"So I suppose." He paused at the door. "My compliments to the Colonel, John. Tell him to think nothing but beautiful thoughts."

Welwyn sat looking after him for some moments with a puzzled frown. Then he sighed, and picked up the telephone.

CHAPTER FOUR

SIR NICHOLAS'S BUTLER, a disagreeable old man with a deceptively saintly appearance, was hovering at the back of the hall when Antony got home and realized, with some surprise, that it was already well past eight o'clock. He had walked home, and taken his time about it; a mistake, as it happened, because Gibbs made something of a fetish of punctuality and had his own ways of making his displeasure felt.

Jenny was out, and he was dining alone with his uncle. While they were at table, Sir Nicholas made no attempt to open the subject that was uppermost in both their minds; but as soon as they were settled in the study with no further interruptions in prospect, he wasted no time.

"It seems you were wrong, Antony, in your interpretation of Welwyn's reaction." His tone was mild, but left his nephew in no doubt of his meaning.

Antony took the cup of coffee which was being offered him, and said with a deceptive air of candor, "I'd better tell you what happened."

"I have been hoping to hear . . . whatever you are able to tell me."

Antony considered a moment, and then launched on his narrative. He caught his uncle grinning once or twice as the tale proceeded, but Sir Nicholas was serious enough by the time he came to the end.

"You were under no obligation to accept this commission. The question of an alternative motive must obviously be considered, but if you think you can help Gerry—''

''No, sir. I think I'd do better with a free hand.''

''Welwyn has put you in an intolerable position—''

''Yes, I think so. I see his point, however.''

''Well, yes. It is his job, after all. But not yours.''

''I'm sorry, Uncle Nick.''

''I can't understand what made you agree—''

Antony got up restlessly. ''Can't you, sir? I'll try to explain if you have the patience to listen.'' He leaned his shoulder against the corner of the high mantel and looked down at his uncle with an expression that was wholly serious. The words did not come easily, even though he had made up his mind that some measure of explanation was inevitable. ''Do you think that if you . . . if you fear something very much, sooner or later it will happen to you?''

''That sounds uncommonly like superstition, Antony.''

''Yes, I know. And I don't really believe it. Only, it does seem to be happening.''

''What are you afraid of?'' His voice was expressionless. Antony looked down at the fire and replied without looking at his uncle, ''Of a man called Ohlendorff, who may very well be dead.''

''In that case—''

''But I don't think he is. I think I saw him . . . yesterday . . . in the square.''

There was a silence. Antony walked across to the window, and back again. When it became obvious that he was not going to say anything more Sir Nicholas said quietly, ''You can't really have thought this—explanation, did you call it?—would try my patience.''

The other grinned at that, a little wryly. ''That's all there is to it,'' he protested.

''I take it Ohlendorff was a wartime . . . acquaintance?'' said Sir Nicholas. And added, impatiently, ''I have noticed before this tendency of yours to shy away from any discussion of your work at that time.''

''But I've just told you—''

''Little enough. It would have been better to say nothing.''

"Perhaps it would. But . . . I couldn't talk about it; you know that, Uncle Nick."

"Why not?"

"Well, no valid reason, now, I suppose. All the same . . . the habit of secrecy dies hard."

"Dammit, boy, I'm not caviling at your discretion. I'm only complaining that you carry it to the length of keeping things from yourself as well. Even Falstaff would have thought that a little excessive."

Antony grinned again, this time with real amusement. "Psychology, sir? I'm afraid I'm a very poor subject."

"Psychology, fiddlesticks!" snapped his uncle. "Common sense, more like."

"What exactly are you complaining of, sir? You're not being very lucid, you know."

"Not that you won't talk; no reason why you should. But that you're afraid to remember."

There was a silence. Antony moved from the fireplace to take the chair opposite his uncle. He said, after a while, "What do you want me to do, Uncle Nick? Write my memoirs?" His tone was bitter, and Sir Nicholas flared to anger again.

"Damn your impudence!" he said. "I've never asked for your confidence, have I? Have I, Antony?"

"You've never needed to, of course. But this is different. I just don't want to talk about it."

"Or even think about it. Don't be childish, Antony! And don't lose your temper with me," he added, seeing the younger man about to speak. "I won't have it!"

Antony bit back the remark he had been about to make, but the look he gave his uncle held nothing of affection, and very little of respect. After a moment he said, coldly, "May I remind you, sir, that this conversation is none of my choosing?"

"You may, of course . . . if you really want to stand on your dignity." Sir Nicholas appeared to have regained his good humor, and his tone was bland. Antony, who could never take himself seriously for very long at a time, smiled reluctantly and relaxed a little.

"You're still not being constructive, Uncle Nick. Having maneuvered me to this point, I suppose you have some idea of where we go from here. I'm not to be childish; I'm not to lose my temper. Very well: what *am* I to do?''

"Give your memory its head, for once. Take your skeletons out and look 'em in the face . . . even if you won't bring them right into the open and set them dancing for the gratification of my curiosity." He paused, hoping for some sign—either of anger or amusement—that his nephew had comprehended this complicated demand. When nothing happened he added, placidly provoking, "Or haven't you got the guts?''

Antony took his time over replying. He said, at last, "It isn't an edifying story.''

"Does that matter?''

"I suppose not." He got up and went back to the window, pushing aside the curtain; all he could have seen against the darkness was his own reflection and the reflection of the room behind him, but he stood looking at it blankly, seeing nothing. His thoughts were racing now, hammering in his head. He said, "I don't think I *can* explain," and never knew that he had spoken aloud. Only now it was equally difficult to keep his mind on the present, and forget . . . and forget . . .

Before ever he had met Ohlendorff, there had been his first encounter with John Welwyn; and perhaps it was true to say that everything that went after had its beginning in that neat, low-ceilinged bedroom in the inn at Ambleside. As he thought of it the smell of the oil lamp was vivid again, and it came to his mind how he had to stoop to the dim old mirror that hung in the most awkward corner of the room; and how, hearing the click of the latch, he had raised his eyes and seen the reflection of a stranger—a slight, fair man who eyed him with disfavor.

"Of course, I didn't know who he was then," said Antony to his reflection in the windowpane. (It had been a boy's face that looked back at him from the mirror of The George's second-best bedroom, but he saw, of course, no difference.) "He said I'd kept him waiting, and he wasn't very pleased about it.''

He remembered, too, how the job he had been doing had dovetailed neatly with the new work assigned to him, making it at once easier and more dangerous. Welwyn had eyed him doubtfully, with all his distrust of these raw young men apparent in his look. But that had been while the tide still ran in his favor: he had gone to his problem with confidence, and completed it to his own and everyone else's satisfaction. After that there had been a brief leave, and a staff job—officially—in London. And he hadn't known then—how could he have known?—that his newly found self-confidence was so precarious.

The leave had been eventful, too . . . that was when he had become engaged to Jenny. A couple of young idiots, no doubt; but why think that, when neither of them had ever had cause to regret it? He turned from the window, and went back to his favorite spot near the fire. "Do you remember, Uncle Nick," he said, as though continuing a conversation already in being, "that's what you thought? Because you said, 'Fools rush in . . .' "

Sir Nicholas disentangled this without too much difficulty, and if he was bewildered by the line his nephew's reminiscences were taking he made no sign. "I approved your choice, but deplored your tactics—as you well know. You should have left me to deal with her father—"

"Yes, I dare say. The trouble was, you know, I'd got over a little too well the idea that I'd taken on a soft job that you'd wangled for me."

"I remember that very well indeed," said his uncle, with a private grimace at the fire. "It had to be done."

"Well, old Conway didn't like it—who would? Jenny didn't either. That was the first time I hurt her, Uncle Nick, and I couldn't help it. But that didn't make it any easier to take."

"Did she ever blame you?"

"You know she didn't. She said, 'If you can pretend, I can too.' But that was long before Mardingly, and the row I had with you, Uncle Nick. Do you remember that?"

"I remember."

"You said, 'I never had much use for a quitter.' "

"Does that still rankle? You can forget it, Antony. . . . I didn't mean it."

"Didn't you, sir?" His tone was detached. It was not this part of the story, Sir Nicholas realized, that held his strained, unwilling attention.

"In point of fact," the older man prompted quietly, "you didn't quit."

"I wanted to. How I wanted to!" Antony sat for a moment, and suddenly there was no longer the high-backed chair, and the fire warming his legs, and the faint fragrance of his uncle's cigar. Only the past had any reality: the bare stretch of moor, the cottage in the hollow, sunrise and sunset; the bright cool days of April, and the cold, cold blackness of moonless nights. He never knew at what point in this nightmare of recollection he began to speak.

Even now there were things that could be said, but more that were beyond the relief of words. He could say, "There was a man I was watching . . . he went to earth in an empty cottage on Pock Stones Moor. I knew there was going to be trouble, I even knew *when*. We waited three days, nearly, before two men came over the moor to the cottage; that meant things were moving, and the date was right, too. One of my companions, a local chap, followed when they left; the other went back to the town to wait for a message." He could say, "Later, much later when he didn't return, it became obvious something had gone wrong. It had, of course . . . they both of them were dead. But I didn't know that, and I didn't know what to do. I waited. I waited too long." He could say, "There was an explosion at one of the big engineering works. Twenty-seven people killed, and if I'd been ten minutes sooner . . ." He could say, "It seemed like the end of the world." But he couldn't explain how the taste of failure was made more bitter by the facile words of sympathy that were spoken by his colleagues; or how the wheels of the train, on the long journey back to town, had caught the phrase and flung it at him as if in derision . . . you DID your best . . . you DID your best . . . you DID your best.

"I remember," said Sir Nicholas, carefully, "that you asked for a transfer after that."

"I didn't want to go on. I don't know why I did, except that Jenny seemed to trust me. And the next job was down at Wellbury. And that was where I met Ohlendorff. . . ." He paused and gulped some of his coffee, and the cup rattled against the saucer as he put it down again. "He was an architect. I was going to say he was posing as an

Englishman, but that isn't strictly acc
ine enough, had lived here for years,
here. Only the name he used was his n.
English, he told me.''

"You seem to have become remarkably in
Nicholas spoke tentatively, and was relieved wi.   ny
smiled across at him, without any real amusen.   ., but
also without restraint.

"That was later. He was quite frank about himself, once
it came to a showdown between us.''

"In Jenny's absence I am compelled to ask you: what
was he like?''

"A big man, good-looking. Fair, but not that startling,
Nordic fairness. With a quiet, rather lazy manner . . . that
was on the surface. And he was clever, no doubt about
that. What happened isn't really important. He was all set
to go back to Germany, with some plans the boffins
seemed to regard as important . . . all in the best story-
book tradition, but you don't think of that when you're
living through it. Well, I caught up with him (and some of
his friends) at Wellbury, in the middle of an air raid. And I
got the plans back—''

"How did you do that?''

"Something I overheard . . . it seemed pretty hopeless
really.'' So he had found himself looking for a house "in
the street behind The Goat,'' and had asked directions of a
sad-eyed man who led him to the heap of rubble that was
all that remained of the public house. "The kids were in
the country,'' said the sad-eyed man, "but Joe and his
missis . . .'' He shook his head, and added what was
obviously the most fitting epitaph he could devise: "They
kept good beer.'' And it was queer that this trivial incident
should come, after all these years, so vividly to his mind
. . . when a moment later he had stood on the landing of
the little, dirty house, and heard the murmur of voices
through the closed door . . . and had known, suddenly,
that there was no turning back now. Success and failure no
longer had any meaning; they were words only, and he
knew their value . . . knew, too, that—whatever the
outcome—this was his job. And always he would stand
like this on the brink of danger, seeing it clearly. The hot

. of anger was not for him, nor any exhilaration. "I
.nt in then," he said, aloud. And now he was glad to
speak, because the words were a refuge. "Only my gun
was empty. . . . They found that out pretty soon."

"You said," Sir Nicholas reminded him, "that you got
the plans back."

"Yes, I . . . if you must have the whole story, I span
them a yarn, and got them to believe it by letting them
think they'd forced it out of me. That was when . . . that
was when I began to be afraid of Ohlendorff."

"And this, I gather, was not your only meeting?"

"No." Antony put up a hand to tug at his collar. This
part must be told, if his explanation was to mean anything.
"Do you remember when we went to France, John and
I?"

"Only too well."

"It was quite an important job: months of hard work, so
that the R.A.F. could have five minutes of merry hell with
the Nazi secret headquarters, somewhere in the suburbs of
Paris. It had its points, too, in the beginning, being very
much my own show because John's French (as you know)
wouldn't deceive a Hottentot into thinking him a Frenchman.
We got settled into an apartment in Paris, and I gave out
he was my idiot brother; once they got used to him,
nobody noticed whether he was there or not, and nobody
expected any sense out of him. Then I landed a job,
broadcasting. That was a fluke, really, but lucky, too . . .
at least, I thought so at the time. It led to our neighbors
thinking I was a collaborator, but it kept the Germans from
suspecting anything. And we worked out a code, so all our
messages went out with the propaganda broadcasts;
that was a big thing, because it is always difficult to
camouflage a transmitter, especially if it's continuously in
use. So everything was going well, until there was just one
week to go . . .

"I'd heard about the new German Kommandant, of
course, and heard he was coming to look over the broadcasting studios that evening. I didn't give it a second
thought, and I was broadcasting when he arrived." He
paused, and for the first time since he had started his story

looked straight at his uncle. "My God, it was Ohlendorff!" he said.

"After that . . . it's a funny thing, I found I was still reading the script, just as we'd prepared it. So I put out the rest of the message in plain language—well, I knew I was done for anyway. I was there ten days, at the Gestapo headquarters, I mean. Only I didn't know then how long it was, or that the day had come and gone for the job to be done, or that it had been successful. I didn't even know whether John had been taken, too." He looked up at his uncle again. "I got to know Ohlendorff even better during those ten days," he said, and his voice was very quiet and very bitter.

"But then you got away?"

"Oh, yes." He sounded indifferent. "They knew I was pretty far gone, and my arm was useless by then. Of course, I had help. I swore to the chap that helped me that I'd never mention his name to a living soul . . . and he believed me . . . and I never have. And John was at the rendezvous. So we came home." He was silent for so long that Sir Nicholas was about to speak when he went on. "A braver man could say, 'That was bad . . . that is over.' I can only think that Ohlendorff may be alive, and that I am afraid of him; and that we shall meet for a third time. And that if I do anything to avoid that meeting, I shall never be free of fear." He paused again, and then grinned at his uncle. "I'm sorry, sir. All very dramatic! But you did ask for it, you know."

Sir Nicholas heaved himself out of his chair and went across to a tray on his desk. He spoke without turning his head. "I'm glad to know what you are feeling. It will help me, at least, not to interfere with what you feel you should do."

"You never have, Uncle Nick."

"I might have tried." He turned from his task, and came across the room with a glass in each hand, and smiled companionably at his nephew. "It is probably as well, for both our sakes, that you have inherited—from your father's side of the family, I am sure—a certain stubbornness of disposition. It would certainly have a deleterious effect on my character if I habitually met with compliance on your part.'' He was talking at random, giving the atmosphere time to return to normal, and added as the younger man took the offered glass, ''That's the *good* Madeira, Antony.''

''I'll treat it with the deference it deserves.''

''Then we had better return to our problem.'' He sat down but did not, for the moment, return to his usual relaxed position. ''From what Welwyn told you, it seems quite possible that this man Morris is alive, and that he killed Dr. Martin; in Gerry's interests, we must, of course, go into this, and Welwyn may be able to help. In return, he wishes to make use of your services with a view to uncovering what is at present a purely hypothetical connection between Morris and—er—a spy ring.'' He brought out the phrase with obvious distaste.

Antony grinned and said helpfully, ''A group engaged in subversive activities. That sounds better.''

''Thank you.'' Sir Nicholas put down his glass and continued. ''So far, we are still in the realms of reason. The rest is guesswork—and borders upon insanity.''

''I realize that. All the same—''

''You said at the beginning, if I remember, that you thought you had seen this man Ohlendorff again?''

''In the square, last night. I had the feeling somebody was watching, but I couldn't be sure, I couldn't see him clearly. The way he moved seemed familiar, and that could be imagination, because talking to John had made me think of the war.''

''Do you really believe that?''

''Not really.''

''Did you tell Welwyn of this?''

''Good lord, no. He'd say I was mad.''

''If you want my opinion . . .'' Sir Nicholas sipped his wine, and shook his head as he set down the glass carefully. ''Well, we'll leave that for the moment. How do you intend to go about executing your commission?''

''Business as usual,'' said Antony. He was suffering the inevitable reaction from so much soul-searching, and was grateful to his uncle for not prolonging the discussion unduly. ''Did Geoffrey have anything helpful to say after I left you?''

"There was one point that may repay consideration in the light of what Welwyn told you," said Sir Nicholas slowly. "This man he spoke of—"

"Teddy Morris?"

"Yes. It is an obvious possibility (if he is indeed back in England) that he encountered the doctor and killed him to avoid recognition. You did not, however, hear the housekeeper's story."

"Only something about times."

"That is not what I mean. Dr. Martin's quarrel with Gerry took place in the late afternoon, and he did not go out again. He had a visitor, however, a man called Benson, a retired solicitor."

"From Tilham? I seem to remember—"

"Yes, an old friend. Now, Mrs. Goodbody says the doctor was distressed by what had happened, and was obviously dwelling on it. The next morning he had a surgery at nine o'clock. Just before eleven, when the last patient had gone, she took him some coffee, and he asked if Gerry had telephoned; he seemed preoccupied, as though the quarrel were no longer the most important thing he had to think about. And he went on to talk in a worried way about crime, and his duty; and said there were, after all, worse faults than Gerry's. And then he tried to phone Benson, whom he had seen the evening before, and seemed upset when he was told he was out for the day."

"The inference being that someone he saw at his surgery . . . yes, I see."

"So no doubt you will find out tomorrow whether Benson can throw any light on the matter. You'll have to take the preliminary hearing; I can hardly leave Hargreaves to young Lorimer's tender mercies. But after that—"

"It sounds . . . hopeful, sir. And the fact he phoned for an appointment with the Colonel . . . Gerry was telling the truth, wouldn't you say?"

"It seems, at least, that the police are wrong about the time the doctor died. But we haven't, so far, tested Gerry's alleged alibi for the time of the phone calls."

"I'll bear it in mind. I say, Uncle Nick," he added, as the older man rose to replenish their glasses, "I wonder if all this does amount to anything. John won't forgive me in a hurry if all I've done is put up an outsize wild goose.''

"I suppose not. That seems to me, however, to be the least of our worries," said Sir Nicholas dryly. And Antony grinned, and allowed the talk to drift to other topics.

But later, when he was alone, Sir Nicholas found—and was aggravated to find—a line of verse repeating itself in his mind. He looked across at a photograph, an old one of his nephew in battle dress, which adorned the top of the bookshelves; and presently . . . " 'God help us,' " he murmured, speaking his thought aloud to the empty room. " 'God help us, for we knew the worst too young.' Though in its context," he added, perhaps as a concession to the lack of sentiment on which he prided himself, "in its context, I must admit, the quotation is not entirely apposite."

CHAPTER FIVE

THE EVENTS of the following day displayed a pattern which Antony was later to consider significant. This was not, however, immediately apparent; sitting down to his notes that evening he was conscious only of being tired and discouraged. The difficulties of the task he had undertaken had become only too apparent, and perhaps it was as well that he did not then realize fully the implications of what had occurred.

He was inclined, for instance, to dismiss his conversation with the police as being of no importance. His mind insisted on dwelling on the subject, probably because it displeased him. Superintendent Briggs was one of the few people he really disliked . . . a wholly irrational feeling, which was mirrored in the detective's own feelings of aversion and distrust.

They met as they were leaving the Magistrate's Court, where Gerry Martin had pleaded "Not Guilty" to the accusation that he had murdered his cousin. Antony was irritated by his client's attitude (an air of false jauntiness which must have seemed the height of callousness to anyone who did not know him; Gerry, it seemed, was not going to make a good witness). He was also puzzled by the fact that the hearing had not resulted in a straight committal for trial but in the prisoner's being remanded for a further seven days at the request of the police. Seeing Briggs and Detective Inspector Sykes leaving the court together, he could not resist the opportunity for comment.

"You have my sympathies, Superintendent. And it looked such a safe bet, too."

Briggs stopped and looked at him. He was a big man, somewhat overweight; with a heavy jaw, a bulging forehead, and cold blue eyes. He did not pretend to misunderstand the remark, but said at last, "Our case is a formidable one, Mr. Maitland. As I am sure your instructing solicitor will explain to you." He spoke slowly, as though giving each word due weight and consideration.

"You appall me," said Antony placidly. "And I thought you were having second thoughts."

Inspector Sykes, following sedately in the wake of his senior colleague, said reproachfully, "Mr. Maitland will have his joke, sir." He was himself inclined to like the younger man, though he knew well enough the violence of Briggs's feelings. There was a certain amusement to be derived from the situation, but it would not, of course, be politic to let his feelings appear.

"You wrong me, Inspector. The matter is much too serious for joking." Antony's tone was judicial, and Sykes recognized—as the Superintendent did not—an echo of Briggs's tone. "It can happen so easily . . . a moment's rashness . . . ill-considered action . . . and there you are! A man arrested, and somehow you've got to show cause."

"I'm sorry to disappoint you," snapped Briggs.

"If you mean you have a case, after all, even though you don't choose to state it . . . why should that disappoint me? If you withdrew at this point, what would become of my brief?" At this point Briggs, who had been showing signs of restlessness, made a growling noise that might possibly have been construed as a farewell and quickened his pace. Antony was dawdling, looking over his shoulder, and finally he stopped altogether, moving aside from the stream of people leaving the court to find a vantage point from which he could watch for Geoffrey Horton. Sykes stopped, too, and eyed him squarely.

"Will you be going to the inquest, Mr. Maitland?" he asked.

"Not I . . . why should I? After all, you've already done your worst. Besides, I've other fish to fry."

"You'll be seeing the witnesses, I expect. The housekeeper . . . the neighbors . . ." Watching his companion's elaborately casual air, Antony grinned and spoke in a friendlier way.

"Come off it, Sykes. . . . What a very depressing picture! Of course I shall see them, but you must know my uncle well enough by now to realize he won't be content with a negative defense."

Sykes smiled back at him. "Would you be?" he inquired.

"Well . . . no. But it's no use laying traps for my tongue, Inspector. You're the last person I'd choose for a confidant, you know." Antony shivered as the wind swept down the narrow street and found the corner in which they were standing; he turned up his coat collar with a rather fumbling gesture of his left hand, saying as he did so, "I can't think what's keeping Horton. He promised to drive me—"

"And I'd better not keep the Superintendent waiting." Sykes did not seem perturbed by the prospect; in fact, he in his turn was dawdling, so that Antony asked shrewdly, "I wonder . . . are you quite happy about the time of death, Inspector?"

The detective shrugged, and his look was deprecating. "The medical evidence is vague . . . as no doubt you already know, Mr. Maitland."

"And you're wondering—aren't you?—about that telephone call. You'd like to ask me what I think the doctor wanted—if that wouldn't sound like an admission on your part that he still might have been alive at four o'clock." He laughed a little, and added gently, "Console yourself, Inspector. I wouldn't answer your query, you know, even if you felt in a position to put it." He turned as Horton came up, and added with apparent relief, "Just in time, Geoffrey. Inspector Sykes is doing his best to influence me by the silent pressure of his personality."

"I shouldn't worry too much about that," said Sykes, greeting the solicitor with his customary serenity. "Our case doesn't rest on what you may or may not tell us, Mr. Maitland; and I'm bound to add 'fortunately,' because I don't suppose you'd give us much help, in the circumstances." And with a briefly sketched salute to the two young men, he moved off in the direction Briggs had taken.

Geoffrey Horton looked after him, and then turned to his companion with a faintly troubled air. "He seems a nice enough chap—"

"I don't like the company he keeps. But what does it matter, anyway," he added, and began to move in the direction of the car park. "Briggs isn't likely to give us any bother this trip."

"There's always the little matter of refuting the evidence the police have gathered," suggested Geoffrey, moving in his wake through the rapidly thinning crowd. Antony's tone as he replied made light of the matter.

"Oh, that!" he said. "That'd still arise if he loved me like a brother. I meant . . . personally, you know. Briggs or another, it's all one." And he did not guess then, nor did he remember later, how untruthfully he spoke.

It was lucky, he considered, that Geoffrey Horton had an appointment for lunch, and could only drive him as far as Dr. Forbes's house, leaving him thereafter to his own devices. His researches were not likely to follow a purely orthodox pattern, and he had no desire at this stage to have to occupy himself with parrying the solicitor's questions.

Looking wearily through his notes that evening, he considered this point and did his best to concentrate on the accurate division of the information he had gained: so little, so very little, that could be regarded as evidence. And even less for John Welwyn . . . or perhaps that wasn't altogether true, but it was all surmise, even looked at in the most optimistic light.

There was, for instance, the odd little story which Mrs. Goodbody had told him. Not much there for Gerry's defense; and though it could be regarded in some sort as a confirmation of his own fears, it wasn't the sort of thing John was likely to take cognizance of . . . not standing alone, as it did, and without even the promise of a positive identification at some future time.

It amounted simply to this: that she had heard his own name spoken between two men in a Streatham teashop, at a little after four o'clock on the day Dr. Martin died. She mentioned it as a coincidence only, and Antony—already bored by the repetition of her evidence—listened at first with no very great interest. He was wondering, in fact, how long Dr. Forbes was likely to be, and her account of the episode had been rambling on for several minutes before his attention was caught.

The fair man had been there when she arrived, seated at a table at the end of the room, which was not at that time very crowded. She had noticed that he consulted his watch once or twice, but not as though he were impatient; after a time he had been joined by another man, younger than the first, she thought, who stood and spoke to him and after a moment or two sat down. This second man had dark hair, but she never saw his face.

"The first thing I heard him say—for I wasn't listening particularly, you know—was something about 'it being no trouble at all.' I thought he sounded impatient, as if the other one was asking foolish questions. And then he said, 'And it wasn't too soon—I heard him telephoning . . .' "

That was the point at which Antony's attention was caught and held. He asked, "What happened then?" and Mrs. Goodbody looked a little startled at the note of rather strained interest that had crept into his voice.

"The fair man didn't say anything, but I felt he wasn't pleased. The dark one said, 'And that wasn't all,' but then he lowered his voice. I thought he was trying to sound impressive. After a while he spoke more loudly again, and that was when your name came into it, Mr. Maitland."

"Can you remember—exactly—what was said?"

"Why, yes, I think so. It was only a word or two I heard. He said: 'After that he called a chap called Maitland; only he didn't get through.' And the fair man said, quite loudly, 'Antony Maitland!' and of course I wondered, having heard the doctor speak of you so often."

But what, after all, did it amount to? She could not even describe satisfactorily the fair man whose face she had seen; and had she been able to do so there was nothing positive, nothing that could be taken to court. Two men had spoken of another, who had made two telephone calls. Even the mention of his own name did no more than suggest that they might have been discussing Dr. Martin;

and how sure would the housekeeper be of what she had heard by the time the prosecution had finished with her?

Dr. Forbes was hardly more helpful. He had been recalled in haste from his convalescence, and seemed in consequence to be regarding life with a jaundiced eye. He allowed Antony to make a list of the patients who attended surgery on the morning of the previous Friday, but made no secret of his impatience with the proceeding, and refused point blank (and in terms of unnecessary vehemence) to provide even the most brief and innocuous information about any of them. The fact that Antony had expected this attitude did not make it any easier to bear; he departed in a disgruntled frame of mind, and started his lunch some twenty minutes later with the list of names propped up against the water jug.

They were all local, that was a comfort, anyway. And mostly women; the men, he supposed, would either be ill enough to be visited in their homes, or well enough to go to work and attend the evening surgery. Four men, in all; they'd better be left till evening, when there was a sporting chance of finding them at home. But the women, unfortunately, couldn't be ruled out altogether. It wasn't likely, but Morris could have had a girl friend all those years ago who had been faithful to him through all that had happened, and all the years between. It wasn't likely, but it would have to be checked. And if he wanted Welwyn to do anything about it, the list must be shortened until it showed some regard for possibilities.

Looking at his notes, he realized sadly that the fruits of his day's endeavor were going to look extremely meager to Geoffrey Horton. Even if the jury were willing to believe that Dr. Martin had been alive at four o'clock, and making phone calls, there was no doing anything with Gerry's alibi. There was the evidence of the neighbor who had seen the accused man go in by the surgery door; but the most exhaustive inquiries up and down the street failed to reveal anyone who had seen him leave again. As for the waitress who had been on duty at the table he claimed to have occupied, she had looked with faint interest at the photographs he displayed—after all, nobody could deny Gerry's good looks—but as to when, or even if, she had seen the original, she declined to be positive. "I couldn't say, I'm shew-ah," mimicked Antony bitterly to himself, and broke his pencil point on the underlined comment "Hopeless!"

To get back to the women patients, he was cursing Dr. Forbes pretty freely by the time he came to the end of the list. Fortunately, only one of them could conceivably be said to fall within the age group from which Morris might have selected either wife or mistress. His explanation was becoming glib by the time he visited her, but he prolonged the conversation and was rewarded at last by the information that the picture on the piano was of her husband. One look was enough to inform him that this was not Morris: an elderly man, with buckteeth and a deprecating smirk. But had he really expected that even the most laborious inquiries would produce the information he was seeking? The probability seemed again as cold and remote as it had done when he spoke with John Welwyn.

By that time it was nearly five o'clock, and only the four male patients remained on his list; and old Mr. Benson, who being retired might already be at home. In spite of himself Antony brightened a little as he got off the bus near Streatham Common and started out to follow the conductor's directions. Something might reasonably be supposed to emerge from Benson's statement; at worst, he had a good and apparent reason for his visit, and could be done with the circumlocutions with which he had sought to explain his questioning of Dr. Forbes's patients.

Theodore Benson had rooms in one of the old houses near Streatham Common, which share with it now only memories of bygone elegance. But it was a well-built house, and if the grounds were overgrown, still they must be green and pleasant in the summer. His sitting room at the back of the ground floor was shabby and comfortable; a french window at the rear led on to a little veranda, with steps down to the garden. . . . "A pleasant amenity when the weather permits me to use it," said old Mr. Benson, who had been sitting in the firelight. He got up to close the curtains as his visitor arrived.

Antony explained his presence briefly, and did not mention their previous acquaintance—which indeed was very slight. Benson waved him to a chair, and seated himself at the other side of the fireplace. "You'll have seen in the papers that Gerry Martin has been arrested," Antony said.

"Oh, yes, indeed. For the murder of my old friend. Such a dreadful affair."

"And Sir Nicholas Harding has been briefed for the defense."

"Now you do interest me, indeed you do. Such an able man . . . now, let me see, you are his nephew, are you not?"

"Yes, Mr. Benson, I'm in his chambers, and I'm deviling for him; so I hope you'll help me."

"Well, yes, of course; one would always wish to help a young man who is starting in his career. But Martin's murder: oh, dear me, that's a very different matter."

"But, Mr. Benson—"

"Now you are about to tell me I mustn't prejudge the case. And you're quite right, too, quite right. Besides, now I come to think of it, I don't know anything about it at all." He sat back, looking triumphant.

"But you knew Dr. Martin," Antony persisted.

"Yes, I knew him . . . oh, for many years."

"I have felt, from what I have been told, that you would be in his confidence, if anybody was."

Benson nodded. "Yes, I think I may say that."

"The police will have asked you about the telephone call he tried to make to you on the morning of his death. Were you able to help them?"

"Guesswork, young man. That wouldn't help the police . . . or you."

"Not directly. But it might lead somewhere." The old man shook his head with an air of vagueness. "Something might have happened that morning. . . . After all, you were with him only the evening before; he wouldn't have been calling up just to pass the time of day."

"No, he wouldn't do that." Benson looked at him then, and his eyes for a moment were clear and intelligent. "I expect there was something he wanted to ask me. Or perhaps he wanted to tell me he had grown afraid of Gerald."

"Well, I shouldn't think—after all, nothing had happened about that since he saw you. It must have been something he wanted you to help him with.''

"You may be right, I really cannot say.''

"But your own ideas . . .'' Benson shook his head slowly, and Antony sat back a moment to deliberate. He must be more open if he wanted results, though it seemed unlikely now that the old boy knew anything of interest. Still, it couldn't do any harm. . . .

"Do you ever remember Dr. Martin speaking of a French family he knew, at Pontoise, in the Compiègne district?''

Benson was silent for so long that Antony decided he had forgotten he was not alone, but at last he said, "Their name was Bonnard. They were . . . very dear to him, I think.''

"Then, he did speak of them?''

"Oh, yes, often. And then, after a time, he did not speak of them again. Only the once.''

"And then he said—?''

"He said he had killed them. He said he had sent a traitor into their home, a young man whom he had trusted; and that he himself had taught this young man all he needed to know to betray them. But that was many years ago; I have never forgotten it, but he never spoke of them again.''

"Did he tell you this man's name?''

"I do not think so. But perhaps I do not remember.''

"You say he never spoke of the Bonnards again; but did he ever mention the man who betrayed them?''

This time Benson did not reply, but turned to look directly at his questioner. "Why do you ask me this? Henry Martin is dead, and his murderer will stand his trial. And I do not think you will help him, or your uncle's case, by digging into a past that is dead and now should be forgotten.'' The look of brightness faded again from his eyes, leaving them vague and clouded. Antony knew the moment had passed, for the present at least, when the old man might have helped him, and he took his leave without very much delay.

CHAPTER SIX

IT WAS COLDER than ever outside. He thought longingly of home, and the warmth of the shabby, comfortable room; but better finish this series of interviews, now he had started. John would be impatient for something to get his teeth into; and certainly he had not much excuse, so far, for calling it a day. It wasn't often that his inability to drive troubled him; tonight he felt impatient with the disability, perhaps because his shoulder was more painful than usual. He was consigning Major Welwyn to the devil, silently but with deep feeling, as he looked around for a telephone booth.

In the event, he was left with only two interviews which had to be written into his notes. Arnold Fidler was sixteen years old, and Wallace Clark was sixty. Which left him with David Condon on his list, and James Maddison . . .

James Maddison and his wife had a nice, newish house, with nice, newish furniture, and a general air of being very comfortably established. Maddison was tall, and obviously putting on weight. He had dark, sleek hair, receding now at the temples; and if his expression verged on the self-satisfied, Antony was inclined to forgive a good deal because of the friendly lack of curiosity with which the other greeted his rather laborious explanation of his presence. Sheila Maddison was a good deal younger than her husband; small and fair, with fluffy hair and a lively manner. She sat on a low chair, and hugged her knees.

"We never dreamed anyone would want to see *us*," she said.

"Well, you see . . ." said Antony; but they didn't seem interested in why he had come. Which, he reflected, with a certain grim amusement, was probably just as well. It was enough that they were, for the moment, on the fringe of an event that was exciting and unusual; Sheila, at least, would probably make the most of the story for weeks to come.

"I'm trying to get a line on Dr. Martin's state of mind that morning. Had you met him before, Mr. Maddison?"

"No, I can't help you there. Dr. Forbes is our regular chap, not that we either of us need him very often. I didn't even know he was away until I got there—"

"Then you can't, I suppose, say if his manner was normal? Was there anything that struck you as unusual?"

"Not a thing. Well, I was more concerned with my own problems, you know; and after nearly an hour in the waiting room I was only too anxious to get it over and get away again."

"Yes, I suppose so." Antony assumed a downcast air. "I hope it wasn't anything serious. . . . Whatever it was took you to the doctor, I mean."

"Nothing but a spot of indigestion." He spoke deprecatingly, and Antony said, because something seemed to be called for, "Damned painful, anyway."

Sheila greeted this rather halfhearted sympathy with a grateful look, and said confidingly, "Jimmy suffers dreadfully sometimes."

Maddison laughed a little at that. "I don't think, you know, darling, that our guest is exactly interested—"

"No, well . . . tell him about the doctor then. You know you said . . ."

Strangely, he seemed put out by this reminder. "Nothing that could interest a lawyer, my dear."

"I assure you—" said Antony.

"Facts, not fancies. Isn't that right?"

"Well, yes. But if you gained a certain impression, that might of itself be a fact, you know."

"There was nothing."

"Something you told your wife." He gave Sheila Maddison his blandest smile.

"It was only that he nearly forgot to give Jimmy his prescription," she said. She sounded troubled, and looked doubtfully at her husband.

"He seemed preoccupied, then?" Antony looked at Maddison as he spoke, and the other gave a rather rueful laugh.

"Women!" he said. His annoyance seemed to have vanished. "You see how petty it sounds, Sheila. After all, the doctor wasn't a young man. He may have been habitually absent-minded."

"It was a dreadful thing to have happened." She seemed anxious to turn the subject now. "I couldn't believe my ears when they gave it out on the nine o'clock news, and I said, 'But that's Dr. Forbes's address!' But you didn't know the name of the one you saw, only Robert said there wouldn't very likely have been two of them, doing locum at the same place."

Maddison smiled at his visitor's look of bewilderment, and said with a trace of apology in his tone: "Robert Pitt is our 'lodger'; he was quite right in his assumption, as it turned out—"

"He's something frightfully important at the Ministry of Supply," Sheila put in. (Antony was beginning to recognize in her a genius for inessentials.)

"—but I wasn't sure till next morning, when there was a picture in the paper." Maddison had probably decided long ago that if he were to allow his sentences to be diverted by his wife's interruptions he might never succeed in completing one again. "Sheila's right, it makes you think, a thing like that. He seemed a nice old boy. The medicine he gave me was the usual muck—" ("But those capsules do *work*, darling, when the pain is bad.") "—and I don't suppose I shall take the advice he gave me. But still."

"Well, I'm sorry to have disturbed your evening." Antony was beginning to find the room stuffy, and even thought of the frosty street outside with pleasurable anticipation. But Maddison waved aside his protests: Sheila was going to make some coffee, surely he had time for that?

And Antony sat back in his chair again, with no more than a momentary regret that his liberation was postponed. He was fishing in the dark, of course, and probably in unstocked waters; but this man was at least somewhere near the age he was looking for, and their talk might seem more illuminating in retrospect, after he had talked to John Welwyn again.

David Condon's domestic arrangements were of a different nature altogether. He was in lodgings in one of the semidetached houses two streets beyond Dr. Forbes's residence; his supper was still on the table when Antony was shown in, but he got up immediately, waving aside the newcomer's protests, and only pausing to dog-ear carefully the book he had been reading. "You're not interrupting me," he said. "Finished half an hour ago." He looked with disfavor at the congealing remains of his meal, and added abruptly, "Take you upstairs. It's a bit cold, but we shan't be disturbed."

He was much more slightly built than Maddison, though he had a heavy pair of shoulders. Antony, following obediently up the second flight of stairs, thought that though diet might have something to do with his thinness, temperament was more probably the cause. Condon seemed full of nervous energy, and his conversation moved from subject to subject as jerkily as his body moved from place to place.

His bedroom was at the top of the house, a pleasant enough room with a sloping ceiling and a dormer window. It was undeniably cold, but Condon busied himself with an old-fashioned oil heater which he dragged out from the corner by the wardrobe. "It'll warm up presently," he promised. And smiled at his guest, so that for the first time the worried look vanished, and he was revealed as the possessor of undeniable good looks. "Why do landladies always have daughters?" he demanded. "This one's fifteen, full of questions. Well, she won't interrupt us here."

Antony was looking about him with interest. The room had obviously been decorated by an amateur hand; he would not have suspected Condon of so much practicality. And there were books everywhere. Following his eyes, their owner said with his customary abruptness, "Got to keep up to date. Can't afford not to in my line of business. Chemist," he added, in answer to Antony's look of inquiry. "Research work. I'm with Hepworth's, in their Croydon lab."

"That must be very interesting," said Antony, deliberately trite. The other didn't appear put out, but gave a bark of laughter and said amiably, "Oh, I'm sure! If it isn't your subject—"

"Well . . . no."

"That's all right then. What's all this about the doctor?" He accepted Antony's careful explanation without comment, and seemed to be giving the matter careful thought. He said at last, "Try everything. Only way . . . I see that. But I don't think I can help you."

"No," said Antony. In spite of himself, his voice reflected his weariness, and the other went on with quick perception.

"Dreary business, is it? I'll tell you what I can and you can see for yourself, but I'm afraid—"

"I shall be grateful," said Antony. And meant it.

"Well, I thought it was Dr. Forbes, you know. I mean, I hadn't been before, so I didn't know it was a locum till we got talking . . . National Insurance . . . you know. He wasn't a young man, and I thought he was worried—no, I really thought that at the time, not just afterward. Only went because you have to before you can get your eyes tested, but he was a proper sort of doctor, I can tell you that. Gave me the certificate, of course; felt he was interested—bedside manner, I suppose—soothing, these days. Said I should learn to relax . . ." How vividly the doctor was brought to Antony's mind by this reference to the brief homilies he was accustomed to give his patients! "My dear boy, if you would only . . ." His expression grew bleak at the memory, and Condon, who seemed to miss very little, broke off what he was saying and asked shrewdly, "You knew Dr. Martin?"

"Yes, I . . . very well."

"But you're acting for . . ." He paused, and obviously revised his sentence. "For the man accused of killing him," he said at length. And added, with a rather engaging frankness, "Got to be careful. Nothing you like better than a good slander action, I dare say."

Antony grinned. He was finding his companion refreshing, but at the same time his talk with John Welwyn was vividly in his mind. "No witnesses," he said, with a show of regret. "But to answer your question . . ." He stopped, and his expression grew blank again. "Well, as a matter of fact, I don't think I can answer it."

"Stupid remark," said Condon rapidly. "Have some beer, and forget it."

"I'm interrupting you," said Antony, but made no move to go. The other disregarded the objection.

"Chance to learn something about your line of business," he remarked. "Too good to miss!"

So he rewrote his notes for Geoffrey Horton, Mrs. Goodbody's statement (the bare facts, and no comment on them); what the neighbors had said, and the teashop waitress, negative information at best; and a brief account of his conversation with Benson. For Welwyn, Benson again, and Maddison, and Condon. He sat looking at the results of his labors for what seemed to Jenny an unduly long time; and after a while she put down her book and said, "You're worried, Antony."

He came back with something of a jerk to the present; pushed the reports out of the way, and picked up the untidy sheaf of papers on which he had made his first notes. He came across to the fire, and scattered the pieces of paper over it so that the flames danced hungrily for a moment. "It's nothing," he said. "A long day, and damn' all to show for it . . ." He saw the disbelief in her eyes, and added, quickly, "Did Uncle Nick tell you I'd been to see John?"

"I don't mind, Antony . . . truly!"

"Don't you, love?" His tone was dry. "May I ask what he *did* say to you?"

Jenny spoke carefully, her eyes on his face. "He said, 'I'm afraid you may have to resign yourself to the fact that your husband is getting mixed up with that gang of thugs in Whitehall again.' " Her anxiety faded as she saw his frown give way to laughter. ''And I'd rather know,'' she added.

''Of course. But there's nothing . . . a watching brief, John said, and that's fair enough.'' Her gaze was steady and disconcerting, and he looked down again at the fire. ''I *couldn't* refuse,'' he said, after a moment, and there was something like desperation in his voice.

CHAPTER SEVEN

THE INTERVIEW with Gerry Martin which Geoffrey had arranged for the following morning achieved little beyond Sir Nicholas's exasperation. Gerry was going to prove a bad witness; so much had been obvious in the Magistrate's Court, and needed no confirmation. And while it might be unreasonable to feel that this increased his own responsibility in the matter, Antony had found before that reason, unfortunately, had sometimes only too little to do with the way he felt.

They came out from the prison into the bleak grayness of the January morning, with Sir Nicholas a pace or two ahead of his companions growling his discontent to himself; of the two younger men, Horton's expression was apprehensive and Antony's resigned. They turned toward the main road, where a taxi might reasonably be expected to be found; Geoffrey's car, a sports model, had been vetoed by Sir Nicholas, and not without cause, his nephew felt. Ahead of them a well-built young woman was dawdling along; Antony noticed her idly, because the disconsolate droop of her shoulders contrasted so sharply with the flamboyance which was evident in her attire. But he was unprepared for her sudden movement, just before they came up to her; she swung round abruptly, and stood blocking the pavement, so that Sir Nicholas had to halt rather quickly to avoid a collision.

"You chaps been to the prison?" she inquired.

Sir Nicholas inclined his head. And added gently, after

a brief pause which invited her to continue if she wished: "Is there any way we can help you, madam?"

"Well, I don't suppose . . . only to tell me how to get in, to see somebody, you know."

"I'm afraid that's not too easy. You see, we're rather by way of being privileged parties. Who was it you wished to see?"

The girl's eyes hardened, and her tone was rough as she replied. "You wouldn't be press, by any chance? Reporters, and such?"

"I assure you . . ." Sir Nicholas seemed a little taken aback. A sudden fancy possessed itself of Antony's mind, and without pausing to reflect on its unlikelihood he came up beside his uncle and interrupted without scruple.

"Are you by any chance Miss Margaret Cooper?" He both expected her defiant "Yes, I am!" and was astonished when it came. A guess if ever there was one, and nothing to go on either. "Poor little Daisy" indeed! She must be at least three inches taller than Gerry. "We've just come from seeing Mr. Martin," he added by way of explanation. "We're his lawyers."

"Oh, I see." She looked uncertainly from one to the other of them, and seemed reassured by what she saw. "There wouldn't be any chance of me seeing him, I don't suppose?" she asked wistfully.

"Not at present, I think. But Mr. Horton here will do his best to arrange it for you. Meanwhile, if we may have the privilege of escorting you back to town . . ." Sir Nicholas displayed no surprise, only pleasure at the unexpected encounter. And indeed there was something very likable about Daisy, quite apart from her more obvious attractions.

"I wouldn't want to trouble you—"

"No trouble at all, my dear young lady. You see, I wished to get in touch with you . . ." They began to move again toward the main road, and Geoffrey grinned expressively at his companion as they fell into step again behind Miss Cooper and her escort. Sir Nicholas was in full flight now, and seemed, thought his nephew undutifully, to be having much the same effect on the girl as an unusually fascinating cobra might have had on a rather simple-minded rabbit.

In any event, they went back to chambers, where Sir Nicholas's clerk, old Mr. Mallory, would have lent an air of respectability to a far more unorthodox gathering. Daisy settled herself in one of the big leather armchairs, and her expression became gradually less wary. Antony threw some coal on the fire, and retreated to his favorite vantage point by the window, leaving the field clear for his uncle. The girl seemed relaxed now, but no sense in confusing her; and Uncle Nick seemed to have taken one of his unexpected fancies to her.

There was a silence, broken at length by Daisy. "You said you wanted me." The sharpness in her tone was more likely owing to nervousness than to impatience. Sir Nicholas smiled at her.

"I'm sure you want to help Gerry Martin."

"Oh, yes, I do!" Her voice betrayed her eagerness, but she added a moment later, "Not but what we might mean different things by that, you and me."

"My only concern, Miss Cooper, is with the case the police have against him."

"You wouldn't be thinking I might be got to give him up, if talked to right?"

"Nothing of the kind!"

"Well, then!" But she added belligerently, before he had time to speak, "Because I'll tell you straight it isn't like that, me and Gerry." She looked into the heart of the fire, and went on slowly. "Oh, I know his faults. He's lazy, and he can't keep a job, and he isn't above borrowing a fiver when pressed . . . and none too particular about paying you back, either. But he's treated me right, treated me like a lady . . . lovely manners he has, you know. And we've had fun together." She looked again at the barrister, and her tone was challenging now. "Not but what I'd give him up any time I thought it would be right for him; but then it wouldn't need no lawyers to make me."

"I'm beginning to think," said Sir Nicholas gravely, "that would be the very worst thing that could happen to him."

She laughed a little self-consciously, but went on steadily enough. "Well, you're not one to blame me for speaking my mind, and it won't do any harm to clear the air."

"No harm at all," said Sir Nicholas cordially. "But what I do want, Miss Cooper, is your account of Gerry's actions—both on the day of Dr. Martin's death and on the one before it." She eyed him doubtfully. "I know all about the quarrel, of course; Gerry told me that himself. But your evidence may be useful—"

"You mean, how he seemed, and that?" He nodded. "Well, I'll tell you one thing. He didn't come back to me that day from doing a murder, like they say. Puzzled, more than anything, he seemed—"

"If you could, perhaps, go back—"

"The Thursday? I wasn't expecting him till evening. But there, I never minded with Gerry. So he said the old man was angry, and maybe he'd stay a day or two and see if it blew over before he went looking for lodgings of his own, you know."

"Was he upset by what had happened?"

"Oh, no. That wasn't his way . . . only to be sorry he was missing a free bed and board, you see. Not but what he wasn't fond of the doctor, but Gerry has his own ways, and no use expecting him to be just like other people."

"Did he think the doctor was likely to overlook the disagreement?"

"He didn't say anything about it till next day, and then just that he was going over to Streatham. But afterward—"

"What time did he get back?"

"Round about five. There's a train direct from Streatham Hill to Victoria, you know." (It seemed obvious that the trend of the police's questions had impressed upon her that this was an important point, for she looked anxiously at Sir Nicholas as she spoke.) "He had plenty of time to have tea, as he said," she insisted. "He said he'd wanted to think things out, but he couldn't have done that if he'd just killed the old man . . . could he?"

"He wanted to think things out—?" prompted Sir Nicholas.

"Well, he said he didn't understand it. He'd expected the doctor to come round, sooner or later; but not to . . . well, to lose interest, sort of."

"Can you explain a little more particularly?"

She spread her hands—an oddly defenseless gesture from so large and self-possessed a young person. "He said the doctor seemed to have forgotten about their tiff. Only when Gerry spoke of it, he seemed to think it didn't matter any more." She paused, and frowned a little, concentrating. "And he said once, when the telephone rang, the doctor snatched it up as if he was expecting a call. But it was just a patient."

"And after that?"

"Nothing, really. Gerry came away after a bit, because they didn't seem to be getting anywhere. It wasn't very long after he got back that the police came. Well, there's nothing else to tell you, really."

"There is one thing I must ask you, Miss Cooper. Did the police search your apartment?"

"Yes . . . later that evening. I couldn't stop them, could I?"

"Certainly not. I'm sure their warrant was in order."

"Well, I didn't have nothing I shouldn't, so I don't suppose it matters. Not but what it isn't very nice—"

"Miss Cooper! You know—don't you?—what I want to ask you."

Antony, watching intently now, saw her hands clasp together in her lap. In the chair he had taken near the desk, Geoffrey Horton stirred with sudden uneasiness. Daisy was staring at Sir Nicholas, and her expression was one of dawning horror. She said, at last, "About . . . about the stocking?"

"Exactly."

"I'd never have let it happen if I'd known, but it was nothing to do with Gerry!"

"Then you must explain to me, so that I can explain to the court when the time comes. You know the police found an odd stocking among several pairs in your drawer, and you must realize how that will sound to the jury."

"I wouldn't have let anything like that happen to Gerry—"

"So now you must help me. Did you know the stocking was there?"

"Of course I did!" She seemed astonished by the question, and suddenly became voluble. "You always buy two pairs of stockings alike . . . any girl will tell you that. Then if one goes of each pair, you still have one pair left."

"That sounds reasonable."

"It's better than reasonable . . . it's true!" said Daisy forcefully.

"Yes, I'm sure. You will have to repeat that in court, you know. You won't mind that?"

"What d'you take me for?" Daisy seemed to have recovered her spirits. "Tell you the truth," she confided, "what I couldn't stick was the feeling I'd let Gerry down."

Antony moved from his place by the window, and came across to the fire. He was inclined to be annoyed with himself that this obvious solution had not occurred to him; but it had been worth it, he thought, to see his uncle's face. He looked down at Daisy and said, "The police took the single stocking?"

"I've been telling you—"

"Yes, I know. But the other pair . . . the pair it matched?"

"Well, they couldn't take those, I'd got them on."

"May we have them?" He glanced at his uncle, and for a moment allowed his amusement expression. "Exhibit A, sir," he murmured.

Daisy was sitting up straight, and seemed to be working out the implications of this request. Presently she looked up, smoothing her stocking and stretching out a shapely leg in a gesture of unconscious coquetry. "Wouldn't it be more effective if I wore them in court?" she said.

In deference to Sir Nicholas's feelings, Antony and Geoffrey undertook, jointly, to persuade her that this was not altogether a good idea.

Antony lunched with Geoffrey Horton, and was grinning to himself when he returned to chambers and pushed open the door of his uncle's room. "He isn't very pleased with us," he confided.

Sir Nicholas sat back and removed his spectacles. "I suppose," he hazarded, "he has become aware that our approach to this case is not precisely orthodox?"

"He'd be a fool if he didn't realize it." Antony was shrugging out of his overcoat as he spoke. "However, if we do get a line on Morris I don't expect John will feel there's any harm in being open about *that*."

"Welwyn will keep you dangling just so long as suits his purpose," said Sir Nicholas bluntly. "We shall have to deal with that as the occasion arises. And speaking of Morris—"

"You want to know how I got on yesterday." He crossed to the desk, and looked down at the spread of papers. "Have you time for a session, sir? It was quite a day."

"There's nothing pressing. Mallory tells me we shall be in court on Thursday with *Procter* versus *Halligan*. But we'll leave that for the moment." He looked up and smiled at his nephew. "Did I detect in what you said just now a certain hardening of your opinion? Concerning Morris, I mean."

"It isn't only Morris," said Antony glumly. "I'd better tell you about Mrs. Goodbody."

Sir Nicholas was looking grave by the time he had heard the story out. "I gather you think the dark man had just come from killing Dr. Martin?"

"Well—don't you? I also think the dark man was Morris; and the other (probably) Ohlendorff. That would account for his sudden interest in me—I mean, I don't suppose he even knew I was alive. But it would be quite easy to trace me, once he knew."

"You still may be mistaken."

Antony shook his head, and said positively, "To my mind, the bit about the phone call clinches the matter. I bet Morris was shaken by what he heard."

"Have you told Welwyn?"

"Not yet. I—oh, well, I think he'd just laugh."

"But you're in this at his suggestion."

"Yes, I know. He thinks if I can identify Morris for him, Morris may lead him to the man he wants. If I suggest at this stage it may be Ohlendorff he'll think I'm halfway to Bedlam."

"All the same—"

"No!" said Antony.

"Well, can we call this Mrs. Goodbody?" Sir Nicholas seemed to be in a mood of unusual compliance. "If we produce Morris, of course."

"Not even that. I don't think her sight is all that good, and she never even saw the dark man's face."

"Then we must take some other line." The older man was philosophical. "What about the doctor's Friday morning patients?"

"I've got a description now—vague enough in all conscience—that could have fitted two of them."

"I see. When you say the description is vague—?"

"I mean it, unfortunately. He had dark hair and brown eyes; was five foot eleven, eleven stone six, and twenty-seven years old. I ask you!"

"I see what you mean. These two men, now—"

"Are both in their late thirties; both dark, though one has a good deal more hair left than the other. Maddison is an interior decorator, married, and has put on weight with the years. A comfortable fourteen stone now, I should say. The other chap, Condon, is a research chemist, and inclined to be scraggy. You pays your money and takes your choice—I'm playing no favorites."

"And Welwyn, I suppose, is investigating both these men?"

"Oh, yes. I had some considerable talk with both of them, and nothing emerged that could be regarded as definite either way. I mean, if somebody who knew them before the war could swear to identity . . . I expect something will turn up."

"But, meanwhile—"

"They both have an alibi, of sorts. Mrs. Maddison mentioned a lodger, a chap called Pitt, Ministry of Supply. He was with Maddison, that Friday afternoon, and they also spent the evening together. John seems to know about Pitt, presumably from the 'check-up' he described so feelingly. I was rather fancying the pair of them as villains . . . until I talked to Condon and he mentioned where he had been for the week end." He paused, and looked at his uncle—who declined to be moved by this obvious attempt to introduce a note of drama. "His chief is Sir Francis Potter . . . the germ chap, you know. Condon says he traveled down to Guildford on Friday morning to stay with him and confer about some discovery he has made."

"That sounds like an alibi that wouldn't depend on one man's word."

"So I thought. But Potter's by way of being a recluse, I hear. So it may be—"

"And I cannot approve of your referring to a person of Dr. Potter's eminence—I believe he prefers that mode of address—as 'the germ chap.'" Sir Nicholas reproduced the phrase with an air of distaste, and Antony laughed.

"Well, you must admit, he makes a fine sinister background," he said. "John was furious; he even accused me of dragging both Dr. Potter and Pitt in as red herrings. . . . I'd quite a job convincing him of my sincerity."

"In the circumstances, I don't altogether blame him. However, what are your plans?"

"I promised to see John early tomorrow morning. He should have some information for me by then. Carr has gone over to Pontoise, where the Bonnards used to live. There's just a chance he might pick up something; after all, the last information they had was when things were still very unsettled."

"I was thinking that perhaps you should hand over your work to someone else for the present. If Welwyn makes demands on your time—"

"I suppose that would be sensible." He did not sound elated by the prospect, but added firmly after a moment, "Derek's pretty full, I think. There's Carter, though. I heard—"

"He looks hungry," said Sir Nicholas. "However, I believe him to be intelligent."

"Yes, sir. So I think. And even the Procter brief wouldn't be very difficult to pick up," he added—and if there was a suggestion of wistfulness in his tone (for Mr. Procter's affairs were of unusual complexity and fascination), his uncle ignored it and went on firmly to more detailed arrangements.

CHAPTER EIGHT

ANTONY WAS PROMPT at Whitehall next morning, and found Welwyn sorting his mail. At this time of day the Major was never at his best, and he returned Antony's greeting somewhat sourly, adding, "Well, what have you got to say for yourself?" in a distinctly aggressive tone.

"Boot's on the other leg," said Antony, perching in his favorite place on the edge of the desk, and thereby disarranging some of the papers and bringing an anguished cry of protest from Welwyn.

"Don't do that! I told you, Carr's away; life's hell without him." He arranged things to his own satisfaction, and then asked, "What do you mean, anyway?"

"I mean, you asked me to come. I thought you had some news."

"So I have, a little. However, you talk first, while I finish with these."

"I told you already." Antony's tone had a suggestion of mutiny, but seeing that the other was not yet prepared for speech he went briefly over his activities of the previous day. When he had finished Welwyn snorted, "Helpful!"

"That's much what Uncle Nick says."

"Well, I'm doing my best to check up on these two men of yours. And whether their alibis hold water." John Welwyn pushed aside his correspondence, leaving it, as far as Antony could make out, in as great disorder as ever. He found a pencil and began to scribble on the blotting pad. "I'm not having much luck with Morris's past," he admitted.

"So you said."

"The trouble is, there's damn' all information to be had about him. The description I gave you came from an old file. Nobody remembers him clearly, I don't think that's surprising. The fellows who were training with him are mostly dead, or abroad and out of reach. He had no family."

"Sounds hopeful."

"There is just one possible source of information, not a very good one. An ex-R.A.F. pilot called Henderson. He was at the Bonnards' farm when they were arrested, and was taken with them. He was on his way out, after escaping. It was pretty bad luck."

"But not for us. Get him here, and let him have a look at . . ." His voice trailed off as Welwyn shook his head.

"Unfortunately, that's not possible. He's blind."

"Oh!" Just for a moment this seemed an obstacle, impossible to surmount. "But I may as well see him, I suppose."

"This afternoon, I thought—if you can manage it." Antony was amused by his companion's attitude; the words were a concession to conventional politeness, but it was obvious from his tone that Welwyn did not really envisage a rebuff. He said meekly, "I'm at your disposal," and John nodded and made a note on his blotter, and went on smoothly to the next item on his own single-minded agenda.

"There's one other thing—"

"Tell me the worst!"

"I told you Carr had gone to Pontoise. He seems to be in difficulties . . . mainly linguistic. He says the locals tell him that Mlle Bonnard did not die, but returned there after the war. When he asks how she survived, and where she is now, they all look at one another and shrug their shoulders. He seems to find it exasperating. However, he's got an idea someone more fluent would fare better."

Antony grinned. "Very likely. I remember Carr's French—nearly as bad as yours."

"It's worth a try, I think." Welwyn ignored the thrust,

and regarded him consideringly. "Let me have your passport, if it's out of date. I'll make all the arrangements."

"Thanks. And what about your end? Have you turned up anything on my two prospects?"

"Very little, so far. Nothing to put either of them out of the running."

"This Ministry chap, Robert Pitt . . . you don't feel there might be anything there, I suppose?"

"I do not. He's been with the Ministry since he was demobbed. Clever chap, considered very reliable."

"And before that?"

"Came from the north somewhere. Sharp's got it in hand, but there's nothing so far and not likely to be, in my opinion."

"I seem to remember," Antony reminded him gently, "being lectured on the virtue of having an open mind."

"Well, there's that. But I don't want you going off at half cock, Antony. We can't afford talk, and a few questions in the wrong place—"

"You make me wonder," remarked the younger man reflectively, "why on earth you chose to drag me into this business at all, since you obviously don't trust my discretion." He got to his feet as he spoke, and Welwyn looked up at him in something like alarm.

"Now, don't go taking a huff! I told you—"

"Forget it," the other recommended. "If you won't allow me Pitt and Maddison as villains, what about my alternative?"

"I don't think much of that either," said Welwyn frankly. "I'll grant you Condon as a possibility if you like, but Potter—"

"He might be somebody's grandmother," said Antony, but seeing that his companion did not take the reference he went on, "If you don't fancy him, have you checked on whether Condon was really at Guildford on Friday afternoon?"

"Not yet. You don't seem to realize," Welwyn complained, "that we have to move delicately. This peacetime operating is the devil and all."

"I'll believe you. There's just one thing, John, about

Friday morning: what do you think the doctor wanted to speak to Benson about?''

"Guessing was never my strong suit." Welwyn's tone was repressive.

"No, but this is interesting. Benson was in his confidence about Morris and what had happened to the Bonnards. That projected phone call adds a little probability to the idea that Dr. Martin had seen and recognized Morris that morning.''

"Do you think so?"

"Yes, I do. Don't be so damned apathetic, John. I say it does mean something.''

"But Benson didn't know—''

"How would he? Anyway, I think you should keep an eye on him, he might be able to recognize Morris, too. In fact, that was most likely why the doctor wanted him: because he himself wasn't sure.''

Welwyn said, "Nonsense!" and Antony grinned.

"You never would encourage my wilder flights, would you? To get back to the point—''

"If you can prove Morris strangled Dr. Martin, well and good. But I may as well tell you now, Antony, I'd want a little time—''

"I see." He picked up his hat, but made no move to go. "If we find him we give him enough rope to hang himself and his associates, too, if any.''

"Exactly.''

"I'll bear it in mind. Of course," he added, with a sudden look of amusement, "we may be barking up the wrong tree altogether.''

Welwyn relaxed and laughed a little. "That had occurred to me," he said.

The next job was to hand over to Carter, who proved competent though uninspiring and—fortunately, Antony felt, for Sir Nicholas's sanity—did not need anything explained twice. Their business together was therefore completed in good time, and Antony was able to leave him, surrounded by notes and documents, and to wish him joy of their perusal.

Even so, it was well into the afternoon before he was

free to set out for Haslemere. He thought Jenny sounded subdued when he phoned her, and he left for the station in no very cheerful frame of mind.

The Hendersons' house was an old one, set in grounds which gave a pleasant air of seclusion. Antony was received by Mrs. Henderson, a gray-haired lady whose undoubted kindness of manner was backed, he instinctively felt, by a good deal of strength of purpose. She led him to a large room at the back of the house and left him with her son.

At first glance it was a strange room, being dominated by a grand piano and otherwise rather sparsely furnished. Long windows opened onto the garden, and near one of these a man was sitting. He got up to greet Antony, and waved him towards a chair. As they seated themselves Antony realized that the room was odd to his eyes because it was arranged to meet the needs of a blind man—stripped of inessentials, bare of ornament. He looked at the piano and then back at his host, who had taken up a pipe and was busying himself with the filling of it: a man in his middle thirties, pleasant-looking and with an air of serenity which was, in the circumstances, surprising.

"I'm a fool not to have realized it. You must be Peter Henderson."

"That's my name. Ought I to know you?"

"No, but I've heard you broadcast, of course."

"I was lucky, to have an interest in music." There was no hint of self-pity in his tone, and he went on with a smile, "My old chief told me to help you and not ask questions, so—"

"I'm looking for information about a man called Teddy Morris. It's rather important, I hope you can help me."

"I will if I can. Is Morris alive then?"

"I don't know. I believe so."

Henderson's expression hardened, then he laughed. "Hatred is not an emotion I enjoy, and I've been at great pains to excuse his actions to myself. Why should his being alive make a difference? It isn't logical, but it's easier to think charitably about a dead man than a live one."

"That's quite natural."

"Is it? But you didn't come here to discuss my feelings. What do you want to know?"

"Everything you can tell me about Morris. Appearance, habits, anything. Start when you first met him, if you like."

"I was already at the Bonnards' farm when he came there; you know the background, I expect?"

"Vaguely," said Antony. "Tell me about them."

Henderson leaned back, fumbled for matches, and relit his pipe. "They were a very united family, that was the most remarkable thing about them, I think; and good, in a simple, unselfconscious way that I hadn't encountered before. There was Madame, little and round—rather like an apple: shiny, and crisp, and not too sweet. She ran everybody around her—me included, within two hours of my arrival. Papa worshiped her. He was a thin, gray man, with a big mustache and a perpetual look of worry; then he would go off into peals of laughter about something quite small, and you realized the worried look didn't mean anything at all. As for the three boys, they all took after their mother, small and very strong, but with their father's habit of unexpected, boisterous merriment. I didn't know them long enough, or well enough, to find out the differences between them; superficially, they were very much alike. I was there two weeks before Morris turned up— there was some sort of a holdup and I'd been told to lie low for a bit; naturally, I was pretty well confined to the house, and saw most of Mme. Bonnard . . . and Madeleine." He lingered a little, unconsciously, over the name, though his voice remained as level as ever. "They were good people—I said that before, didn't I?—kind and good . . . and Madeleine was beautiful. I was going back, after the war; she was very young, but I wouldn't have changed, and I don't think she would have either. But that isn't what you want to hear. About Morris . . ." He stopped again, frowning. "I'll try to be as accurate as I can; he was a big chap, six foot—perhaps not quite; broad shoulders, heavy built but light on his feet. He'd been a commando, you know; he'd be rather the popular conception of one, I should think, very quick and active."

"Hair and eyes?" said Antony.

"Black hair, straight and smooth, the kind that's always tidy. I don't remember the color of his eyes."

"Never mind. How old was he?"

"Late twenties, I should think."

"Can you remember any special ways he had?"

"No . . . no, I don't think so. Only what I've told you, he was always on the go. He liked a drink, but I never saw him take too much. He smoked—chain-smoked when he could get cigarettes. He liked women; he liked Madeleine." He paused . . . and then went on in the same even tone. "He was a pleasant chap, no getting away from it; of course, I knew nothing of the work he was doing, but everyone seemed to think him very capable. He wasn't at the farm when the Germans came, but I thought he was in the same boat with the rest of us. It was very sudden. I didn't have time to get away from the house—once they searched, of course, my presence was enough to damn the family, without anything else. I never saw any of them again." It was now apparent that whatever composure he might bring to his daily life, this retelling of a bitter experience was more of a strain than he would have wished to admit.

Antony prompted quietly, "And what then?"

"They were taking me back; I took a chance, two days later, to make a run for it. I got away; I don't remember much about it except the pain in my head after the shooting. And then, I don't know how long after, I woke up in a loft, lying on hay, with bandages on my eyes. I didn't know what had happened; there was a girl . . . I thought she was Madeleine. I expect I was pretty sick, and I couldn't see, you know. She didn't say much, and when she did speak it was very quietly. Then, one day, someone else came up: the doctor. He'd been before, of course. But not when I was conscious. I was much better then, and when I heard her speak to him I knew it wasn't Madeleine; and after a bit it came over me what had happened. The doctor was trying to tell me gently that I wouldn't see again, and I was asking what had happened to the Bonnards. Only they didn't know. Later they were able to find out that they were all dead. And who had betrayed them." He was silent a moment, and then he laughed—an unconvincing sound. "An ordinary enough story. And not even pertinent to your inquiry. Forgive me."

"As a matter of fact," said Antony, "I'm interested in everything that happened then. Did you pursue any further inquiries? I'm wondering if anybody remains at Pontoise who might be able to identify Morris."

"I did go back, once, when the war was over. I don't think you'd find anybody now who knew Morris; his circle was a narrow one, you know, and the local Resistance was completely scattered when he went over to the Germans. Some got away, but heaven knows what happened to them later. I asked about Madeleine; it was hard to believe she was dead, but the man I spoke to was quite definite. His voice was very bitter when he told me; I thought perhaps he'd been fond of her himself, so I didn't ask him any more."

"Do you think you could recognize Morris's voice after all this time?"

"I'm sure I couldn't. If I'd met him after I was blind it might be different; even so, it's a long time."

"It is, indeed."

"You have my sympathies." There was a tinge of amusement in Henderson's voice now. "Annoying to have only one witness to identify, and he unable to see."

"It only leaves me one other question: do you think Morris would have been likely to gain or lose weight as he grew older?"

"I should think . . . well, come to think of it, I haven't the faintest idea."

"I wasn't very hopeful."

"I'm only sorry I can't be more help." He heard his visitor getting up and added, "Are you in a hurry? Mother was talking of supper, and she'll be glad to meet you."

Antony left some time later, fortified by a warm meal and some pleasant conversation. Mrs. Henderson put her coat on and walked down the lane with him to show him the beginning of a short cut to the station; the opportunity seemed too good to miss, and he asked her bluntly, "Has your son ever spoken to you of Madeleine Bonnard?"

"Many times. I don't think he will ever quite get over

losing her; it is hard to believe, but losing his sight was a small thing to him by comparison."

"I have information—it's second-hand, so it may not be accurate—that she is alive."

"You haven't told Peter?" She spoke quickly, and added, as though to herself, "Hope can be so very cruel."

"I said nothing to him. If it should be true, though—what then?"

"He was told so very definitely . . . and then, surely she would have tried to get in touch with him."

"I've no opinion to give you on that point. I'm going to France tomorrow to try to find her. If I do I shall ask her to come to England to see if she can make an identification for us."

"Bring her to me." She spoke impulsively. Antony shook his head.

"Think about it, first. To speak frankly, there is one obvious explanation of her being alive still; it may not be the true one, but if it is it might not recommend her to you."

"I would not blame her."

"Nor I. But it is not what her life may have been that concerns you, but what it may have made her. It would be very hard on your son to have her restored to him and find she was a stranger."

"But you said she might come to England. If she is alive I must see her."

"I'll let you know, as soon as I know anything myself."

"When I see her I shall know. Mr. Maitland, you don't know what this may mean to Peter."

He smiled at her. "I don't mean to be impertinent, but you remind me of my wife. She'd take on half a dozen dragons any day, on my behalf."

"Well," she said, speaking more lightly, "I hope poor Madeleine won't turn out to be a dragon. Even so, the final decision must be Peter's; I'd like you to know I realize that."

He phoned Welwyn from Waterloo, and found without surprise that a seat had been booked for him on a flight for Paris quite early the following day. It was late when he got home; there was no frost that night, and the air was damp and only pleasantly cool; a small breeze stirred in the trees that grew in the center of the square. He was walking near their enclosing railing, looking up at the sky through the bare, overhanging branches, and fostering a pleasant illusion of being still in the country, when he stopped suddenly, grateful for the shadow and for the invisibility it afforded him.

There was a street lamp on the corner about four doors beyond Sir Nicholas's house; a little beyond that again a man stood, smoking. His outline was clear enough; he was tall and broad-shouldered, and wore a dark coat and hat. That was all that could be said with certainty, but Antony thought again of the quiet figure he had seen four days before, who also, he had felt, was standing and watching—and for no obvious or innocent reason. He had done his best to dismiss the incident from his mind; but now the same uneasiness took possession of him, and though he told himself impatiently that it might well be without foundation he knew that this time it would not be so easily pushed away.

He thought for a moment before he moved and could never have said afterward whether it was fear or good sense that took him straight to his own front door, without further investigation. True, Welwyn's game called for caution, but was that what had weighed with him?

There was a light in the study, but no sound of voices. Antony guesed, rightly, that Sir Nicholas was alone, now, and that Jenny had gone early to bed. He stood a moment, wondering whether he should give his uncle a brief report; then he crossed the hall and went quietly up the stairs.

Jenny lay in the darkness and listened for his footsteps. The wind that stirred the curtains was faintly damp, and she sniffed a little but decided regretfully that not the most violent effort of imagination could invest it with an authentic country fragrance. She heard at last what she had been waiting for. The front door opened quietly, and there was the click of the light switch in the hall. She waited for Antony to come across to the bedroom door.

He didn't come straight away. She could follow his

progress easily enough. First, the hall cupboard, then the
bathroom, then the kitchen door; he was only a moment in
there—she reflected, sadly, that the glass of milk she had
left must have gone down the sink. Then the light went off
in the hall again, and at last he came in.

"You can put on the light, darling. I'm not asleep."

"I can manage, thanks." His voice sounded remote.
She heard him moving quietly about in the darkness, and
said no more until she judged he was ready for bed. Then
she said, "Antony," and he came to stand beside her, so
that she could see him silhouetted against the faint light
from the window. After a moment he sat down on the side
of the bed, and fumbled for her hand; his was unexpectedly cold, and not quite steady. Jenny held it tightly and
wriggled herself into something nearer a sitting position.

After a long silence he leaned forward to switch on the
shaded lamp by the bed. He was very pale, but Jenny was
conscious of a relaxation of strain, as of a crisis passed.
She smiled at him encouragingly, and after a moment he
grinned back at her.

"Well, now." He raised her hand to rub against his
cheek and gave her a look, half rueful, half amused.

CHAPTER NINE

THE PARISH PRIEST of Pontoise was a big man, with the air of one who had been, in his day, an athlete. If his hair was gray now, it was still thick and curly; beneath heavy brows his eyes were blue and mild; he had a fierce beak of a nose, a thin mouth and a jutting chin. Antony eyed him with some trepidation.

"I am seeking Mlle Madeleine Bonnard, Father."

That brought a sharp look and a gruff query. "What do you want with her, monsieur?"

"I am a barrister; it is a question of identification; I believe she may be able to help me. At first it was believed that Mlle Bonnard was dead, but one has told me she lives. After that, I could learn nothing. And so, I come to you, *mon père*."

"And rightly." The curé was suddenly genial. "And was he, too, *avocat*—that other one who has asked for her?"

"My colleague," said Antony.

The priest chuckled. "That is comical!" He paused, contemplating this, and was shaken by a vast rumble of merriment. "My people have told me there is one who asks questions, but they cannot understand what are his reasons. So I, myself, I ask him, 'Why do you wish to know this?' " He spread his hands. "Perhaps he thinks he speaks French? I do not know."

"He does his best," said Antony apologetically.

"Bah!" said the curé. Which seemed adequately to

dismiss the subject. "And is there no other who can make this identification, but you must seek *la pauvre Madeleine*?"

"There is one other, Father. He is blind."

"I see." He added, slowly: "But I do not think I can help you, m'sieur."

"It is a matter of importance, a case of murder. A man is under arrest, I believe wrongly. Without this evidence—"

"You mistake me. Tell me, if you will, when did Madeleine know this person whom you wish her to identify?"

"During the war, Father. He was, in fact, the man who betrayed her family."

"Then I fear it is useless. You must understand, m'sieur, that since the war Madeleine has not been herself, and she seems to have no memory at all of those days."

Antony was silent; there was to be no easy way, and the realization was bitter. He said, at last, "Is there perhaps someone local who remembers this man?" But he spoke without hope, and was not surprised when the priest shook his head.

"Few saw him, m'sieur. The affair has been much talked of, that is natural, but I have never heard of anyone who knew him by sight. Of those that did, most were arrested . . . and those who were arrested died; two escaped, but they were killed later, in another place." He looked searchingly at his visitor. "This has grieved you. Believe me, I am sorry."

"Couldn't I try? Perhaps if I spoke to her—"

The curé shook his head. "I will tell you her story, m'sieur. You know, I see, the background: that her family were of the Resistance, that they were betrayed by an Englishman whom they had trusted and taken into their home."

"Yes. I know that."

"Those were sad days here, and afterwards many were afraid. I tell you this, so you may understand what happened later. The Gestapo came, and very soon we began to hear that Louis and his wife were dead; their sons did not die under the questioning, they were shot about three months after. Of Madeleine we heard nothing. I thought she, too, had died. Then there was a rumor that she was living in Paris under the protection of a German officer. I did not believe it; people will talk, but how should they know a thing like that? I would not listen.

"But the time passes. The war was ended. There was much bitterness, even among families; it was in that atmosphere that she came home. Men who have been afraid, when they have no longer cause for fear, grow angry. They would have ill-treated her, but I heard of it in time. And I still have some authority. So I brought her here. She seemed dazed; I thought at first it was by her reception, but soon I saw that it went deeper than that. I could not find that she recognized anybody, and though after a while she came to accept me the mere sight of any other man would make her tremble. After a while I took her to my sister, who lives ten miles from here; I fear my people here will not easily forgive her for being still alive. She seems happy to work and will answer briefly but sensibly if she is addressed directly. But of the past—nothing."

"Have you no idea what happened to her? I beg your pardon, Fahter; that, as you are about to point out to me, is none of my affair."

"As to that, curiosity is understandable. I should like to know as much as you would, but I fear we never shall."

"Nevertheless, I should like your permission to see her."

"I tell you, m'sieur, it would be useless. I fear it might upset her." The priest shook his head, and Antony added urgently: "Just let me try."

"Very well." His mind made up, the curé rose briskly. "Have you transport?" He glanced from the window, to where Carr sat behind the wheel of an ancient Citroën. "Ah, the car of our good Gaston. If you will forgive me, m'sieur, I will make arrangements and be with you immediately."

The way was bumpy, and the car's springs had seen better days. Both Antony and Carr were glad when their destination was reached; but the curé seemed to take a simple pleasure in the trip, taking no notice of even the most violent ups and downs, but maintaining a smooth flow of commentary on the countryside through which they passed.

It was midafternoon when they reached the farm. The curé went in alone but returned, beckoning, within a few minutes. "My sister has said we may speak with her in the kitchen," he remarked as Antony joined him. "She will feel at home there, I hope. Will you leave it to me, m'sieur?"

"Gladly, Father."

It was dim in the kitchen, after the brightness outside. A girl was seated at the table with a basket of sewing, and she got up as they went in. As his eyes grew accustomed to the light Antony studied her with a sense of shock. Hendrerson had said she was beautiful, and that was true; but she looked, even now, no more than seventeen—a dark-haired, pale-faced girl without a line on her face. For some reason this was more shocking than anything he could have imagined.

"Ah, Madeleine, we come to interrupt your work. Sit down, child. This is M. Maitland, who has come from England to see you." She glanced briefly at Antony, and he could sense her withdrawal, though she sat down again calmly enough. "Now you must listen to me carefully, Madeleine, this is important business that we are about today."

She turned her eyes back to the familiar face of the priest. His statements seemed to cause her neither interest nor concern.

"M. Maitland is a lawyer. He asks that you will tell him all you can of M. Morris, whom you once knew."

Her expression did not change, her voice held nothing but polite regret. "I do not know anything of this, *mon père.*"

"Come, my dear, you must try to remember. Once you knew him."

"I do not know. I do not remember."

Antony had to admit to himself that the curé was a trier. He approached the subject from all angles, but without result. Madeleine's voice grew quieter, her answers even more brief, her expression more wooden. At last the priest threw up his hands in a gesture of despair. "It is useless, m'sieur."

"May I speak to her? There is one question I should like to ask."

"As you will. I do not think she will speak to you."

Antony got up. If he remained at his own side of the table he hoped she would retain a sufficient sense of security. "Madeleine." She raised her eyes to his for a moment, then looked down again at her hands. "Do you remember Peter Henderson?"

"I do not remember."

"Madeleine, listen to me." He leaned across the table, now, letting the urgency he felt show plainly in look and voice. "*Pierre*, who loved you—don't you remember? —and whom you loved, too."

She looked at him now. For the first time some faint expression showed in her eyes, and Antony took what comfort he could from this. But still she did not speak. After a moment he straightened up, though keeping his eyes fixed on her. "Please, Madeleine! I need your help so badly."

There was another silence, but this time she did not look away. Beside him, Antony could hear the priest's heavy breathing and prayed he would not intervene. The girl sat very still, her hands clasped loosely together in her lap, strangely relaxed. "Pierre . . . is dead," she said at last, flatly.

"But you remember him . . . don't you?" he urged. "You remember—"

"No—"

"It was summer when he came to the farm, wasn't it? To your home. And your parents hid him, as they had hidden others before; but this time, for you, it was different." She was still looking at him, but almost without expression. It was impossible that he could communicate to her his own sense of urgency. . . . It was foolish that he should even try. "Think about those days, Madeleine. . . . More than a month, was it not? You forgot the war, and you were happy; just with the small things, just to be alive."

"I do not know. . . . I do not understand—"

"He lied to me then, your Pierre? When he told me you loved him, that was a lie?" When she made no reply he turned to the priest, speaking almost casually. "It is a sad thing, *mon père*, that a man should be so deceived."

"Sad indeed," said the curé. But his eyes were on the girl. She was looking down now, and her hands were no longer still but were busy with the hem of her apron, pleating it, and carefully smoothing out the creases again.

"Perhaps he was wrong about the other things too." Behind the easy tone the priest could hear now the note of strain. And however impervious the girl might be, suddenly for him the issue was clear and vital . . . immensely important. You must be calm, said the curé urgently, but silently, as he watched the girl's face and listened to his companion's voice. Antony was saying, "He told me how they made him welcome . . . your parents, your brothers. When he came to Pontoise as a fugitive. He told me of your life at that time. He told me how Morris in his turn came to you. Was he mistaken in all these things too?"

The silence was heavy between them. After a while she raised her head again and said deliberately: "It is you who are mistaken, monsieur. Pierre is dead . . . like the others."

"But you remember," he repeated, insistently. "You were happy, and then—"

"If you please, m'sieur." She got to her feet as she spoke, and her voice was as calm as ever, but her eyes were troubled. "I cannot help you. I do not understand—"

"So you have told me, mademoiselle. But you have not said 'I do not remember.' That would be a lie, would it not?"

"It is . . . so long ago."

"Pierre would have helped me, if he could."

For the first time she showed a flash of anger. "How can you say this? How can you know all these things? Pierre is dead."

"It is you who mistake, Madeleine. I spoke with him in England, yesterday."

"That . . . cannot be true, m'sieur. Father . . . it cannot be true?"

"True enough, my child. I think we may trust M. Maitland."

"But—Pierre?" She put a hand to her head, looking from one to the other of the two men with an expression of bewilderment. "It is right what you say, that we loved each other, but . . ." Her voice rose; Antony thought afterward that he would never forget her look of horror. "He is alive, and now so much must come between us," she said on a note of anguish. Then, in a low voice she added, "Why do you make me think of these things? I want only to forget." She began to cry.

The curé took Antony's arm, and led him toward the window. "Do not worry. It is well that she should weep; she will be better soon. Tell me, m'sieur, this Pierre you speak of—"

"A pilot of the R.A.F., *mon père.*" His companion made an impatient gesture.

"Why did he never come back?" he demanded.

"He thought her dead. He did come once, and was told so again; whether before or after her return I do not know. Being blind, he did not recognize the tone of the reply for hostility."

"He is blind, then. Does he know she lives?"

"I was not sure myself until today."

"And the little one?" He jerked his head toward the weeping girl. "What now?"

"She will talk to me, I hope. Then I wish to persuade her to come to England. Would you trust her to M. Carr, whom I will leave to make the arrangements? I assure you, he is a proper person to have charge of her."

"And after?"

"How can I say? I have promised Henderson's mother that I will let her see Madeleine. She spoke of wishing to invite her to their home. If it is a matter of giving evidence, it may be necessary for her to remain some time in England."

"Do not think I doubt your M. Carr's respectability, but I must confess, I am anxious. She is like a child, you see, and I have for so long been responsible for her."

"If you will give me a letter, I promise that wherever Madeleine stays in England it shall be delivered to her parish priest, and that I will myself take her to see him. Will that content you, Father?"

"Then I leave all in your hands. But here we are, settling everything between us; let us see if she will, in fact, talk to you."

Madeleine was wiping her eyes. "Do you feel able to talk to M. Maitland now, my child? If you wish he will come back again when you are better."

"If I must speak with him, it will be better now." But at first her words came slowly, as though they must be chosen with care after she had neglected for so long the gift of speech. "You asked me about a man, m'sieur," she went on, turning directly to Antony; the curé muttered "Marvelous, marvelous, marvelous" to himself and subsided into silence. "I spoke truly, that I did not remember; and yet, it was not true that I could not remember, but that I would not. There was nothing I wished to think about, except Pierre. And nobody spoke of him, until you came— even my mother, papa, my brothers. They let me see François; he said he was the last, and next day they shot him too. If I thought of them—I must also think of that. And so, for many years now—I would not remember."

Antony could not speak. The curé seated himself on the edge of the table near her, and took her hand. "It will pass, child."

She looked at him, and spoke wonderingly. "It is as if I had only just known it, *mon père*."

"I know, I know. But one day the grief will pass, and you will think only of the love and joy of your childhood, and be happy to remember. Believe me, Madeleine, I do not lie to you."

"No, Father." There was, however, no conviction in her voice.

"But now you must face all these sad things, and tell us what you remember about this M. Morris."

She shuddered. When she began to speak she kept her eyes fixed on the priest's face, as though she could draw courage from him. "Pierre was already with us two weeks when he came. He was expected, and all the men said: how clever he is, how efficient, how pleasant his manner. Pierre, too, he called him a 'good chap.'" She produced the English phrase diffidently, and looked for a moment at Antony. "Is that right, m'sieur? He said we should call him *Tédé*, and Papa laughed and said, 'like your king Edouard,' but somehow I did not wish to use his name. Even then, I think I did not like him; but it is hard, now, to say when I began to fear and hate him. All the time they were busy, such going and coming, and secrecy and importance. But that did not concern Pierre, he was at home. Then the Germans came.

"It was early in the morning. They came quietly, there was no time for him to hide."

"Do not speak of that, mademoiselle. It is too difficult. Tell me, only, can you describe Morris to me? Could you recognize him again?"

"Is he not dead, then? I had thought he might be. But, of course, I should know him anywhere."

Her description of Morris tallied well enough with the one he had already received from Henderson; she was gaining animation now, and it was not accomplished without a good deal of gesticulation. "But his ways, m'sieur, that is more difficult."

"Well, what struck you most about him?"

"He was lazy, he was very lazy," she stated simply.

Antony said, "What!" and nearly went over backward, chair and all. He looked at her anxiously, for fear he should have startled her, and was surprised to find her eyeing him with a sort of amused indulgence.

"M'sieur is astonished?"

"It is not what I have been told of him."

"No? You have asked your questions, I think, of those who knew him but little. On the surface he was all movement, all energy. But, *au fond*, he did not at all wish to exert himself. More than anything else, I believe, he loved comfort."

"That," said Antony, "opens up quite a new line of thought."

"It is true what I tell you. Me, I know."

"And afterward, did you hear any more of Morris, or what became of him?"

"Oh, yes, indeed." She paused, eyeing him consideringly. "Now, I think I will tell you. And M. le Curé will say, perhaps that I do ill to speak of these things; but it is a part of remembering, and it may be it is best to speak things once, and then to say: that is past, and done. And later, please God, it will be as you say, *mon père*, and grief will pass.''

Antony said, ''I do not wish you to speak of things that sadden you.'' It did not occur to him until much later that perhaps she spoke to him deliberately, in the hope that he would repeat to Henderson things that were bitter to remember, too bitter to speak to the man she loved. But the priest was wiser and held his peace.

''At first, you understand, I did not know it was he who betrayed us. I did not see him until after François was killed, and then I thought he was a prisoner. He laughed when I said that, and told me not to worry about the past; he was free, and I could be, too, if I would do as he said. I thought, at first, there was something they wanted to know; I said, 'They have killed my family, and soon they will kill me, but I will never speak.' I don't know if that was true, it is very hard to be brave. Then he made me understand what he meant, and still I said 'never.' But it was no use; later he went to Paris, and I was sent there, too. I was with him for nearly six months. I fought him, believe me, at first; but he knew that I hated him, and never did he give me the opportunity to do as I wished and kill him.

''It wasn't just what he had done to me, I knew by then all that he was responsible for. I heard them talking sometimes, he and other men who came to our *appartement*. There were a few who looked at him oddly for what he had done, but mostly they applauded him. It is difficult to explain: I do not think he was a malicious man, or that he betrayed out of a desire to hurt others. But the conditions of a worker in the Resistance lack comfort; he found it irksome. In some ways he had courage enough, but he could not face living hard.'' She stopped to study her hearers' expressions. ''M. le Curé, you are not surprised, I think. But you, m'sieur, this appalls you, does it not?''

''Such treachery is always horrible, but for so trivial a reason—''

''Perhaps I mistake.'' She sounded absurdly, to his ears, like a mother soothing the fears of her child. ''It is not important, after all. The rest I do not think will interest you, and I do not think I can explain properly, but I should like to try. I was with him for six months, and after a while nothing seemed to matter any more, nothing seemed real. That was after he had told me about Pierre; he said, 'He was a fool, he tried to escape and they shot him.' That was not true?''

"He was wounded. Perhaps they thought him dead."

"At last he went away—to Germany, I think. Afterward, there were others. And the past went away, and away, until at last there was nothing left at all. But when the Germans went I thought only, I must come home. And you were kind to me, *mon père;* you, and madame, and her husband, who have helped me to stop being afraid."

Antony found nothing to say. The priest patted her hand again, and asked, after waiting politely for his companion to speak first, "Will you go to England, to identify this Morris if he can be found?"

"To England?"

"Do not have any ideas of revenge, my child, though that would be easy enough. I ask you to go to help M. Maitland, who is troubled, and a man who is in prison for a crime he did not commit."

"Then I will go, Father. And I need not be afraid, so perhaps I shall not hate him any longer." She got up. She had been speaking calmly, but she was very pale. "May I leave you now? I think I should like to be alone." She was again on the verge of tears.

Antony watched her go out, and turned to his companion. The priest, too, was staring at the door, and his expression was stern. "You wouldn't blame her—?" His tone was anxious, and the other turned and smiled at him.

"That is an error I am not likely to fall into, my son." His voice was mildly rebuking. "This Henderson, now—?"

"If I'm any judge . . . but I've met him only once, you know."

"When she recovers herself a little there will be questions she will ask."

"You will tell her that he lost his sight?"

"I will tell her. Will she see him, in England?"

"I'm sure she will."

"Ah, well. I must leave all to you. There will be

adjustments, of course—but I pray he will not fail her. I do not understand the English,'' he added, with a shrug. Then with a return of his former briskness he went on, ''Did you not speak of a plane to catch? My housekeeper will have prepared a meal; we must hasten so that you may not leave unrefreshed.''

CHAPTER TEN

THE NEXT DAY, Friday, Antony awoke late after the luxury of having his sleep out. He lay awhile wondering a little wildly what day it was, and puzzling over the other, similar confusions which vex us in the moment of waking. Then the door opened, and the sound of Jenny's light footstep resolved all his questions. He opened one eye cautiously and then, as the smell of coffee became apparent, committed himself to the day's activities by opening the other eye and pushing himself up on his elbow.

"What on earth time is it?"

"Eleven o'clock. I'm glad you've wakened up. I couldn't have let you sleep any longer because of seeing John." She insinuated the tray into a position of comparative safety, and sat down on Antony's feet.

"What time have I to meet him?"

"Not till one o'clock. But he said to tell you not to go there direct. Shall I pour that for you?"

"Please." Antony bit into a piece of toast. "Not to go where?"

"A café in the City. I've got it written down."

"Did he have anything else to say?"

"No. He sounded a bit flat."

"Poor John. Never mind, love, another day or two should see our part of it cleared up, with any luck."

Jenny eyed him reproachfully. "Can you look me in the eye and tell me, truly, that that's the end of the matter for you?"

"Well . . ." said Antony. He sounded defensive.

"I knew it!"

Antony grinned and licked butter off his fingers. "Have a heart, love. Shall I tell you what happened in France?"

Jenny, faced with a choice between her grievance and her curiosity, decided to gratify the latter without any hesitation at all. Antony was brief, but thorough enough. She said, as he finished, "Mr. Carr can bring her here. Then she'll be all right whatever Mrs. Henderson wants."

"I'm afraid that won't do."

"But, why?"

"For the same reason that John wants me to take a circuitous route to the City. A precaution—probably quite unnecessary—but silly not to take it."

"Oh, I see." She was about to say more, but checked herself.

Antony said, with more affection in his tone than in his words, "Yes, love. I know quite well you deserve a medal."

"I don't know what . . ." She changed her mind and smiled at him disarmingly. "You mean, because I didn't even protest about your helping John?"

"That among other things."

"But I never interfere, Antony. Of course, I know you can look after yourself perfectly well."

As I did during the war, thought Antony. Why must we always come back to that? Unconsciously, he had reached for her hand, and found it without much difficulty. He said, with seeming irrelevance, "I did my best to play fair, Jenny. I hated that bloody ambulance, but I never tried to persuade you to give up driving it." She looked at him uncomprehendingly for a moment and then suddenly laughed with a carefree note that he had not heard since the night of Dr. Martin's death.

In spite of his late awakening he was first at the meeting place, which was a drab but genteel café with a dreary black-and-white tiled floor, walls which had been painted buff color—but not for some time—and a series of cramped booths which he knew from experience gave only an illusion of privacy. A table in the corner at the far end seemed, however, to be reasonably suitable, and at this he seated himself. A tentative suggestion that he should wait until his friend joined him was received by the waitress with such arctic displeasure that he took the menu meekly and ordered "Today's Special."

When John Welwyn arrived, late and unrepentant, he found his colleague gazing despondently at his plate. "Don't," he said in hollow tones, "don't whatever you do, order the special."

Welwyn seated himself. "What is it?" he inquired with interest.

Antony prodded a pale, soggy mass gingerly. "It called itself fish pie," he replied doubtfully. "What we do at the call of duty!"

John became aware of a breathing behind him, and hastily asked for a sausage. This arrived, fat and pink, and swimming in watery gravy. Antony suppressed a grin. "Now good digestion wait on appetite," he remarked. "What on earth made you choose this place?"

His companion looked round vaguely. "I'd never been here," he said.

"That," said Antony, "is obvious."

The waitress retired to a distance, and leaned against a serving table.

Welwyn said severely, "Where's Carr? I told you I needed him."

"Carr, I hope, is making things hum. I told him you needed the fair Madeleine over here at once if not sooner; of course, his command of the language being what it is, they may have palmed him off with tickets to Australia—"

"The trip went well, then?"

"Excellent well. If we can produce Morris, she can identify him. Our interview was not without interest; real 'sleeping beauty' stuff, John."

Welwyn took a moment to digest this, and then eyed him in alarm. "You haven't been philandering, Antony?" he inquired.

"Nothing like that."

"I'm relieved to hear it. You'd better tell me . . ."

The story did not take long in the telling. "Well, that's

something," said Welwyn. "If we can once identify Morris, we shall be getting somewhere."

The pudding was too heavy, and the custard too thin; the coffee came out of a bottle. As they sat over the latter, they again got down to business. "I know a good deal about your two prospects now," said Welwyn. "And none of it much use," he added sourly. "Maddison was born at Keswick but left in his teens to take a job in Lancaster. From there he went to Preston, to Middlesbrough, to Leeds; never very long in one job. Only relations parents, both died during the war. He joined up early on, aircrew, a gunner. Did three trips, then copped a packet, and had to bale out. Rest of the crew got theirs. He spent the rest of the war in a POW camp. Came to London when he was demobbed; started his own business, married, and seems to be doing well. We're still working on it, of course."

"For further installments of this thrilling story, see this magazine next week," said Antony gloomily.

"Yes, well . . . I don't know what you were expecting. Condon comes from Exeter, good family, good education. Still some cousins down there . . . say they wouldn't recognize him; they haven't seen him for eighteen years, when his mother died. He did his service in the army—"

"Don't tell me he was a prisoner, too!"

"No, but he isn't out of the picture either. There's a hiatus, and we haven't found so far whether there's any possibility of identification 'before and after.' "

"How did that come about?"

"He was acting as forward O.P. officer with one of the artillery regiments in Normandy, and just disappeared. He was posted missing, and by the time he turned up again his unit had moved on, and he was sent home to hospital. We'll get more in time, of course."

"This year, next year—" said Antony.

"Yes, I'm afraid so. There's just one thing, though—"

"Not a genuine, copper-bottomed fact?" said Antony hopefully.

"No, I'm sorry. Just a story that Condon has some odd-looking visitors at his digs."

"Any description?"

"They looked 'as if they were up to no good.' "

Welwyn's tone was expressive. "And it's no use cross-examining me," he added. "I don't even know if there was one visitor, who kept on coming round like a stage army; or if there was a constant stream of odd-looking people."

"Well, were they Trotsky and Co., or Herman and Co., or just plain, honest English spivs?"

"The last, I should think. At least, if anybody had been inquiring in Condon's direction with a foreign accent, or even in flawless English but hiding behind a suspicious frill of whiskers, I think we'd have heard about it."

"You disappoint me. You'll go on digging, won't you?"

"For my sins," said Welwyn sadly, and the younger man grinned at him.

"Endless ramifications," he murmured. "What fun for you!"

"Well, it is a bore," agreed John. "But you never know what might be a line."

"No, so I'd better tell you about Mrs. Goodbody." Antony's air of candor was not particularly convincing. "I forgot to tell you . . ." He went into some detail, but without comment; Welwyn took his time to consider the story, but finally pronounced it interesting but irrelevant. Antony opened his mouth to mention Herr Ohlendorff, and then closed it again without speaking. He said, instead, "Did you do anything about keeping an eye on Benson?"

"Yes and no. Nothing to report there, I'm afraid."

"And to hark back to Condon—"

"We're doing all we can. Things are more tricky than ever at the moment." Welwyn's expression was suddenly bleak. "An attempted 'bomb outrage' at the Russian Embassy, of all places—and we heard of it from their security people."

Antony whistled—a vulgarity which brought an even more pained expression to the face of the waitress, who had been waiting to clear their table for some time now. "Genuine?" he asked.

"I'm pretty sure of it. They'd have had their complaints a good deal more pat if it was a put-up job. But there's been some mudslinging none the less—well, you can imagine."

"Death, where is thy sting?" said Antony, with sympathy.

"So you see, I want action." He turned to signal to the waitress, who came with more alacrity than she had previously shown but frowned a little over the two cups still full of cold, muddy coffee, apparently regarding them as an insult, personally directed.

Antony got up. "I'll be getting on, then." The waitress left the bill and departed with a tray of dirty crockery. He added, with an air of studied casualness, "John, do you remember Ohlendorff?"

Welwyn was startled. "I could hardly help it. But why think of him?"

"I don't know. Don't look so doubtful, I'm not holding out on you. I expect it was going to France . . . no, that's not right, I was thinking of him before. I got the feeling someone was watching the house, waiting in the Square at night. I thought of Ohlendorff then."

"But why?" Welwyn sounded querulous, and Antony replied rather vaguely.

"I also thought of him when I heard Mrs. Goodbody's story."

"Oh, stuff!" said Welwyn, disgusted. Antony grinned at him.

"Well, at least," he said after a moment, "you can't say I didn't warn you." He stood for several seconds, staring rather vacantly into space, and then looked again at the older man. "Forget it, John. No doubt I'm being foolish." He raised his hand in casual salute, and left abruptly.

John Welwyn looked after him with a puzzled expression. There was little about the young man who had just left to remind him of the ragged, filthy scarecrow, half-dazed with pain and lack of sleep, who had emerged somehow (God alone knew how) from the clutches of the Gestapo in Paris to chart and steer a course to the sea in as crazy and unlikely an escape as any ever undertaken. It was no wonder, he supposed . . . not that he believed for a moment . . .

Welwyn shrugged and prepared to leave in his turn.

*   *   *

Antony, having decided that it was only fair to his digestion to give it every assistance in coping with a singularly horrible meal, made his way westward leisurely and on foot. He looked in at chambers, and was surprised to find that his uncle was in, but that Mr. Carter had gone out of town. "Good heavens, already? I didn't think they'd reach that business till next week."

"An earlier case on the list was settled out of court," Mr. Mallory told him. "Mr. Carter had to leave in something of a hurry."

"I hope he had everything clear," said Antony, worriedly.

"I have every confidence in him, Mr. Maitland. A most conscientious gentleman, with a great gift of concentration."

Antony could think of nothing to say in reply to this, and went in to find his uncle.

"I thought you'd be still in court," he said.

Sir Nicholas got up from his desk, and went to one of the chairs by the fire. "We got through surprisingly quickly. I'm glad to see you back, Antony."

"Are you, sir? By the way, I'm glad to hear you've got hold of such a paragon."

"Young Carter? He's extremely able, and suits Mallory down to the ground." He gave his nephew a sudden, companionable grin. "But why didn't you warn me? I find him very hard going."

"I thought you might." Antony was complacent. "But you've assured me so often that what you need is someone who keeps his mind on his work—"

"Hm," said Sir Nicholas. And the younger man plunged in a hurry into an account of his activities during the past two days.

CHAPTER ELEVEN

IT WAS A LITTLE after eight-thirty when the phone call came from Benson. "If you could come over, Mr. Maitland . . . something has occurred to me . . . I am sure you would be interested." He sounded excited, a little flurried, but nothing like as vague as he had seemed at their previous meeting. Antony put down the receiver presently, a little bewildered by this sudden demand for his company.

"It's Benson, love, I'd better go. I'll get a taxi, I don't want to have you waiting about."

"What a nuisance, darling. Do you think it will take long?"

"No longer than I can help," said her husband firmly.

He occupied himself on the journey by speculating on the nature, and possible value, of his errand. On the last occasion the old man had seemed inclined to hostility—not to himself, but to the cause he was representing. He had seemed vague, too, at times, but perhaps that had been because he did not wish to answer questions. Had he had a change of heart? Or had something really come to his mind that had changed his attitude towards the whole affair? It was useless to speculate . . . and impossible not to do so.

The same sense of excitement which had been evident in Benson's voice showed in his manner as he greeted his visitor. He had been hovering, evidently, and had the front door open almost before Antony's finger left the doorbell. But when they were in his room again he wasted a good deal of time fussing over the younger man's comfort, offering him a drink ("I have a nice little sherry which I am sure even Sir Nicholas—and I am persuaded he is a connoisseur—would not despise"), and generally showing such a disposition to avoid the subject of the meeting that Antony was hard put to it not to display his impatience.

He accepted the drink, which was indeed a pleasant one, and Benson settled himself at last, and gave him another of those bright, disconcerting stares of his. "You want to get to the point, and I don't blame you, Mr. Maitland, I don't blame you. You must realize that I have given the matter we spoke of a great deal of thought, because I wouldn't wish to be unfair to anybody. You do see that, don't you?"

Antony nodded cautiously, not quite sure what he was agreeing to. The old man went on eagerly: "It concerns that unfortunate young man."

This was merely bewildering. "Gerry?" he said, and Benson shook his head impatiently.

"You asked me whether Martin had ever spoken of him, and I was unwilling to tell you. I have remembered his name . . . it was Morris, Edward Morris."

If Antony hadn't been concerned to wonder at his companion's choice of adjective, he might have been conscious of a sense of anti-climax. No good denying that he had come here hopefully, but this was old stuff. He said, with an attempted lightness, "I should have thought, sir, that it was his victims who might be designated 'unfortunate.' "

Benson bowed his head. "Very true, young man, very true indeed. But who more unhappy than a traitor; a man who betrayed not only his country, but the friends who trusted him?" His tone was sententious; Antony began to have an uncomfortable feeling that he was being laughed at. Certainly, Benson seemed to be a bit of a humbug, but perhaps his mannerisms of speech were merely habit.

"Do you think it might have been about Morris that Dr. Martin wished to speak to you on the day of his death?"

The old man looked astonished, perhaps at being asked so leading a question. "I have no reason to think so. You must take my word for it, Mr. Maitland, I have no idea in the world what he might have wanted to say to me. I thought you would be interested in what I had to tell you. When you were here before you seemed unaccountably interested in uncovering the past.''

''I was, I am. Please go on, sir.''

This was quite enough invitation for his host, who embarked on the familiar tale of Morris with a good deal of gusto, and some circumlocution. It was the story of his treachery as seen by Henry Martin, from his own brief, tragic participation in the affair to the blurred outlines of what had happened at Pontoise as he had gleaned them from those few of ''his boys'' who had lived to tell the tale. Antony, listening with half his attention, was conscious once again of regret for the upright old man, whose efforts to help his country had recoiled so bitterly on the people he loved. For the rest, it was a wasted evening, but no doubt Benson had meant well. He thought, idly, ''The way to hell is paved with good intentions.'' And suddenly was conscious that the house was very quiet, and that he himself was uneasy.

He was alert on the instant, trying to analyze the reason for this disquiet. Benson's voice was droning on, but there was in the room a definite feeling of tension; as though his inconclusive talk were leading to some climax, some hidden purpose of which he knew nothing.

He moved a little, suddenly restless, and was aware of Benson's sharp attention. ''I am boring you, Mr. Maitland?''

''Far from it, sir.''

''Another drink, before I continue? Yes, I am sure you will take another glass.'' He got up, but before he could take their glasses from the round table that stood on the rug between them there was the sound of someone tapping on the glass door that led to the balcony. Benson exclaimed impatiently, and then went down the room, saying over his shoulder, ''Nothing important, my boy; one of my neighbors. If you'll excuse me for a moment . . .''

The only light in the room was a standard lamp behind Benson's chair. The far end was almost in darkness, and though it was possible to see that the newcomer was a man, it was not possible to recognize him. Antony heard them speaking together, Benson's voice a little shrill (was there a note of relief in his tone?) and the quiet voice of the stranger. He knew now that this was the moment he had been waiting for, ever since he had first suspected the presence of a watcher in Kempenfeldt Square. And what he had feared against all common sense, against all reason—so that, except for the brief candor of his talk with Sir Nicholas, he had dismissed the thought as often as it had intruded itself upon him—had now come about. The voice was recognizable beyond all doubt, though he had not heard it for so long, as that of Ernst Ohlendorff, sometime German Kommandant in Paris. What he was doing here, and where Benson came into the picture, were points upon which he could not concentrate just then; he got up quietly, and backed across the room, without knowing what he was doing until he came up against the heavy oval dining table that stood by the wall opposite the window. He stood still, then, fighting a sense of panic. He could leave, he supposed, but he knew as the thought crossed his mind that flight was the one course not open to him.

Benson backed from the glass door, and a tall man followed him into the room, pausing for a moment to find the light switch with obvious familiarity. There had been no mistaking the voice, and the change in his appearance was subtle rather than startling, but the thought crossed Antony's mind that they might have passed in the street some day, and he would have been none the wiser. The hair made a difference, of course, no longer cut *en brosse;* and darker, he thought . . . yes, definitely darker. And the mustache was equally misleading, a droopy, half-apologetic affair, quite unlike anything Herr Ohlendorff would have permitted himself. But the greatest change was in his manner, no longer harsh and unbending, but casual and quietly competent. And you might have thought him a pleasant, friendly man.

Benson was displaying some agitation, and addressing the newcomer in German. "You said you must see him. I thought you would never come . . ." Ohlendorff turned on him with impatience, saying, in English:

"Spare yourself the trouble, my friend. Captain Maitland speaks German quite as well as I do—and rather better than you, if you will forgive my saying so." He turned to

Antony, and smiled; his eyes were cold and watchful, his voice pleasant and friendly. "Good evening, Captain."

"Good evening," said Antony. His voice was expressionless, but after a moment he smiled. "Not captain, though. I left the army years ago."

Ohlendorff waved that aside. "What else should you be doing in this affair?"

"I'm a barrister, hasn't your friend here told you?"

"A convenient tale, no doubt. However, deception is surely unnecessary when old friends meet. You disappoint me, I had expected some show of surprise when I came in."

"I heard your voice before I saw you. In any case, I wasn't exactly surprised."

"Then why didn't you make a run for it?"

"Run?" asked Antony, politely mystified. "Why should I?"

"I was afraid that your memories of our previous acquaintance might not be so pleasant as mine. I'm glad to know I was mistaken."

"As a matter of fact," said Antony, lying blandly, "when I heard you at the window I said to myself: 'There's Ohlendorff, I bet he won't be fool enough to come in.' And here you are!"

Ohlendorff looked amused. "And now I suppose you will tell me that the house is surrounded, and I shall be arrested as I leave?"

"You've only forgotten one thing: there's a microphone concealed behind the whatnot."

Benson seemed startled, and looked round a little wildly, as if the room had suddenly become unfamiliar to him. Ohlendorff said reassuringly, "Take no notice of what he says; Captain Maitland is a most facile and imaginative liar."

"Dear me," said Antony, pleased with the tribute. "Coming from you, that's praise of a high order."

"Oh, I don't pretend to be in your class, my dear fellow. But enough of that. I felt it was time we had a little talk." He added, turning again to Benson, "Hadn't we better sit down? And, if I may make a suggestion, the curtains . . ." Benson shrugged, and obeyed. He had the air of one who has lost all control of the situation, and poured himself another drink before he came back to sit again in the chair he had previously occupied. Antony moved behind the armchair, and perched himself on a pouf in the chimney corner, his hands clasped around his knees. Ohlendorff sat on the arm of the sofa. "I should have inquired after your health, Captain Maitland. From all appearances it has improved greatly. When last I saw you . . ." He was observing the other closely and, seeing that he tightened his lips slightly at this thrust, was well satisfied that he was not quite so calm as he wished to appear. "But that is a long time ago, after all. Let us speak of more pleasant things."

"Such as why you wished for this reunion, for instance?"

"Do you find it surprising?"

"Well, I don't know your present identity, of course; but I do know who you *are*."

"Yes, indeed. But just at the moment, if you will forgive me for bringing up a disagreeable subject, you are hardly in a position to do anything about it, are you?" He withdrew his hand from his pocket, and displayed a small caliber automatic. "In case you are under any illusion, Captain Maitland. I must take my precautions, after all."

Antony hugged his knees. The gun was . . . only to be expected; but the hand that held it wore a surgeon's glove. Which seemed to argue an uncomfortable degree of forethought. "I hope you're not going to ask me to put my hands up. I'd hate to disoblige you, but it can't be done."

"Then the injury was permanent? Your right arm, if I remember. Well, it makes no matter. But I should advise you against making any sudden movement."

"I'm quite comfortable. In any case, I'm not armed."

"No?"

"I told you before, I'm a barrister. It is not customary to go about armed."

"We won't argue the point, though I think it is—may I say?—a legal fiction." Ohlendorff seemed pleased with his joke, and Antony suddenly threw his head back and laughed. Benson stirred uneasily at the sound, and said fretfully, "I don't understand all this."

"Patience, my friend."

"I'd rather like to know the point myself," said Antony. "Why did you want to see me?"

"It seems probable that my colleague, Morris, is in a fair way to being unmasked. That is a pity, but what really concerns me is your participation in the affair."

"An unfortunate coincidence," said Antony politely.

"I fear you will find it so. You realize, of course," said Ohlendorff, his tone apologetic, "that it has become necessary for me to kill you?"

"I've realized that for some time, but I thought you'd prefer to stage an accident. Are you proposing to shoot me here? Won't you find the body a little inconvenient?"

"That need not concern you, after all."

"But it concerns me," said Benson, coming into the conversation with sudden violence, very much at variance with his previous manner. "Why didn't you tell me what you knew of Maitland? I know you said he was dangerous because he could recognize you, but I'd no idea he was anything now but what he claimed to be."

"I did not wish to worry you. You should thank me for my consideration."

Antony laughed again and proceeded to prod at what seemed to be a sore place. "You didn't answer my question. Is he also to thank you for presenting him with my corpse for disposal?"

"No doubt he would, if I intended anything so stupid."

"Stupid, yes. But on your present form . . ." He spoke deliberately; for some reason anything in the nature of schoolboy repartee infuriated Ohlendorff as no amount of verbal fencing could do. He had not expected, however, quite so violent a reaction; he could not know, after all, the depth of hatred which their two previous encounters had engendered. The German came across the room, suddenly furiously angry. Antony let his eyes rest for a moment on the gun, and saw that it had a silencer. He looked up calmly into his enemy's face, and knew that any move at this moment would be his last. Ohlendorff towered above him, and began to speak, low and very fast, in German.

"I do not like insolence, Herr Maitland. Do you not remember?" Antony sat very still. "We have met again now, for the third time, and I think it will be the last. And this time it is I who will laugh."

"You know," said Antony, eyeing him reflectively, "you're losing your grip. In the old days you'd never have wasted time on heroics." Ohlendorff struck him across the mouth, and then—suddenly losing all control—hit him again and again.

Benson got up from his armchair and crossed to stand at Ohlendorff's side. He said, thoughtfully, "If you want him to talk you'll have to do better than that," and his prim tone was strangely at variance with his words.

Ohlendorff had recovered his equanimity. "I should be glad indeed if I thought he would talk to me. There are things he can tell me that I very much wish to know."

"That should be easy," said Benson—and laughed for the first time since the arrival of his second visitor.

"Not so easy. I know Captain Maitland of old. He is a very ingenious young man. No doubt he will talk. He talked once at Gestapo headquarters in Paris; in fact, he talked for ten days—not all the time, you understand, but whenever he was conscious—and every day the story changed. And still I do not know what was truth and what was lies, or how he tricked me at the last."

"If you'll forgive the interruption," Antony broke in. "You're welcome to any information I can give you—free, gratis, and for nothing."

"You see!" Ohlendorff backed away again, to his former position on the arm of the sofa. His eyes were watchful. "If you wish to find your handkerchief, Captain Maitland, you may do so. Your lip is bleeding."

Antony extracted the handkerchief and dabbed his mouth. "I didn't remember that you wore a ring," he said.

"This signet?" Ohlendorff extended his hand, and regarded it complacently. "It is a souvenir. I must remember to tell you . . ."

Benson had moved back across the hearth. He said now, impatiently, "This is all very well, but it's getting us nowhere."

"You feel we should be getting down to business?" Ohlendorff's tone was courteous, but his eyes never left Antony's face. "Perhaps you are right. In that case, I'm sorry to trouble you, but can you think of some excuse for getting your good landlady out of the house for half an hour? I think you said your fellow guests were creatures of habit and would be out this evening?''

"That's right. But you said . . .'' He broke off, glancing at Antony. "Oh, very well,'' he added, and went out of the room.

Ohlendorff said apologetically, "I'm afraid my colleague has no finesse. He still imagines I propose to question you with violence if necessary. I assure you, I wouldn't attempt anything so clumsy. At least, not here.''

The room was suddenly very quiet; outside a car door banged, and the engine came to life noisily. But all that seemed very far away. Antony felt chilled, in spite of the warmth of the room. Now was his only chance, while briefly they were alone together; but the gun never wavered, nor the watchful gaze of his enemy. And he knew that there was no chance at all.

"I quite appreciate your need for privacy.'' He spoke his thought, and his voice was level. "Even a silenced gun is not quite silent.''

"Precisely!'' Ohlendorff beamed at him with every appearance of affectionate approval. "While we are waiting, perhaps you would like to tell me how you came into this affair. Just as a matter of interest, you know.''

"It's very simple: Dr. Martin was a friend. And my uncle, as no doubt you've heard, is defending Gerry Martin.''

"And you are in Sir Nicholas Harding's chambers. No doubt you find it a convenient camouflage.''

"Have it your own way. But that is all my interest in the matter . . . the case for the defense.''

"But you weren't surprised to see me, Captain Maitland,'' Ohlendorff reminded him gently. "That rather spoils your story, I'm afraid.''

"You forget, I saw you watching me in the square.''

"It was dark, I do not think you could possibly have known—''

"That's true enough, but something put you in my mind. Your figure, your walk? I don't know. If it hadn't been for that I'd have thought there was nothing in it but

Morris trying to save his own skin. And I still don't know your racket."

"I am sure your friend Major Welwyn will have told you rather more than you admit."

Antony compressed his lips again at this sign of the other's efficiency. "I did ask some questions," he said warily. "And got warned off the grass for my pains."

Ohlendorff shook his head at him sadly. "More lies, Captain Maitland?" He broke off as Benson came back into the room and spoke without looking at him. "Is it arranged?"

"She has already gone. And the others, as I said—"

"Thank you, that's very satisfactory."

Benson shut the door, and went over to his chair. "Do you progress?" he asked as he seated himself.

"Captain Maitland has been telling me a fairy tale. A nicely constructed story, but not, I fear, the truth."

"Tiresome of him." Benson spoke negligently. He seemed preoccupied. "Well, then . . . what's the next move?"

Antony, whose eyes were fixed intently on Ohlendorff's face, saw the change of expression and knew for a moment more sharply the fear of death. He braced himself to meet it, as the German's grip on the gun tightened.

"This!" said Ohlendorff. "This is next!" And, turning sharply, he shot Benson through the head.

CHAPTER TWELVE

"I ADMIT," said Antony, mildly, "I was tired of his conversation myself. But wasn't that rather drastic?"

"He had served his turn." Ohlendorff spoke indifferently. He had resumed again his watchful pose, and though the younger man had had presence of mind to scramble to his feet, that was all he had time to do before the gun was again covering him.

"I'm not weeping for him," Antony pointed out. "Apparently he was as big a scoundrel as you'd be likely to meet on a day's march. Present company excepted," he added.

Ohlendorff flashed a smile but spoke abstractedly. "It is all a question of viewpoint, after all. He has been useful in his day, but now . . ." He appeared to come to a decision, and added with more energy, "I am gratified that I have caused you amusement, Captain Maitland, but now I have done what I came to do. Let us go?"

"Us?" said Antony.

"That is what I said. I do not need to remind you that I have a gun, and that I am prepared to use it."

"May I ask where we are going?"

"You will know soon enough. I have a car in the next street, and one of my colleagues, which simplifies matters a little. Perhaps before we start I should warn you: I shall kill you without hesitation if you make it necessary. Also, I am up to all the tricks; you are thinking that at close quarters you may have a chance to turn the tables, but I think you will find it difficult. To be successful, there should be an element of surprise, and I assure you I am looking for trouble.''

Antony said slowly: ''I suppose you must want me alive, for the moment anyway.''

''Don't deceive yourself, my friend. My desire for your company stops short of the foolhardy. I have too much at stake to take risks.'' His eyes met Antony's and held them. He added, softly, ''At the first sign of opposition I shall kill you. Do you understand?''

''Oh, yes. That's only sense.'' He sounded hopeless, and Ohlendorff laughed with real amusement.

''You may spare your pains, Captain Maitland. I know you too well.'' Antony achieved a bewildered look, and he added impatiently: ''This fade-away air; I have noticed that when you sound most despairing, or appear to give way to panic, you are generally up to no good.''

''You give me credit for more cunning—and more courage, I think—than I possess.''

''No.'' Ohlendorff eyed him consideringly. ''You are not a fool, and you would be foolish indeed not to be afraid. But I do not think you will display your fear unless you choose. However''—he was suddenly brisk—''we have wasted enough time. We will go the way I came in, and I must ask you to precede me.'' Antony hesitated, and the command was repeated in a decidedly peremptory tone.

He moved then, not hurrying himself, and being careful to keep his eyes fixed on his enemy's face. Somewhere between them, a little to the right of a direct line of progress, was a coffee table; a round tray of beaten brass, on a light framework that had been made to support it. If he could make contact with that, something might be done, though he was no match for Ohlendorff if it came to fighting, and he knew it. Now, with his right arm useless, he must place his reliance on getting hold of the gun.

His foot caught against the coffee table; he stumbled with exaggerated clumsiness, and as Ohlendorff's eyes involuntarily sought the cause of the disturbance Antony grabbed at the tray, left-handed, and spun it in Ohlendorff's direction with all the force he could command. The gun went off, and there was a resounding clang as the bullet ricocheted off the heavy metal, to bury itself harmlessly in the wall. Ohlendorff had staggered backwards. Antony aimed a kick at the hand that held the gun and had the doubtful satisfaction of seeing the weapon fly harmlessly out of reach. He followed up with his left, but Ohlendorff, though the blow rocked him, had now regained his balance and countered with a couple of quick punches which did their recipient no good at all. He managed to hook his leg round that of his adversary, to bring him down; but Ohlendorff grabbed him as he lost his balance, and they fell together heavily. The ensuing scrimmage left Antony underneath. He felt his enemy's hands at his throat, jabbed with his left into Ohlendorff's side, producing a grunt of pain but no relaxation of pressure.

Looking up he saw, hazily, Ohlendorff's face above him; all the veneer of calmness was gone, leaving nothing but hatred and the exultation of fulfilling it. He had no longer strength or will to fight back. As he lost consciousness his last thought was, strangely, one of pure curiosity: will he finish me this way, or will he use his gun?

Antony returned to painful consciousness to find himself lying full length on Benson's sofa, with two strange and unfriendly faces looking down at him. Somewhere, very far away, a voice said: "He's coming round." And another voice said, speaking curtly: "Better leave him then, till Sykes gets here." He tried to speak himself, but the faint croaking sound he achieved was ignored; both faces disappeared, but after a moment the younger of the men came back and, propping his head somewhat roughly, put a glass to his lips. The touch on his head was agonizing, and almost sent him back into unconsciousness again; but the drink did him good, and he was able to whisper: "Thank you" as the glass was withdrawn and the good—if rather taciturn—Samaritan went his way. He lay back quietly then, trying to arrange his thoughts. Now he was aware of a confusion of sound in the background; there must be several men in the room. And someone had spoken of Sykes; in that case these chaps were probably police. But what had happened to Ohlendorff? And, come to that, why was he still alive?

Sykes arrived at this point; Antony heard the comfortable north-country voice, calm and questioning, and the curter tones of the local inspector answering him. For the moment, it all seemed very far away, nothing to worry about, no concern of his.

". . . glad you've been so quick." That was the curt voice. "We took some photographs, but we thought you'd like to see everything as it was."

"Thank you, yes." There was a pause, and then he went on, "If you could give me some idea—"

"Neighbor called us in. Came round to visit Benson . . . some idea of a game of chess, he said."

"I see. And Benson—?"

"That's him," said the local inspector, abruptly; and there was a pause. "Sitting in his chair, he was, just as you see him, when his friend arrived; he's the star boarder, I gather, lived here several years now, a very respectable old fellow."

"Had the neighbor—"

"Hargreaves."

"Had Hargreaves come here by appointment?"

"No. Said it was a sudden decision. Fellow *he* was expecting hadn't turned up."

"And how did he get in?"

"By the french window. Came through the garden; quickest way, he lives in the house that backs on this one."

"And the window was open?"

"Well, no. Wouldn't be, on a night like this." He paused, and went on a little stiffly, as though Mr. Hargreaves's tale embarrassed him. "One queer thing, he says he heard a sound like a . . . like a gong, when he was coming down his own garden."

"And when he got here?"

"He tapped on the glass, and listened. Something moved, he says. Says it sounded . . . furtive." The inspector's voice was scornful. "Probably an afterthought, that bit. Then he heard a door close. He waited a moment, and then tried the latch."

"And the window opened, and he went in and found Benson dead." Sykes was not giving his full mind to the account of the visitor's actions. His tone was absent, and the other man said hurriedly, almost defensively, "This other one was lying on the floor; seemed to have cracked his head against the edge of that brass tray thing."

"Yes," said Sykes, but it was clear that his interest had been recaptured.

"I thought at first he was dead, too; he seems to have been throttled pretty efficiently, but he was showing signs of life just before you arrived. The doctor had a look at him, of course, doesn't seem to think there's much harm done though there might be a slight concussion. The landlady says Benson was a close friend of Dr. Martin—would have it there must be a connection; that's why I got on to you."

"I'm very glad you did. It's a right puzzle, you know; *this* is one of the defense counsel, name of Maitland. He's also a friend of the accused man . . . makes it seem queer like, doesn't it?"

"It does, indeed." The curt voice sounded startled. "What do you make of it, then?"

"Give us a chance, lad." Sykes was unperturbed. The other small sounds of activity had stilled since his arrival, and now Antony had the impression he was moving quietly about the room, examining everything methodically as he did so, and murmuring to himself from time to time as one thing and another struck him as noteworthy. "Aye," he remarked at last. "Well, now. Benson seems to have died peacefully; no signs of a struggle about *him*. Have you found the gun?"

"Behind the sofa. It's the right caliber, anyway. No prints worth mentioning; they're blurred out of all recognition."

"What does the landlady say?"

"Mrs. Nightingale? She says Benson told her he was expecting Maitland about nine o'clock. She thinks she heard him arrive about nine-fifteen but isn't sure. Her rooms are in the basement. Later on, Mr. Benson went down to ask her to take a note to a friend of his. She says he knew she liked a walk of an evening, so she wasn't at all surprised at the request."

Antony's brain was clearing a little now, and it was at

this point that the difficulties of his position began to dawn on him. One thing was clear, he could do no talking until he had seen Welwyn; in any case he wouldn't have wanted to . . . what was important was to get Ohlendorff. At the moment he had no ideas how this should be accomplished, but no doubt when his head stopped aching things would seem easier. It seemed most likely that he was the only person who could identify the German without delay, though no doubt in time any number of people could be found who had been familiar with his appearance, at least, in Paris. But they couldn't afford to wait. John had been pretty evasive when he had asked him what action he had taken about Benson; it didn't seem likely . . .

A low-voiced conversation had been continuing between the two policemen. Sykes said now, "To my mind Benson was shot before all this struggling took place. Is that how you see it?"

"That's what I thought. But who shot him, that's what I want to know?"

"Let's see if Mr. Maitland has come to his senses yet; he ought to have something to tell us."

Antony thought, "Here we go again!" He swung his feet to the floor and sat up dizzily. The two policemen were pulling up chairs to face him. Sykes appeared friendly as ever, but the other man looked severe.

"Well, now, Mr. Maitland, I hope you're feeling better."

"A good deal better, thank you." Antony cleared his throat and tried again, but the words still came hoarsely.

"Well enough to talk to us? It's quite important."

"Yes? I—I don't understand, I'm afraid." He looked across at Benson's chair, where the activity now centered more busily than ever. "What happened?"

"That, Mr. Maitland, is what we are hoping you will tell us."

"What's happened to Benson?"

Sykes eyed him appraisingly. "If you *don't* know, Mr. Maitland, I'd better tell you. He's been shot."

Antony put a hand to his head, which was indeed throbbing painfully. "I suppose you mean he's dead?" he inquired. "I don't see why," he added vaguely.

This brought an interruption from the local inspector.

"It is a usual consequence of being shot through the head," he said. His voice was harsh with suspicion.

Sykes raised a hand, and said, "Wait a bit now, Mr. Wallace," in a soothing tone. He turned again to Antony. "So you see how important it is for us to know what happened here this evening."

"I had to see Benson on business; he telephoned me." That was true enough, anyway. "I came about nine, perhaps a bit later. We were talking."

"And then—?"

Antony looked worried. "I don't know," he said helplessly.

"Are you trying to tell us that you don't remember?" Inspector Wallace might have called in a colleague from Scotland Yard, but he had no intention of completely relinquishing the conduct of affairs.

"That's right." He caught Sykes's eye and essayed a smile in his direction. "I'm sorry, Inspector, really I am."

"That's as may be," said Sykes.

"But it's preposterous! Do you want us to believe that you don't remember all this fighting that's been going on; that you don't know who killed Benson—or even if you did it yourself?"

"I don't care much what you believe. All I'm saying is, I don't know what happened."

Sykes intervened again. "Now, sir, you can see for yourself there's been a battle royal in here. From the look of you, you were in the thick of it. Surely you remember that?"

Antony shook his head. "Sorry," he said again. "My throat hurts," he added helpfully.

"I expect it does. Someone tried to strangle you."

"Oh," said Antony. "You seem to go in for rough sports in Streatham," he added reproachfully to Inspector Wallace.

"Then we'll go back a bit." Sykes spoke hastily. "What was the nature of your business with the deceased?"

"You must see I can't tell you that. I came here on Gerry Martin's behalf, and you represent the prosecution, after all." (And that was also true.)

"That's all very well!" Inspector Wallace erupted into the conversation again. "This is a case of murder!"

Antony looked at him. "So is the other. There is also the small matter of a man on trial for his life."

"It's my belief," said Sykes, with the first signs of asperity he had so far displayed, "you're quite enough recovered to come to the station and make a statement."

"If you like, Inspector."

"On second thoughts, it's no more trouble to go down to headquarters. On your way home, you might say; and we can get a doctor to have another look at you." Sykes spoke with an air of elaborate reasonableness. "Could you arrange a car for us, Mr. Wallace?" As the local man took himself off, he turned back to Antony. "Now, sir, can't you tell me what this is all about? I'm bound to have more than this to report to the superintendent, but you look as if you ought to be home in bed."

"I can't help you, Inspector. Are you arresting me?"

"You know better than that, Mr. Maitland. But I must say I don't think Superintendent Briggs will be satisfied with your statement as it now stands."

Antony leaned back and shut his eyes. He said wearily, "It's lucky, then, that satisfying Briggs is not one of my major ambitions." He was very pale, and Sykes regarded him anxiously.

"Think it over, Mr. Maitland," he advised, and his tone was urgent. "You may feel your attitude is justified, but . . ."

Antony opened his eyes again. "Don't spoil it, Inspector. Almost thou persuadest me—that you don't think I shot Benson." There was mockery in his tone, but Sykes ignored it.

"Did you?" he asked bluntly.

"No, I didn't. I don't expect Briggs will believe me, but at least I don't see how anyone can prove I did."

"All I want is the truth, sir. And while we're on the subject, Benson's landlady has a story that the old man was afraid of you. Says he called you 'the devil himself.' What about that?"

"Oh, lord!" Antony looked rueful. "A small legal joke, I imagine. I can well imagine him thinking up the phrase—a reference to the fact that I was 'deviling' for my uncle when I visited him. But as for being afraid of me—''

"Hm." Sykes sounded doubtful. "Well, that's very specious, Mr. Maitland—''

"The truth so often is."

Inspector Wallace came back at this point, to announce that a car was now at his colleague's disposal. Antony sat up, and looked about him. "I'd better phone my uncle." He gave Sykes the glimmer of a smile. "I'll need him if you're proposing to third degree me."

"Now, sir," said the detective, automatically, but beyond that he refused to be drawn. "We'll get in touch with Sir Nicholas on your behalf when we get back to town," he said. And ushered his charge out firmly to the waiting car.

For one reason or another Antony's message was somewhat delayed, and it was almost three o'clock next morning before Sir Nicholas arrived at New Scotland Yard. He was by this time furiously angry, partly from his own anxiety, partly from the necessity he had been under to invent a tale that would satisfy Jenny when her own worry became apparent; and he favored his nephew with a bitter and comprehensive denunciation of his character, attainments, and behavior over the past twenty years, which the younger man was in no mood to appreciate. The account of the night's events did little to appease him, and at the end of it he asked coldly, "I suppose it was essential that you should lie to the police?"

"I couldn't tell them the truth."

"You could have told them a good deal more of it than you chose to do."

"You mean about Morris?"

"Not even Welwyn labeled that secret."

"I know. But you know what it is with statements to the police. One asks the questions, and someone else takes down the replies; then yet another brings the typed statement in for signature, and probably someone else files it after that. And before you know where you are the papers have come out with headlines like: 'Streatham killing said to be work of international spies,' and the whole country's in an uproar. After that Colonel Wright commits ceremonial hari-kari, and John looks for a suitable barn to hang himself in.''

Sir Nicholas smiled at that and sat down rather heavily at the bare table that stretched down the center of the room they were using—a waiting room of sorts, but with no allowance made for comfort. ''I still think you should tell them at least part of the truth.''

''Uncle Nick, I can't!'' Antony sounded desperate. ''It would be throwing away our only chance . . .''

Sir Nicholas eyed him consideringly. ''That's all very fine, *if* you find Ohlendorff. Even tomorrow it will be too late to go to the police with half the truth.''

Antony frowned in an effort to concentrate. ''Do they mean to arrest me?'' he queried.

''I don't think so, I don't think they could substantiate a charge. But a recital of tonight's events won't sound well, you can make up your mind to that. And there's Benson's inquest to face . . .''

There was a pause while Antony grappled with this pronouncement; he was, perhaps, too tired to think clearly, but as the full impact of what his uncle said hit him he looked up, appalled. ''This is awful, sir. There's pretty well bound to be a scandal; I can't involve you.''

Sir Nicholas got up. There was no trace now of the anger he had shown when he arrived. ''Don't worry about that, I have something of a reputation, after all.'' He went to stand by his nephew and rested a hand lightly on his shoulder. ''Don't look so wretched, my dear boy. We're a long way from being finished yet.''

Antony twisted to look up at the older man. ''I've got to get out of here,'' he said urgently.

''Very well.'' Sir Nicholas paused on his way to the door. ''I'll have you out of this in ten minutes, on one condition. That you come home with me and get some sleep.''

''I ought to see John.''

''That will have to wait till morning. What do you think I've been doing this past two hours? He isn't at home, and when I rang the private number they were . . . evasive.''

''Oh . . . well,'' said Antony. ''All right, Uncle Nick, it's a bargain.''

CHAPTER THIRTEEN

Sir Nicholas was as good as his word, and half an hour later they were back in Kempenfeldt Square. Antony managed to get upstairs quietly, dropped all his clothes on the bathroom floor, and rolled into bed without more ado. Jenny said, "Mmm?" and snuggled down against him, but without rousing. He was too weary to lie long awake, but his sleep was uneasy, and he awoke unrefreshed.

It was broad daylight now, and the first thing he saw was Jenny's face. She was kneeling on the bed beside him, still in her nightdress, peering at him anxiously and uttering agitated squeaks. When he opened his eyes she became a little more coherent.

"I didn't mean to wake you, truly I didn't. But, Antony darling, your face!"

He put out a hand to find hers and cleared his throat. "Don't worry, love. I expect it looks worse than it is." His basso profundo growl startled them both. Jenny jumped and then said tragically, "Someone tried to strangle you, don't deny it. Your throat is a mass of bruises."

"Don't exaggerate, Jenny. I promise you I'm not hurt, not in the least."

"But what happened? Uncle Nick told me you'd gone on to see John—"

"I'll tell you in a minute. What about a drink?"

Jenny scrambled off the bed. "Of course. Will you have coffee, or something for your throat?"

"Coffee will be fine."

He got himself up as soon as she had disappeared and tried to take stock of the damage he had sustained. There was a lump at the back of his head that was sore to touch, but his mind had cleared—thank goodness for that, anyway—and the slight headache that persisted would most likely disappear with the promised coffee. The mirror told him that his face was bruised and his mouth cut and swollen; on the whole, that looked worse than it was. Two of the bruises on his neck were dark and ugly-looking; when he got his tie on, they wouldn't show. As for his arm, it was a little stiffer than usual, but nothing to worry about. Altogether he'd come off pretty light, physically; mentally, he had taken a beating he wouldn't get over in a hurry. If that had been all, but there was Jenny's share in it too; and somehow he had got to tell her . . .

Ever since he came back from Paris he had been haunted by what he had seen in her eyes, in one brief, unguarded moment. That had been early in 1944, and Jenny was in hospital; she had lost the child she carried, and the doctors had said there couldn't be another, and she was too weak to pretend any more. She had said in a shaken voice, "I thought you were dead. They told me . . ." He had gone to her then, and somehow afterward all the memories were entangled: of the nightmare, that now he felt had never really ended, and of Jenny weeping against his shoulder because she had feared him dead. So that he could never afterward remember what had happened without remembering how she must have felt when she heard of the interrupted broadcast; of his voice saying, "I have been recognized"; and of the long silence that followed.

They sat at the table by the window, with the tray between them, and somehow the tale was told. They were still talking when the telephone rang, and the nightmare came closer again. It was Inspector Sykes, bland as ever and only as apologetic as he felt would be polite. He would be at the Streatham house with Superintendent Briggs at ten-thirty. They would be grateful if Mr. Maitland could make it convenient to meet them there.

Antony demurred; Sykes was insistent. Antony gave way then, though with a bad grace, and left Jenny to phone for a taxi while he went to get dressed. She came to the bedroom door, presently, and said with a doubtful look, "Antony, oughtn't you to take Uncle Nick with you?"

"Well, I'm not going to. It'd do too much violence to his feelings. Besides, he's got a conference."

He arrived at Streatham in good time for his appointment. The taxi stopped short of his objective, and he had paid it off and was walking on to the gate when a police car passed him, and drew up at the curb. Superintendent Briggs got out, followed a moment later by Inspector Sykes.

Antony's stride faltered for an instant, and he went on with rather a sour smile to himself at this reaction: after all, he could hardly turn tail. Sykes saw him first and greeted him with his customary amiability. Briggs turned and said sharply:

"You're in good time, I'm glad to see."

"And very puzzled," Antony retorted. "We went over things pretty thoroughly last night, I can't see what remains to ask. No doubt you'd like a case against me; it's a pity the laws of evidence aren't more accommodating."

Sykes intervened before the superintendent could find words to answer this piece of impertinence, saying in his quiet way, "Are you feeling better, Mr. Maitland?"

"Much better, Inspector."

"Then may I ask if your memory shares the general improvement?"

"Ah, that's another story. As far as I can tell, it's gone for good."

"That would be a pity. If I might suggest, sir," he added, "we may as well go inside straight away. The—er—scene of the crime might stimulate Mr. Maitland's memory." He encountered a furious look from Antony and continued placidly, "I'm sure he will have no objection."

"No objection at all," said Antony bitterly.

Briggs approved the suggestion and led the way into the house. The room where Benson had died was dusty and had the slightly degenerate air that comes so quickly from disuse. Antony said: "Does it matter where I go? Have you finished here?"

"Yes, we've finished. Sit where you like."

He had no special desire to sit down, so wandered round aimlessly until he was standing with his back to the table, and leaned against it as he had done the previous night. Both the detectives eyed him expectantly, and after a moment's silence he laughed uneasily. "I'm sorry to be a disappointment to you. The shock treatment doesn't seem to be very effective."

"Take your time," said Briggs, with ominous politeness. Sykes walked round the end of the sofa and took up his position where Ohlendorff had been the night before.

"Perhaps we can help Mr. Maitland," he remarked, and looked again at Antony. "If Benson had not been moved—and there were no signs that his body had been in any way disturbed—he was shot by someone who sat here."

"That's very interesting," said Antony, with polite indifference.

"Can you remember where you were sitting last evening?"

"When I first arrived? In this chair, here in front of me."

"And later?"

"I told you, Inspector, I don't know."

Briggs interrupted again, saying impatiently, "The room has been examined for fingerprints."

"So I should suppose. That sounds like a warning, Superintendent. Don't say you found mine in some incriminating position!"

"Not precisely. We'll go back a bit. You arrived. You sat in this chair. Where was Benson?"

"Opposite."

"In the same chair he died in?"

"Yes. Always supposing you're right when you say he hadn't been moved."

"Very well. Then he offered you sherry?"

"He did, and I accepted."

"Where did you stand your glass?"

"On the table. The one whose top is on the floor there."

"And where exactly was the table at that time?"

"As far as I recollect, just where the base of it is standing now."

"And did Benson also put his glass down on this table?"

"I believe he did."

"You then went into this mysterious matter of business?"

"Not mysterious, Superintendent. Merely private."

"The effect seems very much the same," snapped Briggs.

Sykes said suddenly, from his seat on the arm of the sofa, "Did the other man not drink when he came?"

Antony looked at him reproachfully. "You travel where I cannot follow. Was there another man?"

"Someone attacked you, after all. It couldn't have been Benson."

"I suppose not. Have you found any other evidence—?"

"Some unidentified fingerprints. Granted, they may not have been made last night. But, as I think I told you, Mr. Maitland, according to the evidence Benson was killed before you fought; we are therefore bound to postulate the presence of another man."

Antony shrugged. "Seems reasonable enough."

"But I should like to make it quite clear to you," said Briggs, taking over again, "that I don't believe a word of this tale of yours about losing your memory."

"Partial amnesia following a blow on the head is not uncommon, I believe."

"The doctor informs me that in that event the period of forgetfulness would most likely cover only what happened immediately before the blow."

Antony said slowly, "So if Benson was killed first, and *then* I was knocked out, I ought to remember the shooting?"

"Awkward, isn't it?" sneered Briggs.

"Not particularly. I'll guarantee," said Antony, more cheerfully, "that for every doctor you produce to back your opinion, I'll produce at least one of my way of thinking."

Briggs exclaimed with impatience. Sykes said peaceably, "Well, expert evidence is awkward, at best. But you must see, sir, that your story does not completely cover the facts as we now know them."

"It didn't cover them last night, either, from the way you went on," Antony retorted. "And all you knew then was what I told you."

"For a member of your profession, your conduct has

been—quite extraordinary," said Briggs, substituting a milder phrase at the last moment for the one that had been in his mind. "And as for this tale of yours—"

"Just a moment, Superintendent." Antony spoke softly. "There's a limit to what I will take from you. You have already accused me of lying. Just what is your insinuation now?"

Briggs said, blustering, "I have merely asked for explanations which you do not seem prepared to give. That being so, you can hardly take exception to my placing my own construction on events. For instance . . ." He paused, and Antony inquired, in a dangerous tone, "For instance?"

"I don't believe what you say about the reason for your coming to see Benson."

"But, my dear Superintendent, I haven't said anything!"

"You have implied that your silence is due to professional secrecy, or some similar claptrap; I think, Maitland, that you will not explain the reason for your call here because you dare not."

Antony looked at him for a moment, and a phrase Sykes had used to the local inspector came into his mind. ". . . one of the defense counsel . . . queer, isn't it?" He said, very gently, "So I was conspiring with Benson to produce false evidence on Gerry Martin's behalf. With all due respect, I don't understand how this slanderous theory helps you to explain his death."

"I admit," said Briggs, at his most pompous, "that the full pattern is not yet clear. But every scrap of truth we find will help."

"A beautiful thought," Antony approved. "I think this is where we part company, Superintendent. I told you I'd stand just so much, and now I've reached the limit."

Sykes, in a mild voice, said, "I shouldn't go yet, Mr. Maitland." And added, as Antony, who had been eyeing the superintendent, swung round angrily to face him, "You haven't told us yet what you know of Dr. Martin's desire to telephone Benson on the day he died."

This time he nearly got under his adversary's guard. "Nothing, I'm afraid," said Antony, after a pause. "I asked Benson, of course, as you must have done yourselves. He wasn't helpful.'' He reflected, suddenly amused, that this was exactly true.

"He didn't tell you, last night?"

"He did not, Inspector. Not that I remember."

Sykes shrugged. Antony said tartly, "You seem to know so little of what happened that I'm rather surprised at the tone you've seen fit to adopt with me."

"After all, Mr. Maitland, we *do* know you were here."

"What exactly is it you believe? From what you've told me, it seems you have two possible theories. Either I shot Benson, and after that some third person appeared and attacked me; or the said third person did both jobs. Faites vos jeux, messieurs! You pays your money, and you takes your choice."

"You're very helpful," said Briggs sourly. "Unfortunately, neither theory will fit the facts, as I expect you know."

"The human memory is very fallible," said Antony. "Very fallible," he added, startled. "I said I was leaving, didn't I? Good day, gentlemen."

He started toward the door, but was brought up short by the superintendent, who said, "One moment, Maitland. I haven't finished with you yet." His tone was peremptory. Antony turned slowly, and said with as incredulous an air as he could assume, "I beg your pardon!"

"You heard me very well, I think. There are still a number of questions I wish to ask."

"I think not, Superintendent. I told you before, I've had enough."

"You will go when I choose, Maitland. Not before."

Antony turned on his heel. Briggs was now so enraged that Antony was almost in expectation of being detained by force, but it was Sykes who reached the door and barred his way with a faint air of apology.

"I wouldn't do that, sir, really, I wouldn't. I'm sure the superintendent wouldn't want to detain you, but if you were to force his hand—"

"Detain me?" said Antony, swinging round again on Briggs with the light of battle in his eye. "Are you thinking of charging me with murder?"

"Not at this present. If there had been prints on the gun

now—" He paused for a moment, gloomily contemplating the omission. "But I'll put it bluntly: either you killed Benson, or you know who did. I shouldn't need to remind you that the charge of being an accessory to murder, even after the fact, is a serious one. If you persist in your attitude—"

"It's a nice point. Can one be tried as accessory to a murder 'by some person unknown'? I must ask my uncle about precedents."

"Damn the precedents!" said Briggs, too angry now to remain on his dignity. "Either you'll stay and answer my questions, or you'll leave under arrest."

Antony crossed the room to stand with his back to the empty grate. He was very white, so that the bruises on his face showed up startlingly. He was making a violent effort to control his temper, but even so he stammered a little as he said, "You give me no choice. But I can't promise to know the answers, I'm afraid."

"Very well." Briggs sounded grim. "Let us go back to your theories. Both, I believe, were based on the assumption that you were the victim of an attack."

Antony glanced about at the disorder that was still apparent, though the fragments of glass had been removed. "Of course, I might have had a fit. But I don't think I could have strangled myself." He raised inquiring eyes to meet the detective's skeptical gaze.

"That was not my point. Perhaps, Inspector Sykes, you will be good enough to tell Mr. Maitland what we have found out about the happenings in this room last night."

"Certainly, sir." Sykes had left the door now, and was standing behind Benson's chair. "We have agreed that you sat here with Benson, talking, and drinking sherry; and that the table was on the rug between you. And while you were talking someone came into this room by the glass door behind me."

"Holmes, you astound me! I'll grant someone came in, if you like; but how can you know when, or how?"

"We feel the assumption is borne out by the evidence; you may prefer to call it intelligent guesswork."

"Go on guessing, Inspector."

"Here I can be more precise. The newcomer sat on the

arm of the sofa there, and you changed your position, I think. At some time you must have stood near that table: your prints were on it, as if you had stood with your back to it, gripping the edge. At some time, too, you sat on that—that stuffed thing near the hearth.'' He looked inquiringly at Antony. ''Any comments, Mr. Maitland?''

''No comments.''

''Well, we'll presume you all sat there talking. At what point did Benson leave the room to speak to his landlady?''

Antony smiled gently, but did not reply. Briggs fumed visibly, and even Sykes was not altogether unmoved. ''We have Mrs. Nightingale's evidence on this point,'' he went on, ''that he did go out to speak to her, saying that his affairs with you would detain him longer than he had expected, and asking her to take a note to a friend of his who lives nearby. At some time after she left the house, he was shot.''

''By someone sitting on the arm of the sofa, you said? How can you be sure of that?''

''The shot was fired from a point too low to have come from behind the sofa—too low for anyone standing, in any case.''

''Unless he was a dwarf,'' Antony put in. ''You know, that seems to strike a chord.''

''Mr. Maitland!'' Briggs had walked to the table for the express purpose of pounding it with his fist. ''This is no time for foolery.''

''There's no pleasing you, Superintendent,'' Antony complained.

''We'll return to the point, sir, *if* you please,'' said Sykes. And was interested to note that Antony went back, without apparent thought, to the precise spot from which he had made his original deviation.

''Are you assuming that the newcomer shot Benson, or that we changed places?''

''On the whole, I think it more likely that the other man shot him. I have an open mind, though,'' he added, with the air of one making a concession.

''Proceed, Inspector. Your narrative interests me strangely.''

"I hoped it might, Mr. Maitland. It was at this point, I think, that the fight was started."

"But not by the other man," interposed Briggs. "You threw that brass tray at him."

"Dear me." Antony's tone was mild. "What a reputation for violence I am acquiring. But—I hate to spoil your story—but wasn't that rather strange behavior, as between accessory and principal?"

"Not so strange, perhaps, if he was threatening you with a gun."

"Extremely strange, in that case. I always make a point never to throw anything at a man with a gun. It's so dangerous," said Antony, earnestly.

Sykes suppressed a smile. Briggs said, harshly, "We have your prints from the table top: the left hand holding it, as you never could have done while it was in place, and tips of your right-hand fingers right underneath. There is also the mark of a bullet, which we must assume was fired when you took this drastic action; and the bullet itself, which was embedded in the wall above the door."

"It seems a pity to have forgotten so exciting an episode. I must have been mad," Antony said, with conviction.

"Well, as to that, sir, no doubt you had your reason." Sykes's pause was purely routine. "Very good reasons, I imagine, to prompt you to physical violence—handicapped as you are."

Antony tightened his lips, but declined the gambit. Instead he remarked, with an air of candor, "Well, the more I think of it, the more unlikely this story of yours seems to be."

Briggs, who had been listening to this exchange with ill-concealed restlessness, broke in to say: "Then perhaps you will enlighten us as to what really happened. That's what we want, after all."

Antony looked suddenly weary. "How many more times must I say it? I don't know. I don't remember."

"Well, Mr. Maitland," replied Sykes, with his air of unshakable courtesy, "you can't be more tired of saying so than we are of hearing it." He glanced at the superintendent, who said, ominously, "Very well, Maitland! Very well! You will, of course, be called at the inquest on Tuesday.''

"Of course," echoed Antony. He shifted his weight from his right foot to his left, and looked from one to the other of the detectives. "May I go now?" he inquired.

Sykes, at least, realized that this was as near an admission of defeat as they were likely to get. And he did not think that, even now, he would get any reaction to his questions that was not calculated. He looked at Antony reproachfully. "Perhaps when you have had time to consider your position—''

The superintendent intervened at that point. He said to Sykes, "We're wasting our time, Inspector."

"Did no one ever explain to you the difference between 'can't' and 'won't'?"

"I can recognize it as well as the next man," Briggs replied.

"Is that all, sir? Then if Mr. Maitland would like to be getting along—''

"We won't keep you any longer, just now," Briggs agreed.

At any other time the incongruity of this sudden relapse into conventional politeness would have caused Antony some amusement. Now he only wanted to get away. He managed a faint smile as he made his farewells and had the small satisfaction of seeing the bland look on Briggs's face replaced by one of anger.

CHAPTER FOURTEEN

IT WAS A GRAY morning, and though the frost was gone the breeze was chilly and there was a smell of rain in the air. Antony went up the stairs toward chambers and shivered a little as he did so, though he was too preoccupied to be conscious of feeling cold. Old Mr. Mallory was hovering, and greeted him with a politely incurious look, that ought to have amused him, and the information that his uncle had that moment returned from his conference.

Sir Nicholas glanced up as his nephew went in and opened his mouth to speak, but, taking a second and more searching look, evidently thought better of it. This time Antony did summon a smile, and said, "Thanks, Uncle Nick," as he crossed the room. He stood at the window, looking out, and after a moment added in a tone that was flat with exhaustion, "I couldn't take any more just now."

Sir Nicholas waited, and presently coughed a little, inquiringly. Antony turned. "I asked John to meet me here. Do you mind?"

"Of course I don't."

"I've been out to Streatham, at the urgent request of the police. It wasn't awfully amusing."

"I see," said Sir Nicholas, carefully.

Antony leaned back with his shoulders against a tall mahogany bookcase. "Jenny said I should have taken you with me, but honestly I don't think it would have helped."

"When," inquired his uncle, pertinently, "is the inquest?"

"Tuesday. I didn't get the impression that they meant to ask for an adjournment."

"I take it the police attitude is still hostile."

Antony grimaced. "They were kind enough to say they didn't think I killed Benson, but if I don't reconsider my position I'm liable to be arrested as an accessory. I suppose that's fair," he added, thoughtfully. "It's near enough the truth, from their point of view."

"They couldn't make it stick," said his uncle, positively. "It's a damned uncomfortable position, but they can't prove you remember what happened."

"It'd be enough if they could convince the jury; and bad enough, anyway, even if I got off."

"No, no, they'd never try it. No evidence: except that you were there. And no motive could be shown."

"Ah, well, perhaps I got rattled for nothing." Antony spoke with more energy, but he did not sound convinced. "I must say, sir, I'm not looking forward to the inquest." Sir Nicholas recognized the appeal, in the tone if not in the words, and his expression became a little grimmer.

"I don't suppose so. Can Welwyn do anything about it, I wonder? A postponement would be something." He turned his head, listening. "That sounds like him now. Come and sit down, Antony. You'll do no good with this restlessness."

Antony came obediently to the chair he usually occupied. Welwyn came in, with a more than usually harassed look. He said, without preliminaries: "I got your message, but I didn't realize how bad it is. Have you seen the papers?"

"We have not," said Sir Nicholas, impounding the copy that was being waved at him and putting it down firmly under a glass paperweight. "Nor do we wish to."

Welwyn looked a little stunned at this regal pronouncement, but rallied to ask, "When's the inquest?"

Sir Nicholas nodded his approval of this grasp of essentials. "On Tuesday. And I should like to know what you intend to do about it?"

"Do?" Welwyn sounded astonished. "Me?"

Sir Nicholas fixed him with a stern eye, and proceeded to point out to him just where the responsibility lay for the occurrences of the previous evening. He finished, "I know nothing of how these things are arranged; but it occurs to me that if you do not wish to be frank with the police there must be some channel—"

Welwyn interrupted. "Yes," he said. "Yes, of course." He looked from Sir Nicholas to his nephew, and his manner held an unaccustomed awkwardness. "If we find Ohlendorff, now . . ." He shrugged his shoulders. "Otherwise . . . there are difficulties."

"Perhaps you would care to be more explicit?"

He got up again . . . and again looked from one to the other of them. "It's damned awkward," he said, uncomfortably. "The thing is . . ." He moved a little, so as to face his former colleague more directly; still he hesitated for a moment, and then went on with something of his customary directness, "Antony, did you kill Benson?"

Sir Nicholas, who was watching his nephew, saw him whiten, though he had been pale before. He sat very still, looking up at Welwyn; only his hands gripped the arms of the chair still more tightly, and his eyes were suddenly bright and very angry.

"D-don't you trust me, Welwyn?" His voice was unemotional.

Welwyn said, with sudden violence, "D'you think I'd blame you? I know nothing of the circumstances. Only I must know."

Antony became aware that his uncle was standing behind him, gripping his shoulder. He said, indifferently, "I didn't kill him."

Welwyn relaxed his strained attitude a little. "You wouldn't lie to me," he said with relief.

"Does that make a difference?" Sir Nicholas's tone was stiff, and he had to make an obvious effort to refrain from further comment.

"It would have made things even more complicated; and, goodness knows, they're bad enough anyway. Wright backed me up, he took the matter up with Selkirk—I'll say this for him, he never lets one of his own chaps down. It's this business of Ohlendorff; they don't like coincidences—well, I look twice at them myself. If we can produce him, well and good. But they want some proof you're telling the truth.''

''The police know someone else was there.''

''Yes, but they don't know it was a German agent. As for Selkirk and company, they think it may have been Morris, but—''

''I suppose you are trying to imply that Antony is suffering from hallucinations? I should spare your efforts to be tactful if I were you, Major.''

''Well,'' said Welwyn doggedly, ''I know myself he had Ohlendorff on his mind, since the French trip at least . . .''

Antony stirred. He felt his uncle's hand tighten on his shoulder and said, ''It's all right, sir. I'm too tired for heroics.'' He looked at Welwyn. ''All this means, no action will be taken? Unless, as you say, we find Ohlendorff.''

''I did my best, Antony.''

''I'm sure you did. But that being so, I'd better tell you where it leaves me.'' He glanced across at his uncle, and for the first time that morning there was a glint of genuine amusement in his eyes. ''Briggs told me to reconsider my position, and this seems as good a time as any.''

''Go ahead,'' said Welwyn.

''I have lied to the police, because I felt my first duty in this matter was to you. But I am not prepared to repeat those lies on oath, on Tuesday, or at any other time. That being so, I shall have no alternative but to refuse to answer questions; the consequences won't be pleasant, and perhaps that isn't important, but I think it entitles me to know one thing: what if I don't keep silent? What if I tell the truth?''

Welwyn met his look squarely, and something of the puzzled honesty in his eyes made Antony remember how much they had been through together. John was a good friend; and he had always known, after all, that where his work was concerned he was completely ruthless. He felt no resentment at what Sir Nicholas obviously regarded as a betrayal; it would take more than a few bitter words to break the bond that was between them.

''That's not so easy to answer.'' Welwyn looked at Sir

Nicholas, and then turned to find his chair again. He spoke with obvious sincerity, picking his words, and making a transparent attempt not to overstate his case. "I won't pretend finding our man—Ohlendorff or another—is of earth-shaking importance; but it is important, for all that. He's a clever man, and a very dangerous one, and we won't catch him if there's any publicity. You know that. What's worse, perhaps, is the effect of another spy scare in the newspapers: the Morris affair is one thing, fairly easily digested. But affairs are pretty tricky, with all this talk about the rebirth of the Nazi party; and no one wants to give our friends the Russians the chance to make capital out of our troubles."

"That's very clear," said Sir Nicholas, and for the first time since Welwyn's arrival his voice held a note of cordiality. They both looked at Antony, who in his turn gazed at the floor. Welwyn had not reminded him of the oaths of secrecy he had taken in the past, and for this he was grateful; he wondered just how difficult he would find it to recall them himself had it not been for the added inducement of his own score with Ohlendorff . . . and even there he was torn two ways. At last he said, still not raising his eyes, "All right, John, I'll play it your way. Don't you agree, Uncle Nick?"

"You'll have to go to the devil your own way," said his uncle, testily. "Good heavens, boy, you can't expect me to encourage you."

"Of course not." Antony looked up, and his expression was a trifle bewildered.

Welwyn said, bluntly, "I never expected your agreement, Sir Nicholas."

"Why will nobody ever take what I say at its face value? I did not agree. I specifically said . . ." He broke off, then, and looked at his nephew. "You see, neither of you two young idiots have bothered to consider the real answer to the question. If Antony tells the truth, without official backing, who'll believe him?"

"Well, there is that," said Antony, deflated.

Welwyn left the subject without further ado and demanded firsthand details of last night's events. He listened attentively as Antony embarked on his recital: a quiet, fair man, who had just got his own way, and found it a surprisingly unsatisfactory circumstance. Antony completed one part of his tale, and went on to his recent talk with the police. "And there you have it," he concluded.

Welwyn, as was his custom, took his time to digest the information. He said at last, "I don't see that it takes us very far."

"At least you know now who you are looking for," replied Antony, a little tartly.

"In a way. But until we identify Morris—"

"When is Madeleine arriving? Have you heard from Carr?"

"They're due in tomorrow evening, and that has been pretty quick work."

"Yes, it has, really. But it doesn't leave much time—"

Sir Nicholas interposed quietly: "What steps have you in mind, Welwyn?"

"That we should try to trace Benson's murderer. The only leads we've got are your two suspects for the other affair. Can you give me any more guidance, Antony?"

"I could ask you to play my hunch, but I think it's too risky. I think you must treat both possibilities equally. And, if you will forgive the criticism, more seriously than you did my tip about Benson. You'll pay particular reference to the gentlemen who provided alibis for them, won't you?"

Welwyn nodded. "That certainly."

Antony said thoughtfully, "What's the betting Mr. Pitt is weekending in the country?"

"He is," said Welwyn. He spoke quietly, and Antony looked at him inquiringly.

"Everything under control," he remarked. "I should apologize, I suppose, for my strictures—"

"Especially," said the other man firmly, "as we've sounded the gentleman out about the alibi and he's inclined to be vague about times. Not nearly so certain as Maddison was, I'm afraid."

"I shouldn't let that worry you. As for the other . . . whatever Herr Ohlendorff has been doing in England, he hasn't been masquerading as Sir Francis Potter."

"He might be in contact with Potter. Or directly with Condon. The trouble is, the field is so wide."

Sir Nicholas had been sitting quietly, intent on the discussion. He got up now, with a movement more abrupt than was usual. Antony looked up at him inquiringly. "Does something strike you, sir?"

"Forcibly. But first I have some questions to ask." He walked to the window and back again, with a restlessness completely uncharacteristic, and came to a stand looking down at Welwyn, whom he addressed formally.

"Tell me, Major, you have no objection to Morris being exposed, and his misdeeds made public, provided"—he held up his hand as the man he was addressing opened his mouth to speak—". . . yes, I am coming to the proviso; provided that your chances of discovering Ohlendorff are not thereby prejudiced." He paused, and then added with an inflection of sarcasm, "For the purposes of my argument I must ask you to bear with my assumption that Ohlendorff is, in fact, the man you want."

Welwyn eyed him warily; Antony, with interest. The former said slowly, "Accepting your premises, I think I may say there would be no objection. But—"

"Then may I outline a possible course of action to you?" Sir Nicholas had no intention of allowing himself to be diverted. "I may add," he went on, with a tight, unamused smile, "that I intend to do so, with or without your consent."

"Then I must listen." Welwyn spoke lightly, but his eyes were intent.

"You have agreed that Ohlendorff must be anxious to—shall we say—dispose of Morris? Do you think," he added, turning to his nephew, "that he is likely to take any action during the week end?" Antony hesitated. "How much does he know, for instance, of your activities?"

"He knew I'd been in touch with John. I don't think he placed much reliance on my denials. But he didn't mention Madeleine, and he would have done if he'd known about her because he was trying to demonstrate how much he knew. He's planning to get rid of Morris, but I imagine . . . well, he'd probably prefer to kill me first." He met his uncle's look steadily. "That's also on the agenda, sir. I thought you realized."

"You must forgive my stupidity," said Sir Nicholas bitterly. "I have not your experience in these matters."

"No, sir. Well, I can't be sure, of course, but I think it's unlikely that Ohlendorff will make any immediate move."

"But if we could arrange matters so that it was obvious that Morris was about to be publicly identified, wouldn't that bring him on the scene? He must be extremely averse to seeing Morris exposed to questioning." He turned again to Welwyn as he spoke.

"It is at least possible." John was still cautious, but his interest was held now.

"And if your department has got the man it wants, Wright and Selkirk will be willing to intervene so that Benson's inquest may pass without awkward questions?"

"*If* we've got him—and before the inquest." His tone was skeptical, but Antony (who had been eyeing his uncle) intervened, to ask eagerly, "Uncle Nick, what are you going to do?"

"I am going," said Sir Nicholas in his most dulcet tones, "to call the police bluff. They asked for an adjournment, did they, to prepare the evidence? Well, they'll need their evidence, I'll see to that. I shall put on the defense— full scale—in the magistrate's court on Monday."

Welwyn was momentarily speechless. Antony muttered, "Have at thee!" under his breath, and added, aloud, "Can we do it, sir?"

"We'll have a damned good try," said Counsel, firmly. And sat back to watch the effect of his suggestion on their visitor.

John Welwyn was still doubtful. "It's risky," he said. And then, more definitely, "I don't like it."

"I don't see that," said Antony. "There are three possibilities—that's right, isn't it, sir?" Sir Nicholas nodded. "First, we may merely demonstrate to the court that there was once a man called Morris, who (if he were still alive) would have the best of reasons for killing Dr. Martin; the second—that, plus an identification; third, in addition to the foregoing, we may also bring Ohlendorff out from cover—well, you couldn't complain about that, could you?"

"Naturally not, provided the matter were then handled with discretion. But—"

"Patience, John. I just want to point out that neither the first nor the second possibility does you any harm that I can see."

"You needn't labor the point, Antony. Major Welwyn has already agreed that there is no objection—"

"I don't like it," said John again. "I can't agree—"

"But I don't want your agreement, my dear fellow. You may think my action ill-advised, but how do you propose to stop me?"

"Anyway, nothing is really changed," said Antony. "I've already agreed to fall in with your wishes at the inquest; unless we get Ohlendorff, we shall proceed as arranged."

There was a little more discussion, but Sir Nicholas showed no sign of shifting his ground; he parried all Welwyn's arguments with a bland facility that sent the latter home, at last, in no amiable frame of mind, and muttering darkly to himself about damned, pigheaded lawyers.

Antony returned from accompanying him to the door, and said with a poor attempt at lightness, "He isn't happy, I'm afraid."

"Major Welwyn's emotions are, I'm glad to say, a matter of the greatest indifference to me," said Sir Nicholas, on his dignity. "Tell me, Antony, how sure are you that you know who Morris is?"

"Well . . . pretty sure."

"We'll have to call both those men . . . Maddison as well as Condon, of course. And if you're right, one of them will be bewildered, and one of them will be in something of a panic; which is all to the good, as it probably means he'll get in touch with his principal. You'll have to handle their evidence: I hope you've no objection to making a fool of yourself in public."

"Console yourself, sir. Compared with what people will think after the inquest on Benson—"

"Very well then. I'll talk to Horton, and try to explain

matters to him. He'll have to see Gerry . . ." He paused with his hand on the telephone. "But I don't anticipate any opposition there," he added.

"I'll bet you don't!" said Antony.

CHAPTER FIFTEEN

OF THE REMAINDER of the week end, the only thing that
later was clear in Antony's mind was the visit Peter Henderson paid to Kempenfeldt Square that evening. He arrived alone in a taxi, at about six o'clock, and Antony took
him into Sir Nicholas's drawing room and led him to a
sofa by one of the long windows. There was a moment of
silence, then Henderson said sharply, "Are we alone?"

"We are."

"I left my mother at the hotel. I had to talk to you.
Maitland, you've seen her?"

The afternoon had been a confusion of plans and opin-
ions, and Antony was still in this world of unreality; a
world where Madeleine Bonnard was no more than a lay
figure—a witness whose only importance was her ability
to make, or not to make, the desired identification. He was
conscious of the effort he made to bring reality into focus:
to see her again as a person with a life to live and feelings
to be hurt. He said: "I found her with the help of the
curé—living with his sister, on a farm about ten miles
from Pontoise."

"Is she well?"

"She seemed very well, in health, at least. But in spirit,
I can't hide it from you, she has been hurt almost past
enduring. She will need . . . great kindness."

"You don't mean—her mind?" His anxiety was painful.

"No, not that. She seemed to forget the past for a time,

because she did not want to remember. Until I spoke of Pierre.''

As always, it was Henderson's hands that betrayed him, clutching painfully at the arms of his chair. He said: ''She wanted to remember me? But—does she wish to see me?''

''I think . . .'' (For once in his life, Antony was floundering badly.) ''I think she both hopes—and fears—to see you.''

''Because I am blind.'' The words came quickly, almost hopefully.

''No.''

''Then, am I right—?'' He stopped short and then went on with determination, ''Am I right when I think . . . she is alive . . . because of Morris?''

''I—forgive me . . .'' Antony paused and then spoke with decision. ''I have no right to speak of what she told me, though I have wondered whether she hoped I should tell you. But—yes—that is the reason.''

The blind man turned his head away, almost as though he could see through the window what was going on in the square below. After a while he said, quietly: ''I have forgiven him so much: his treachery; her death (as I thought); my blindness. Can I forgive him this?''

Antony did not speak. After a long moment Henderson went on, ''You did not know her. But . . . do you think I shall find her altered?''

''She seems a young girl still. I cannot think you will find her changed.'' He was picking his words carefully, and Henderson smiled, but his voice when he replied was scornful.

''You're thinking of Morris. Do you think I care for that? Only that he has hurt her.'' After a moment he added, ''My mother will look after her, she has promised that at least. Afterwards—it must be Madeleine's choice. But I pray she will still be the same.''

They spoke for a while after that, and then Henderson left; and Antony went back to the discussion in the study, which showed no signs of ever reaching a conclusion. It was, in fact, two o'clock on Sunday morning before Geoffrey Horton left; Antony was too sleepy by then to stay long awake, but he spent a restless night—his thoughts a treadmill which his mind plodded uselessly, even while he slept.

Welwyn phoned while they were breakfasting and had nothing helpful to report. Madeleine was already on her way, and he had made careful arrangements for her safety. The other activities they had discussed were all in hand; and none of them, he added sourly, showed any sign of paying dividends. Antony sympathized in an absent tone that did little to soothe his former colleague.

After that the day dragged along, and he would have welcomed even the repeated tedium of yesterday's conference. Sir Nicholas was irritable, and Antony, guessing the reason, submitted docilely enough to a program which gave little opportunity for the execution of any plans Ohlendorff might have formed for his undoing.

Geoffrey reported after lunch that both Condon and Maddison had been duly notified of the hearing the following day. But Antony felt now that the plan was too vague, too haphazard. He went to the magistrate's court on Monday morning without any real hope that Sir Nicholas's stratagem would be successful.

The hearing was before the London Stipendiary Magistrate, Mr. Nolen, a cheerful, bird-like little man who seemed to appreciate quite as much as did the members of the Press the unexpected treat which Sir Nicholas's opening remarks held out before him. The most he had hoped for was a brief statement of the Crown's case, and here was defense counsel promising to bring evidence in refutation. He settled down happily to listen, after a quick, inquisitive look at Sir Nicholas's junior, who seemed to have met with a nasty accident.

Antony was feeling a little self-conscious. Wig and bands would have hidden the worst of the damage, but here he was denied so much camouflage. He felt the eye of the leading Crown counsel, Bruce Halloran, fixed on him sardonically, and gave him in return a rather sheepish grin. Halloran was one of the most eminent of Treasury counsel, a friend of Sir Nicholas who had proved a good friend to the younger man also on several occasions. Now he wondered just what he was making of the set-up, for the defense's decision was unusual, even if not exactly without precedent.

Gerry Martin, when he appeared, made an unexpectedly good impression. He was excited by the turn events had taken, and consequently less on the defensive. Antony saw Daisy sitting at the back of the court, and wondered briefly what would be the outcome of that affair. The girl flushed as Gerry's wandering eye met hers; and seeing the young man's expression soften momentarily, Antony could not help but wonder whether—as he had feared—it was, after all, Daisy who was going to get hurt.

The proceedings opened slowly; well, they had known the strength of the police case, and it sounded no better as it unfolded under Halloran's expert encouragement. Inspector Sykes gave evidence, when his turn came, with all his customary placidity. Antony glanced across at Superintendent Briggs, and thought he looked both angry and complacent. A queer mixture, undeniably, and perhaps he was only imagining the anger; there was no doubt about his self-assurance as he listened to the prosecution witnesses who followed each other in quick succession, and with only the most perfunctory of challenges from the defense.

The magistrate adjourned for lunch when the last of them had been heard; Sir Nicholas lingered to speak to Bruce Halloran, and Antony took the opportunity to look over the spectators who were filing out. There was only one door to the room for the use of the public, and by the time his uncle was ready to leave he was able to assure him with reasonable certainty that Ohlendorff had not been among those present. Sir Nicholas gave him a cold look but made no comment. He was preoccupied today, and just for the moment his intense concentration on the means had all but obscured the end in view. Antony envied his single-mindedness and ate his lunch in a depressed silence.

When they returned to court it was the turn of the defense. Sir Nicholas was aiming at a definite effect, and built up his tension skillfully. First there was Daisy; questions about times, questions about the matching pair of stockings; she gave back look for look when Bruce Halloran rose to cross-examine, and he did not press his questions. The next witness was Maddison, who seemed to be in a bad temper (as well, indeed, he might); he was followed by Condon, who obviously was pursuing his own train of thought, even while obligingly—and without the faintest show of surprise—answering what was put to him. In both cases Antony took them through the direct examination, with a display of ineptitude which he hoped convinced the court that some deep-laid scheme on the part of the defense was being ruined by the junior counsel. He found Halloran looking at him and frowning and thought perhaps he hadn't succeeded as well as he had hoped. Sir Nicholas scowled and fidgeted and called his own clerk, Hill, in something of a hurry when the business of signing Condon's statement was over and the witness had stepped down. Briggs's expression unmistakably darkened as he heard the four o'clock phone call sworn to; he looked with raised eyebrows at his subordinate, and Sykes shrugged slightly and looked blank.

Halloran made short work of his part of the questioning; nobody could have said the evidence was impressive, but Sir Nicholas had got the court to the stage of wondering what exactly he was at. Today he was concerned only with the effect he could create. He asked for his next witness: "Mlle Madeleine Bonnard" with admirable clarity, and then fixed his eyes on the door by which she might be expected to enter the court. But Antony looked at the group of people who had already given their evidence, and tried to decide if either of his two "possibles" could indeed so well be hiding a sudden terror. Could Morris be here and give no sign of fear? Her name he could not have forgotten, still less her face. And as she reached the witness box Madeleine's profile would be clearly seen by each of the previous witnesses; though she, being half turned from them, would have to make something of an effort to look in their direction. Antony had ample opportunity to study the two men, during the troublesome business of swearing an interpreter. But still there was no sign whether he was right or wrong in his belief that Morris was in the court. And still there was no sign of Ohlendorff.

Certainly Sir Nicholas, and the spectators in whom he had succeeded in arousing an interest equal to his own, were getting their money's worth out of Madeleine. As he turned back to look at her, Antony realized he had forgotten how lovely she was. She was quietly dressed, and seemed unexpectedly self-possessed. And when Sir Nicholas spoke to her she turned to him with a friendly, confiding look.

"Your name is Madeleine Bonnard, and you live now at Callens, in Compiègne; but before the war, and for some time after it broke out, you lived at Pontoise, on your parents' farm?"

"All that is true, m'sieur." She was looking around her now, and her eyes lighted on Antony, first with a smile, and then with a look of anxiety. She turned back to Sir Nicholas. "*Ce pauvre* Monsieur Maitland! You will forgive me, I had looked to see him, but no one tells me he has been injured."

"*N'importe*, mademoiselle," said Sir Nicholas quickly, before the interpreter could get going on this artless speech. He turned apologetically to the magistrate, who looked at the witness with benevolence, and assented without argument that the last remarks need not appear on the record. Antony saw the reporters scribbling and frowned at Horton's look of amusement. The court settled again to the slow business of question and answer.

"Will you tell us what you remember of Dr. Henry Martin?"

"But yes, m'sieur, he was my parents' friend. He would stay with us—oh, every summer until the war came. I remember him well. He loved our country, and he would walk, and walk, and in the evenings he would play chess with Papa: it was summertime, *bien entendu*, but my brothers were grown men and could do all that needed to be done on the farm, and in the fields."

Halloran got up here, in his leisurely way. "I should apologize, I feel, for interrupting so charming *une histoire*. But—is this relevant?"

"I claim the court's indulgence. The relevance will emerge."

"In the fullness of time, no doubt?" Halloran's tone was dry.

"Precisely!"

"But meanwhile . . . your worship, I must protest at this attempt to—to beguile the court with irrelevant matter."

"Your worship, I submit that it is my right to call whatever witnesses are necessary—"

"Does my learned friend suggest that the motive for Henry Martin's death is to be sought in France—in the days before the war?"

"If my friend will have patience he will see more clearly than he likes what I suggest—and what I will prove."

This exchange had been conducted at top speed, and Nolan—unable to find a chance to interrupt—was waiting with an air of exaggerated patience for its conclusion. Now he said, as both learned gentlemen paused for breath and looked at him expectantly, "I cannot allow your objection, Mr. Halloran. The defense may proceed."

"Your worship . . ." Halloran began, but caught his opponent's eye fixed on him sardonically and sat down again with a reluctant grin. Sir Nicholas turned back to Madeleine, who (obviously puzzled) eyed him doubtfully and spoke more slowly when she resumed her story.

"He came each year, and the year of the war he was with us in August."

"And after the war started. Did you hear from him again?"

"But yes, one came to us from the Resistance, and spoke his name, and so it was arranged that we might help them."

"Could you tell us a little more clearly, mademoiselle, what you understood had happened?"

"I understood that he had spoken of us in England . . . that we were well-disposed . . . that we were not collaborators."

"And then, did you meet someone who had known your old friend, who spoke of him, perhaps, to your parents?"

For the first time she paused, and Antony saw then how hardly held was her air of self-possession, how thin the veneer of calm. She said, very slowly, "He came from England to join our underground; he spoke of his training in London, and of information Monsieur le Docteur had given to him; and of how he had spoken of us with great affection.''

"His name, Mlle Bonnard?"

"Edouard, m'sieur. Edouard Meurice. He said one should call him Tédé.''

The translation here took a little longer than usual, as it was necessary to spell the second name. They got it right between them at last, but while this was going on Antony had taken the opportunity of looking again at the man he suspected; and now he saw that his guess had been the right one. There was still no outward display of fear that any disinterested observer could have seen. Antony (far from disinterested) saw it in the man's eyes, in the hand that tugged at his tie, in the set expression of his face. He looked back at Madeleine, but she had her eyes on his uncle and was speaking again in that slow, painful way, "After that . . . the days passed. And they were busy with great plans. And then . . .''

"I am sorry to distress you, mademoiselle.''

"That does not matter.''

"Then you will tell us, what happened after that?''

She spoke very low now, but clearly still, and so slowly that Antony felt the services of the interpreter could not possibly be needed by any of her hearers. "We were betrayed. The Germans came—''

"Whom did they take?''

"From our home: my parents, my three brothers, and an English airman who was in hiding till we could send him home. Of our friends in the Resistance I have heard that all but two—''

"And you also were arrested?''

"But, yes, m'sieur.''

"And then—?''

"I did not see them again—only, once, my brother François. But I heard that they died, and I do not believe that they told *les Boches* any of the things they wished to know. François said, too, that they were dead—and the next day they shot him, also.''

"And what happened to Morris?''

"It was he who betrayed us, m'sieur. I had thought you understood.''

"Forgive me. It is a thing I must prove, ma'm'selle: to the court, and—most difficult of all—to the very skeptical gentleman who is sitting opposite me." He waved a hand in Halloran's direction, and Nolan, too, directed a piercing look at him as though daring him to interrupt. It was plain, however, that by this time Halloran was quite as fascinated as were the rest of Madeleine's audience.

"Then I must tell you. And these gentlemen will forgive me that I seem to speak of my own affairs, and that, perhaps, the tale seems long in the telling." She looked down a moment, and then fixed her eyes on a point just above Sir Nicholas's left ear as she began again to speak. She was flushed now, and Antony wondered just what an effort this careful calmness was costing her. "I know it is true that he betrayed us, because he said it himself. He came to me, not long after they shot François. I thought him a prisoner too, and I said to him 'I am sorry for it, m'sieur' . . . after all, he had been our guest. He was not at the house when the Germans came, and I hoped he had gone free. I thought perhaps they had let him come because now he must die, too. But he laughed." She closed her eyes suddenly, as though the sound of that laughter was more terrible to her than all that had gone before. "He said: 'I'm a free man, *chérie*. I've come to help you.' " She opened her eyes again, and looked full at Sir Nicholas for a moment. "He spoke French very badly, m'sieur, But that was not why I could not understand him. I thought only that he had told to the Germans things that they wished to know . . . and how could I blame him? But I said, 'If they kill me, I will never speak' (and I do not know if that was true). He laughed again and said did I not understand? No one should hurt me, but he was offering me freedom. He took my hand. And he said . . ." She was speaking very low now, and her voice was wry, as though the words had a bitter taste to them. "He said . . . he . . . loved me."

During the pause that followed Halloran made as though to rise, but thought better of the idea. Antony took another look across at the men who had given evidence. Condon was aloof as ever, with a little frown of concentration between his eyes. Maddison was sweating a little (but the atmosphere in the court was heavy); he was also listening quietly. He turned then to where Sykes had been sitting and saw his place empty, though Briggs was still in the chair he had occupied since the beginning of the hearing. Someone had given Madeleine a glass of water. It looked yellowish and must be flat, but she seemed grateful and, after she had sipped it, took up her tale again without any prompting.

"I did not like it that he should speak so, and I tried to pull my hand away. But he held it tightly, so I said . . . even if that were true . . . how could he help me? He said, 'They'll do anything I want,' and when I told him not to believe their promises he said I didn't understand. He said he had known before he left England what he would do . . . and he boasted that he had found all the details of our organization before he went to the Gestapo . . . and he did not see that what he had done was horrible. He thought I should be grateful to him that I need not die, too, and that . . . nobody . . . would 'hurt' me." She looked up at Nolan, and then at Halloran, before asking quietly: "Is that enough for your proof, m'sieur? Must I go on?"

"I think that is enough. Now I must ask you—"

"Your worship!" Halloran had heard her tale with interest; but if he suspected there was more to come, at least he had every intention of giving his adversary a run for his money. "I must ask your permission to inquire of my friend what he thinks he has proved by this evidence."

"And I ask nothing better than to tell you. With your worship's permission?" Sir Nicholas turned an inquiring look at the magistrate, who smiled back impartially at the two leading counsel.

"As both you gentlemen seem, for the time being, to be in agreement, I shall be very pleased to hear what the defense has to say."

"Very well." Sir Nicholas's voice was very serious now, and he turned toward Halloran as he spoke. "I think you will admit motive. A man who did what Morris had done would have the best of reasons for killing the one person he knew could recognize him . . . would he not?"

"I will grant that . . . if you feel it has any importance. *If* Morris were alive . . . *if* he were in England . . . *if* his path crossed that of Henry Martin—then, I concede, this argument would have some validity.'' He turned back to look at Nolan. ''When this witness took the stand, your worship, I protested that her evidence had no bearing on the case. I appreciate my learned friend's anxiety to present some sort of case in this court.'' He paused for effect, and added dramatically: ''But what sort of defense is this, that depends on a string of 'ifs'?''

''That is what I wish to show you.'' Sir Nicholas now spoke very gently. ''Morris is alive . . . he is in England . . . he met Dr. Martin on the day he died. Do you still admit the validity of my argument?''

''Prove it!'' Halloran's words were a gauge thrown down, and Sir Nicholas bowed his acceptance of the challenge.

''With your worship's permission.'' Counsel for the defense turned again to his witness. ''Mlle Bonnard, would you know Morris if you saw him again?''

''Without doubt, m'sieur.''

''Then look about you, mademoiselle. Will you tell the court whether you see him here?''

''Willingly, m'sieur.'' But she looked at him for a long moment before turning to obey his request. There was no doubt now about the tension in the court. Antony found himself holding his breath—tormented by one last moment of doubt—before he saw her stiffen, and heard her voice again, with its false note of calm. ''He is there: m'sieur.''

She was looking down at the benches where the witnesses were sitting. Sir Nicholas moved a little to see where she was pointing.

''Thank you, mademoiselle. Let me be sure there is no mistake. The gentleman by the aisle? Would you mind standing up, Mr. Maddison, so that the court can see you?''

CHAPTER SIXTEEN

AFTERWARD, Antony's recollection of that moment was in the form of a series of pictures, each vivid and complete. He saw Nolan leaning forward, his eyes bright with interest; Halloran's look of incredulity, changing to a reluctant belief as he followed the direction of Madeleine's pointing finger; Gerry Martin, whose bewilderment verged (even in that moment of tension) upon the comical; Superintendent Briggs, looking round anxiously to see where his subordinate had got to; and Maddison, getting up shakily and looking round him for the help that, clearly, could not be forthcoming. It was in that moment that Antony saw him clearly, for the first time, as Teddy Morris: the man who had sacrificed his comrades and his benefactors, not for any high ideal, but for the sake of his own comfort; and who had killed again, without a second thought, when his security was threatened. Previously, it had been rather Condon's quick and imaginative perception that had made him believe he must look elsewhere for Morris. The lack of malice was horrifying; even a hint of sadism would have made the man more understandable, but this was absent too, even from his dealings with Madeleine Bonnard; here was nothing but a bland, overweening egotism, a total blindness to any rights but his own.

The clarity lasted only a moment. Maddison, after that one, despairing glance around the courtroom, was clutching at the tatters of the air of disinterested attention which he had worn throughout the hearing. He said, ''I don't understand . . ." and then fell silent again; the words had come thickly, and it was obvious that he found difficulty in speaking.

Sir Nicholas said, "Don't you, Mr. Morris?" and his voice was scornful. He turned again toward the bench, and looked up at the magistrate. "I have no more to say, your worship. That is the case for the defense."

The words rang out clearly in the quiet room, and at once it was quiet no longer. There was a mutter of talk, of conjecture, and the tension was broken in a wave of uneasy movement. But Antony was conscious only of a dull feeling of despair. Of the points he had enumerated to Welwyn, the second had been fulfilled to admiration. But as for the third . . . the bait had not been taken, he could be sure of that now. And tomorrow there would be the inquest on Benson to face, and his promise to John Welwyn to fulfill.

He glanced around again and saw Sykes by the door, his face as placid as ever. And then he looked at Madeleine and forgot his own anxiety when he saw her expression.

He went to her without thinking, momentarily regardless of the courtroom etiquette which should have kept them both in their separate places. (But Sir Nicholas had the court's attention . . . Sir Nicholas and Teddy Morris between them.) She turned to him eagerly and put out her hands to him. He gave her his left hand and she clutched at it; there were tears on her cheeks, and for the moment she was lost in a horror of recollection.

Antony did not speak, and after a moment she looked at him and said, "That is how *they* felt . . . they were caught, and they were frightened. I cannot bear to see that look, even though it is he that looks so. I thought I should be glad when he was taken, but I cannot be glad to see anyone so frightened." She shut her eyes again for a moment, and added almost in a whisper. "Like a rat in a barn, when the boys go in with their dogs."

Antony was more shaken himself than he would have admitted. There was a cold-blooded quality about this that had its own horror. Madeleine opened her eyes again and looked past his shoulder with an air of fascination at the group which had gathered around Maddison. As he watched, her expression changed from the reluctant pity she had felt a moment since to bewilderment, and then to horror.

Antony turned to look, and as he did so the crowd shifted and Maddison, who had been almost surrounded, was clearly in view. His expression had altered now; he no longer looked hunted . . . only stupefied, as though something was happening beyond his comprehension. He looked full at Madeleine and still there was only surprise in his face. Then his head jerked, his body twisted as he fell, and somebody called out in alarm.

Before the confusion became complete, Antony had moved. He released his hand from Madeleine's and made for the other door by the shortest route (an unconventional one, that disregarded obstacles), but everyone was too preoccupied to pay any attention. Outside the door, the official on duty gave him a curious look. Antony said urgently, "Has anyone left in the last few minutes?" and when the man gave him a positive denial muttered, "Someone ill . . . a doctor . . ." and made off down the corridor. He did not stop to consider where he was going until he was on the pavement outside, and found the sun struggling with the clouds for the first time in several days. Then he paused only a moment before he set off again, briskly; and when he succeeded in hailing a cab, it was to pursue his northward route with greater expedition. He was so sure now that he hardly troubled to think it out as he went. Robert Pitt, who lived with the Maddisons and claimed to have been with his landlord on the afternoon of Dr. Martin's death . . . Robert Pitt, who worked at the Ministry of Supply . . . Robert Pitt who had been given a clean bill by John Welwyn as the result of the extensive check-up he had described so feelingly; but then, whoever said that Ohlendorff was a fool, or would leave his tracks uncovered? If he, like Teddy Morris, had assumed another man's identity on returning to England after the war, his plans would have been deep-laid and left as little as possible to chance.

What had happened to Morris in the courtroom was a question Antony could not yet answer, but that Ohlendorff was behind it he did not doubt. He was making for the Ministry offices in St. Giles' Court, and felt now that this was a journey he should have made long since, that he had been wrong to allow Welwyn's urgent plea for caution to stand in his way. Well, he hadn't been sure; but now his actions were governed by an utter certainty for which there was no explanation—except, perhaps, intuition, of which he had a profound distrust. If he was wrong, he was no worse off; while if he was right . . .

The thought brought him up abruptly. The cab had drawn up across the street from the Ministry building, and he paid it off absently. If he was right, he had only to take the few remaining steps across the road to be committed without remedy to seeing Robert Pitt. The alternative was to phone Welwyn's office for assistance. Come to think of it, that must be done in any event; they would have a car in the court here, in about a quarter of an hour. Meanwhile, the sensible thing was to remain on watch, but he went toward the telephone box with his mind already quite clear as to what he would do. He told himself that he had taken the decision because his quarry might leave the building by another entrance, and smiled a little sourly at this attempted self-deception. He was going in now because there was nothing he wished less to do; because he hoped to find Ohlendorff but feared the encounter much more than he hoped for it.

He made his call to the familiar number in Whitehall, checked briefly (in the comparative privacy of the telephone booth) on the gun with which Welwyn had provided him, and then walked firmly back toward the door of the Ministry building and went in.

There was a long room with a desk running the length of it. Antony addressed the clerk in French, and could not remember afterward when he had reached the decision that this was the most reasonable course. "Monsieur Pitt, y est-il? Je veux le voir de suite!"

The clerk managed well enough, once he had adjusted his mind to the fact that the visitor, in spite of looking an ordinary sort of chap, was so unorthodox as to speak no English. "Est-ce que Monsieur Pitt vous attend déjà, monsieur?"

That evoked some gesticulation, and a rush of words. "Non, mais il s'agit d'une affaire d'urgence, d'une circonstance pressante imprévue dont il doit être averti sans délai.''

''Je suis presque certain qu'il refusera de vous voir dans ce cas,'' said the clerk doubtfully.

''Dites-lui, s'il vous plaît, que je m'appelle Légère, et que nous sommes de vieux amis.''

The man turned to the switchboard. He sounded apologetic, but Antony guessed he would be willing to make something of an effort to avoid the need of conversing indefinitely in the French language. ''Someone to see you, Mr. Pitt. Monsieur Légère . . . says he knows you. Yes, sir, I'll ask him.'' He looked across at the visitor. ''Monsieur Pitt dit qu'il ne se rappelle pas de vous, Monsieur.''

''Veuillex lui dire que j'ai passé quelque temps chez lui il y a longtemps à Paris, et qu'il ma'a prié alors d'y rester plus longtemps . . . mais que je ne pouvais pas le faire; aussi que nous nous sommes rencontrés encore une fois récemment chez un ami commun ici à Londres.''

The message was relayed fairly enough. A moment later the clerk put down the telephone, and gestured to a commissionaire. ''Monsieur Pitt est libre maintenant, et il sera bien content de vous revoir.''

It was evident that Robert Pitt's place in the ministerial hierarchy was reasonably high. His office was on the first floor, and opened from a well-appointed hallway. The commissionaire knocked and threw open the door; Antony went past him with his hand in his pocket and heard the door close behind him.

Robert Pitt was seated at his desk: an impressive piece of furniture in an impressive room. His right hand was hidden under a file he had apparently been studying, but Antony was sure enough that it held a gun. He laughed a little. ''Stalemate, Herr Ohlendorff?'' he said.

The other seemed amused. ''The ubiquitous Captain Maitland! I thought I could not be mistaken,'' he remarked. ''I gather you have me covered.''

''That is correct.''

''You will forgive my curiosity . . . is your gun really loaded, Captain?''

''It is.''

''On a previous occasion, if you remember—''

"I remember," said Antony. "This time, however—"

"In that case, it is indeed stalemate. Perhaps I may suggest that we discard our weapons for the time being. I am sure each one of us would infinitely prefer not to shoot the other . . . not under present circumstances."

"I'm inclined to agree, but the odds are too heavy against me, now, unarmed." Antony moved a little, instinctively, so that the door was no longer directly behind him. "As you say, I would prefer not to shoot you—not here, not now—but (as you said yourself when we last met) my disinclination to do so stops short of the foolhardy."

"You are learning wisdom with the years," said Ohlendorff, politely.

"Caution . . . perhaps."

"Then we must continue to maintain this inconvenient degree of vigilance." Ohlendorff spoke lightly, but his eyes were watchful. "May I ask why you have come here?"

"To learn where you got your signet ring . . . why else?"

Ohlendorff laughed at that. "To be sure, I promised to tell you. Won't you sit down, Captain Maitland?" He waved his left hand invitingly; the right was still covered by the inverted file. "Or couldn't you shoot me with sufficient facility from a sitting position?"

"I'm afraid not."

"Then you must forgive my seeming discourtesy. As for the ring, you may call it a souvenir. It belonged to Robert Pitt."

"And what happened to Pitt?"

"He died."

"Of course he did!" Antony sounded impatient. "But where . . . and why?"

"He died at an inn, about ten miles from the prison camp from which he had escaped. He had been wounded, and that was as far as he could get. The good people at the inn asked my advice. The war was ending, then; should they care for him and produce him, strong and healthy, to speak to their kindness when your compatriots arrived? I talked with him—he thought I was also an escaped prisoner, you see, and so he talked freely. After that, he died; it was more convenient. Ernst Ohlendorff was buried, and

in due course that area was 'liberated'—as it chanced, by
the Americans—and Robert Pitt was sent home.''

"As easy as that?"

"He had no relations, except an aged grandfather. Most
fortunately the old man died before the end of the war,
otherwise something would have had to be arranged. As
things were, it was only a matter of avoiding the district
around Durham—which in any event I had no desire to
visit."

"Risky, all the same."

"For a few months only. After that, I was well enough
established and the name not an uncommon one. And with
the slight but effective changes I made in my appearance—''

"I see. I suppose you're right."

"Events have proved me so. And I have certainly been
more comfortable, in my dull but useful job here, than I
should have been if I had stayed in Germany."

"Useful!" said Antony. "Useful to whom?"

Ohlendorff smiled broadly. "Why, to me, my dear
fellow. Who else? I did not know, of course, that our
paths would cross again. If I had known—''

"A lot of things would have been different, I imagine."

"Indeed they would. I first heard of you again the day
Dr. Martin died, from my late colleague, Morris."

That was when the interruption occurred. The door at
the side of the room opened, and a pretty young woman
came in with a pile of papers. She came across to the desk,
and said firmly, "I'm sorry, Mr. Pitt, but it's nearly five.
Will you sign these? You said they should go tonight."

For the first time, Ohlendorff's eyes left his enemy's
face. If he was discomfited, he gave no sign. He said,
"Yes, of course, Miss Armitage," and pushed away the
file with the gun still hidden beneath it, and took up his
pen. Antony drifted, as inconspicuously as possible, toward
the desk. The girl gave him a sharp look, as though
suspecting him of undue curiosity. The few minutes it took
for "Robert Pitt" to go through the pile of correspondence
seemed an age to the younger man. At last all were signed,
and his hand went out almost before the girl's back was
turned. She did not look round, however, and a moment

later the gun was safely in his pocket, and he was backing away from the desk again.

As the door closed, Ohlendorff looked at him quizzically. "Your round, Captain Maitland." Antony thought, resentfully, that of the two of them it was his adversary who was the calmer, but he said without change of expression, "You were saying . . . your *late* colleague?"

"He is dead . . . at least I trust so. I have been out of town for the week end, but surely by now——"

"You gave him poison?"

"Does it surprise you?"

"Hardly that. You did not know, then, that he had been called to give evidence at the magistrate's court today?"

Ohlendorff frowned. "He could know nothing against your client," he said slowly, thinking it out.

"We called him, for the defense," said Antony. "And a later witness identified him, quite positively."

"He said there was no one——"

"There was one person who knew him. Perhaps he had forgotten her. A girl called Madeleine Bonnard."

"Madeleine . . . well!" He thought a moment and then said, almost briskly, "So he has been arrested?"

"He collapsed. From what you tell me, I suppose he died."

"It seems most likely. There is an irony about it which should appeal to you, Captain Maitland. The capsules which Dr. Martin gave him——"

"You made a substitution——?"

"Quite a simple matter," said Ohlendorff, deprecatingly. "And bound to be effective sooner or later. His nerve was going," he added, and paused, as though no further explanation could be needed.

"I see," said Antony. "And Benson?"

"If you will sit down, I will tell you about it. Come, Captain, surely you can afford to relax now, with a positive arsenal in your pockets!" He had kept his hands before him on the desk, and was fiddling with his fountain pen, but casually and with no air of tension. Antony backed cautiously toward the chair. Ohlendorff's look of amusement deepened. He said, "I shall be interested to know your plans, in due course, and how you propose to termi-

nate this interview. Meanwhile, I gather you wish to put
in a little time?'' He nodded, approvingly, as Antony
finally managed the difficult maneuver of seating himself
without ever relaxing his watchfulness. ''If you are comfortable, Captain . . .'' and Antony smiled back at him,
but couldn't flatter himself that he did so with any air of
real amusement.

''Quite comfortable, thank you. Please go on.''

''You were asking about Benson. He had quite outlived
his usefulness, you know. But before the war—''

''So long ago?''

''Now, why should that surprise you? It was he who
suggested to Morris the course he should follow—and
instructed him how he should set about it.''

''But, why should he—''

For the first time Ohlendorff showed signs of emotion.
''How often have we talked together, and still you do not
understand!'' He sounded impatient. His hands were idle
now on the desk in front of him. ''I told you once—do you
remember?—that Germany was my country.''

''I remember.'' Antony's voice was expressionless.
Ohlendorff smiled suddenly.

''Doubtless you remember, too, what you called me on
that occasion? It is your weakness, Captain Maitland, that
you could taunt me then, when you were in my power; but
you would not repeat it now . . . when you hold the gun.
It is your weakness . . . and you think it strength!''

''S-strength or weakness,'' said Antony (and heard with
annoyance the faintest tremor in his voice; for indeed he
remembered, only too well, the occasion of which the
other spoke), ''you were telling me about Benson.''

''I was saying, as I chose, so did others. And not only
my countrymen. Benson had his dreams, no doubt. And as
Martin trusted him, others trusted him also. I said he was
useful. And Morris, too, came to us.

''Then the war ended, and I have told you how Robert
Pitt came home. I had no plans then, but afterwards of
course . . . matters developed. I was able to get in touch
with others of my way of thinking. Benson helped me
willingly enough; Morris, because he was afraid. Things
went smoothly enough, until that day.

"Morris did not know until he was in the surgery that Dr. Forbes was away. Even then, he could not be sure that Dr. Martin had recognized him. He was in something of a panic, but he behaved sensibly enough; he went on to his own office and telephoned to me." He paused and looked at Antony with the now familiar air of amusement. "You can guess my advice to him, Captain Maitland?"

"You told him to take no chances," said Antony promptly. "And in the interests of speed and silence you added, perhaps, a suggestion that it would be a happy thought to buy some stockings for his wife."

"That was his own idea. He was no novice, after all, in the art of killing. After we had talked it over I phoned to ask about the doctor's surgery hours; it was not very difficult to learn something of his arrangements. I'm sure the housekeeper never even remembered the conversation. In the afternoon, I waited in a teashop, and Morris joined me there some twenty minutes later. From my point of view things could not have fallen out better; he overheard the doctor speaking on the telephone: first, ringing your headquarters; and then putting through a call to you. If he had been in doubt what he should do, that must have decided matters. He killed Martin before he could complete the call, and rejoined me in my dreary café.

"You can guess that, spoken in that context, the name Maitland immediately made me think of you. I made inquiries, and made it my business to find out something of your activities. Morris and Benson, of course, had now outlived their usefulness."

"So I imagine."

"And if only I had managed to dispose of you as well . . ." Even then, his tone was light, with a trace of derision which might have been self-directed.

Antony said flatly, "I have wondered, of course, why you left me still alive."

"It was quite unavoidable." Ohlendorff, thought the other man resentfully, might have been apologizing for some slight social lapse. "I was not the only one of Benson's visitors, you see, who came by the french window. I heard steps on the veranda; there was really no time . . . even if I had found the gun quickly, a shot would merely have hastened his entrance. So, being under the unfortunate necessity of leaving you alive, I judged it more artistic to leave also the weapon that killed Benson.''

''So that the police might think . . . yes, I see. And had you intended that Robert Pitt should disappear?''

''I have my preparations made, believe me. But I hoped it might not prove necessary. I hoped—to be blunt with you—that I should find you before you found me. It's surprising how much one can get away with, as you very well know.''

''And that's the whole s-story.''

''I think so. Now *you* can enlighten me, Captain Maitland. You must have known I would guess who was visiting me . . . I have not forgotten Antoine Légère, whom I knew so well in Paris. That being so, you also knew I would have you covered when you came in. If my secretary had not made so ill-timed an entrance, what did you propose to do?''

''I meant to take a chance of shooting the gun out of your hand while we were talking.''

''And damn the consequences? How very ruthless of you, Captain. And what a risk!'' Antony was silent, and after a moment the other went on incisively, ''And now— the next move. What do you propose to do? For your convenience,'' he added, glancing at his watch, ''it is now nearly twenty past five.'' He got to his feet as he spoke, and the younger man followed suit, so that they faced each other across the wide desk. ''I take it you are giving my colleagues time to leave—and yours time to take up their positions outside?''

''You're quite right. I must thank you for filling in the interval in so entertaining a fashion.''

''So now you wish me to come with you?'' Ohlendorff spoke softly. ''And if I will not?''

Antony allowed himself the smallest of gestures with the hand that held the gun. ''Of course,'' he said, ''I shouldn't shoot to kill.'' For all the effort he made, his voice was strained, and the other laughed.

''Should I admire your moderation, Captain Maitland? Why *don't* you shoot me and make sure I shan't escape you? You've a fair chance of getting away with it, after all. Have you nothing to avenge?''

"I didn't come here for vengeance."

"Ah, no, I forgot. It just isn't done!" Ohlendorff's tone was full of mockery. "I had come to consider you a brave man, but I see you are as weak and foolish as your fellows."

"It doesn't require much courage to pull a trigger."

"No?" He seemed to ponder the point. "A little resolution, perhaps," he suggested.

"As you said the other night, Herr Ohlendorff: it's all a question of one's point of view."

"Well, certainly, it seems to me unenterprising. Here I am, at your mercy; a lot might happen between this room and the street."

Antony did not answer. He held the revolver firm, and his eyes were steady; Ohlendorff was determined to taunt him, obviously hoping to distract his attention, to get a chance to come in close. The talk was uncomfortably like some of their previous interviews, but he felt no desire to cheapen his victory . . . if it was, indeed, to be a victory; he felt at that moment no confidence in his own ability to handle the situation, in spite of the gun he held.

"Have you nothing more to say to me?" said Ohlendorff, softly. "You say you do not wish for vengeance, but I think perhaps you do not remember very well all that has been between us."

"I remember," said Antony again. And this, indeed, was true.

"Then I do not understand you. Granted, it might be unwise to shoot me; your standing with the police does not seem from the papers to be any too good."

"No."

"My apologies. But that is just one more thing between us, is it not? Are you so forgetful? Unless—can it be that you are still afraid of me?"

"Still?" said Antony.

"Did I mistake your feelings? You had cause to fear me, I think."

"You must remember, Herr Kommandant . . . the English are an unimaginative race. In any event, why should I fear you—now?"

"For the sake of the past. For the sake of—Paris, shall

we say?'' Ohlendorff's eyes were intent; Antony dragged his attention from the words he spoke and tried to concentrate on the possibility of his making a move. This was not easy; all the horror and fear that this man had ever inspired were crowding in on him. He stood very still and tried to ignore the illogical feeling of panic that possessed him. Ohlendorff laughed—perhaps his expression had betrayed him?—and began to speak again. And walked round the desk.

Antony stood his ground, and achieved an air of indifference as he spoke. ''I wouldn't do that, if I were you,'' he said. Ohlendorff stopped, and looked at him intently.

''My congratulations . . . I believe, at last, you mean what you say. You would shoot me in the arm, I suppose? And still I might accompany you. But you deny me the mercy of death.''

''The decision is not mine, whether you live or die, mein Herr.''

''And you hope to avoid a scandal?''

''If possible. I have been told the French, among others, would be glad to have news of you.''

''A charming prospect. Do you know, my dear Maitland, I think I must refuse your flattering invitation.'' His hands twisted suddenly on the cap of the pen which he still held. His left hand went to his mouth. Antony made a movement, but the German laughed and put both his hands in his pockets.

''You still have the opportunity of stopping me taking the poison, Captain Maitland . . . but only if you shoot to kill.'' He paused and looked at his companion with a twisted grin. ''Humane to the last, I see . . . if you call this humanity.'' His voice achieved a sneer. ''I should be sorry to think that you lived to reflect at ease upon your undoubted virtue,'' he added. And shot from his pocket.

As Antony fell he heard a sound he could not then identify, a harsh gasping not easily to be forgotten. He hesitated for a moment on the brink of darkness; then there was nothing more, and he did not hear his enemy fall, nor the last more terrible sound of the final convulsions which shook Ernst Ohlendorff as he died.

CHAPTER SEVENTEEN

WHEN SIR NICHOLAS returned to his home the following afternoon, rather earlier than was his custom, he made his way directly upstairs. As he hesitated before knocking on his nephew's door the sound of laughter came to him from within, and he smiled a little to himself to hear it. He tapped lightly, and a moment later Jenny appeared.

"Come in, Uncle Nick. We're dying to hear what you've been doing."

Sir Nicholas followed her into the living room. "Why, tidying up, my dear. All the loose ends your husband left behind him." Jenny pulled a face at him.

He crossed the room in his leisurely way, and was about to address his nephew, who was reclining on the sofa with a bandage round his head, when his eye was caught by an enormous bunch of lilies which were arranged in Jenny's tallest vase. "Good God!" he said, taken aback.

Antony waved a languid hand, but could not repress a grin. "That is John's idea of a peace offering, I gather."

Sir Nicholas burst out laughing. Jenny eyed the flowers, and said doubtfully, "I suppose it's his idea of a joke. Aren't they awful?" she added, with more enthusiasm, and perched herself on the arm of the sofa.

Antony said, lazily, "You see us, sir, worn out with our endeavors."

"Yes, Uncle Nick, we have had a day."

"So has Gibbs, he isn't very pleased. But I hoped he hadn't let anybody in."

"It was just the telephone, and I daren't not answer in case you rang up."

"Mostly newpapers," said Antony. "And Jenny's Aunt Carry, wanting to know what the hell."

Jenny giggled. "Well, she did ask some awkward questions. And she phoned four times, Uncle Nick. But the last time she was quite amiable, so I knew the inquest must be over and the result all right, and Antony took the telephone to pieces."

"That accounts for it. I thought you were both asleep." Sir Nicholas turned to his newphew. "How are you feeling now?"

"A trifle pale, sir." He dropped his airs suddenly. "Don't hold out on us, Uncle Nick. What has happened?"

"That seems rather unfair, as one or other of you has been talking ever since I arrived. However, I won't keep you in suspense."

"First then, what happened in court after I left? Jenny wouldn't tell me anything."

"I didn't know much. And you weren't fit—"

"I did feel pretty lousy," Antony admitted.

"Well then! But you aren't telling us, Uncle Nick."

"Oh, I am to be permitted to speak?" said Sir Nicholas. "As you seem to have left your friend Ohlendorff armed, he not unnaturally shot you. You were lucky to escape with a scalp wound."

"Lucky!" said Antony, sitting up indignantly. "You ought to have my headache."

"I still say it is less than such negligence deserved."

Jenny said, "Uncle Nick!" And he turned and smiled at her reassuringly.

"He's all right, my dear."

"Yes, I know." She moved away from them and went toward the window, blinking a little because she suddenly wanted to cry. It wasn't the first time she had waited for news, and she wondered a little desolately whether it would be the last, or whether the pattern must repeat itself. But at least, Ohlendorff was dead. She heard her husband's voice, carefully casual, and was grateful that both men were, for the moment, ignoring her.

"Couldn't we take my carelessness for granted, and get to the facts, sir?"

"Very well. I was, I admit, too absorbed to notice immediately that you had left us. When the uproar had subsided—and that wasn't quickly, by any means—and Maddison had been removed, we were left to conclude the business of the day with a strong sense of anticlimax. Halloran suggested that we should ask Nolan to adjourn overnight; I agreed, tossed the whole affair most improperly into Horton's lap (we owe that lad some sort of an explanation, incidentally), and departed almost as unceremoniously as you had done."

"I doubt it."

Sir Nicholas acknowledged this interruption with a small, tight smile. He was obviously already absorbed in his narrative. "I found Welwyn in one of the offices, with young Carr and Mademoiselle Bonnard. She was talking nineteen to the dozen, and the others trying to calm her down, to get some sort of sense out of what she was saying. She turned on me, and started off faster than ever. Il me faut les faire attention . . . ces imbéciles . . . Monsieur Maitland se trouve dans une situation périlleuse . . . something must be done . . . but immediately! No, you had left her without any explanation. But you had said one word when you saw Morris fall . . . a man's name . . . if something had happened to Morris he was at the bottom of it . . . and now if you were following him, you were in danger too. At this point Welwyn positively shouted her down. 'WHAT MAN?' he demanded at the top of his voice, and I wish you could have seen her look of bewilderment at this unreasonable attitude. 'But, monsieur, I am telling you. Herr Kommandant Ohlendorff, whom I have known in Paris!' "

"At this point," said Antony, "it is John's face I'd like to have seen."

"He said, 'Are you sure, mademoiselle?' And I thought she was going to explode into speech again, but she looked at me, and I think she saw this was serious. She just said to Welwyn, very quietly, 'I cannot mistake, monsieur,' and when he insisted on reminding her that you had just muttered something and rushed away, she added impatiently: But I know the name well. Ernst Ohlendorff. I am his mistress, during three—four months, after Tédé has gone to Germany.''

Antony said, ''Oh, lord!'' and Jenny turned from the window and came back again to sit on the arm of the sofa. ''I hadn't thought of that one,'' he added.

''Neither had Welwyn. He appeared embarrassed and swore under his breath. Madeleine just looked at him, with her chin up, and then she began to cry. She'd had enough to make her, heaven knows. So we left her to Carr's tender mercies, and departed to a find a telephone.''

''Poor Carr. Still, I don't suppose he'd understood a word she was saying.''

''I don't suppose so. But I was grateful; she'd convinced Welwyn some action was needed, and I will say for him—when he gets going he really gets things done. He'd bullied some official into lending him a telephone, before I had time to send a message to Mallory. He phoned his office and was told of your message, and that a car had left for St. Giles' Court. He got on to Wright then, and so far as I could tell got carte blanche to deal with the situation as he pleased. So we took a taxi up to the top of Shaftesbury Avenue.''

''Had you seen Mallory, sir?''

''Unfortunately, no. My dignity was offended,'' said Sir Nicholas austerely, ''by the necessity of chasing across London after you without a hat, and with my brief in my pocket.'' Antony grinned, and Jenny choked back a laugh. ''Yes, very amusing. But to continue . . .

''We joined Welwyn's men in the car, and waited. After some time a police car drove up, and the occupants went into the Ministry building. That decided Welwyn. He took one of his men and followed. I waited. After a time another police car arrived; I recognized Briggs and Sykes as they went in. Then came an ambulance, followed closely by what I took to be a number of press cars. The wait began to seem very long. Presently Sykes came out, apparently to effect a diversion. While he was talking to the press men, two stretchers were loaded into the ambulance. Welwyn returned then. He told me the office cleaner had thought the room empty and gone in. She'd found you on the floor, unconscious and bleeding pretty freely. Ohlendorff lying half on top of you, dead.''

''Poor old dear.''

''As to that, Welwyn said she was quite an imperturbable old lady . . . said it was nothing to the blitz.''

''It was the poison, I suppose?''

''Oh, yes—'the usual thing,' '' Welwyn said. ''He must have swallowed it as he fired at you. I wonder if he meant to, or if he intended to make a run for it after you were dead.''

''I wonder,'' said Antony, reflectively.

''So then I came home to Jenny, and they smuggled you in about half an hour later, after leaving Ohlendorff's body at the hospital mortuary. Officially, you are suffering a collapse occasioned by your injuries last Friday night. You were never anywhere near St. Giles' Court, of course.''

''Of course not.''

''I do not pretend to know how these things are arranged. Robert Pitt has killed himself . . . one of his more senior colleagues will be induced to hint at overwork; the Ministry people will be the last to want a scandal, as you can imagine. If there are rumors about a visitor, we must hope he will not be connected with you. I don't suppose you gave your own name?''

''I gave the name I used in France . . . Légère. And I spoke only French to the clerk and to the commissionaire.''

''What admirable forethought.''

''I'm glad you approve. About that, sir—''

''You must not think I blame you, my dear boy, for wishing to see the matter through yourself.'' (Antony's hands clenched suddenly.) ''But I'm not quite clear how you were so sure—''

''I knew I might be making a fool of myself. But I *was* sure—ever since I talked to Madeleine—that Maddison was our man, so naturally I wondered about Robert Pitt. And when I say I was sure, it wasn't very clever really: I mean, I was sure it wasn't Condon.''

''Yes, I see. And I think I understand your motive well enough in gate-crashing at the Ministry. But what—what on earth possessed you to give the fellow a chance to shoot you? You must have known he would be armed.''

"I took one gun and I knew he might have another; but I daren't go close enough to find out—this damned arm of mine might have encouraged him to tackle me, you know. But I thought he couldn't get a hand to it while I had him covered."

"How did it happen, then?"

"He tried . . ." Antony cleared his throat, but his voice still sounded a little hoarse as he continued. "He tried to call my bluff. Then he saw I meant what I said and intended to take him—alive. I could have shot him, you know, but that would have been his victory . . . I don't know if you understand that. He had the capsules in his pen, and when he put one in his mouth that took all my attention . . . I just didn't notice that he'd got a hand in his pocket."

"Well, never mind that now," said his uncle, with fine inconsistency.

"Can they get away with it? This tale of Pitt committing suicide, I mean?"

"Oh, I think so. Who would suspect anything so fantastic as his real identity?"

"Well, there is that. What happened this morning?"

"First, the magistrate's court. Halloran formally withdrew, and Gerry was discharged. In a few days' time Maddison's inquest will be held and the press (I sincerely trust) will be satisfied that they have pieced together the true story. I couldn't wait to see what happened, I had to get to Benson's inquest. (Really, this affair reminds me irresistibly of the last act of *Hamlet!*) The verdict was 'Murder by some person or persons unknown' and I was put to no greater inconvenience than that of relating to a sympathetic court the story of your sufferings following the attack on you in Benson's rooms. It made a harrowing tale—my apologies for your absence were really quite superfluous."

"And they let it go at that?"

"What else? I rather think that, too, will be put down to Maddison's score in public opinion—and in the circumstances it doesn't seem to matter greatly."

"But who gets the blame for killing Maddison?"

Sir Nicholas smiled. "Obviously, it was suicide," he said.

"He wasn't the sort to kill himself. He—"

"I am sure," said his uncle, unconvincingly amiable, "that your reading of his character is masterly. But in the circumstances it might be advisable to keep it to yourself."

"Yes, of course. But—"

"It is really quite simple. Condon actually saw him take a capsule, soon after Madeleine came into court . . . at least, he saw him fumbling in his pocket and then put his hand to his mouth. If the pain which caused him to visit Dr. Martin in the first place was in any way nervous in origin, the sight of her might well have brought it on. But there is no need to stress the fact that he thought he was merely taking something to relieve his dyspepsia."

"Ohlendorff said it was ironical," remarked Antony, thoughtfully. "And the fact that he happened on the poisoned capsule just at that moment . . . oh, well, I suppose the coroner will play ball?"

"This predilection for slang!" Sir Nicholas was moved to protest. "Your association with Whitehall is over, and a little professional dignity would not be out of place."

Jenny said tentatively, "I was thinking, we might go away for a while . . ." But the suggestion trailed off as she encountered Sir Nicholas's look of outrage.

"Are you suggesting that Antony should leave town in the middle of the Hilary term?"

"Well, yes, I suppose I am." She both looked and sounded guilty.

"Nonsense!" said Sir Nicholas. He turned a compelling eye on his nephew. "I'll send up a copy of the Saintsbury brief, and the relevant documents. The case should come on about Monday next."

Antony began to laugh, and though he protested it was noticeable that a gleam had come into his eye. "Are you proposing that I should appear in court, bandage and all?"

"The doctor," his uncle informed him, with the air of one producing an ace from up his sleeve, "says the bandage should be off by the week-end."

"Well, I think it's too bad. He isn't nearly well enough—"

"Oh, yes, he is, my dear. Ask him." Jenny turned inquiring eyes on her husband, who said, "Fit as a fiddle, my love."

"Truly?" said Jenny.

"Truly." A thought struck him. "But what about Carter, sir?"

"Carter," Sir Nicholas informed him with satisfaction, "has gone on circuit. I am sorry to be uncharitable about so excellent a young man, but I really cannot stand being bored by him any longer."

"You said he looked hungry, Uncle Nick," Jenny reminded him.

"Yes, well, I expect I can still find plenty of work to recommend him for; he's very able, so I shan't outrage my conscience. But it must be out of town," he added firmly, and turned to glare at his nephew, who met his look with one unnaturally innocent. "I know it's your idea of humor, but I don't want to hear any more of the subject," he said.

spond to posted messages, most of which were hostile.

Occasionally, she lurked in the Internet's chat rooms, monitoring the funny, pathetic, outrageous, and just plain stupid exchanges. The American voters, in all their varieties! Grady used an anonymous, androgynous pseudonym, HANDLER—a shortened version of her Secret Service code name—to disguise her identity during her forays on the Internet.

A couple of nights after Jerry and Jane's Cafe Dalat dinner, the First Lady was in her computer cubicle, searching databases and archives for the name of the administration official Dan McLean had been investigating.

It had been surprisingly easy for Jerry Knight to convince Grady to take part in Jane Day's scheme. The First Lady relished a challenge and welcomed almost any adventure which allowed her to break out of the stuffy confines of her life as a President's spouse. Even if the adventure could hurt her husband.

If Jane Day's theory was right and someone in Dale's administration had concealed the existence of American prisoners in Vietnam at the end of the war, the President would certainly be tarnished by the scandal.

Grady hoped her computer search would disprove Jane's conjecture and support her own theory that Dale had been the intended target of a conservative-hating assassin.

It was quiet on the third floor of the White House, except for the clack of her keyboard. The President was away making a speech. Louisville? Indianapolis? Somewhere like that. Grady had sent her attendant home and notified the Secret Service agent in charge of the night detail that she was in for the evening.

She sat in front of her computer screen wearing green satiny warm-up pants and a white T-shirt emblazoned A WOMAN'S PLACE IS IN THE CORNER OFFICE. She was barefoot, her scarlet toenails unconsciously scratching at the carpet.

Her search went quickly at first. Using her security code and her expert knowledge of computers, she called up the names of all the officials in Dale's administration above the rank of deputy assistant secretary, 4,378 names. Then she assembled a similar list from Richard Nixon's administration in 1973, when the United States withdrew its combat troops from Vietnam and the North Vietnamese supposedly repatriated all the U.S. prisoners they were holding.

Next, she tapped a few keys, instructing the computer to find names which appeared on both lists.

The machine found more than 250 matches. That said something about the longevity of government bureaucrats, she thought. Too many names to screen.

On the assumption that only an official of the Pentagon, State Department, Central Intelligence Agency, or White House staff would have written a memo about prisoners in Vietnam, Grady instructed her computer to ignore all the government agencies except those four in 1973 and to match that limited list against the list of current Hammond administration officials.

The computer whirred, then displayed the list of matches. Down to forty-three names. Still too many, though. She had to narrow it further.

Grady decided to play a hunch, that someone who dealt with foreign policy and intelligence matters in 1973 was not likely to be serving in the Agriculture Department or Interstate Commerce Commission twenty-five years later.

She reprogrammed the computer to compare a list of officials in the Pentagon, State Department, CIA, and White House in 1973 with a list of officials in those same agencies in Dale's administration, and to display the matches.

In a few seconds, the machine printed a list of ten names on the screen.

Two of the names drew her attention immediately.

One was Gregor Novasky, Dale's national security adviser. He had been with the CIA in 1973, assigned to Henry Kissinger's negotiating team at the Paris Peace Talks.

The other name that drew her attention was Dale's. He had been a deputy assistant secretary of State for International Organization Affairs in the Nixon administration.

Grady got up and walked across the long, deserted central hallway of the third floor to the kitchen. She removed a Samuel Adams beer from the refrigerator, popped the top with a silver opener engraved with the presidential seal, and returned to her computer cubicle, her bare feet making no sound on the carpet.

She drank the beer straight from the bottle.

Could Dale have written a memo avowing that all the American prisoners had been returned, when, in fact, they hadn't been?

She didn't want to believe it. Dale was a Korean War hero. He never would have betrayed American soldiers. But the worm of doubt gnawed at her conviction.

He was so accommodating. She could imagine Dale writing such a memo under pressure from his superiors, who didn't want anything to interfere with Nixon's plan to withdraw American troops from Vietnam, even the inconvenient matter of unaccounted-for MIAs. With Watergate already unraveling, Nixon's need to bolster his popularity depended on ending America's participation in the unpopular war. The issue of missing Americans had to be resolved. Or covered up.

The pressure for such a memo would have been intense.

Dale was so accommodating.

Maybe his opposition to Clinton extending diplomatic recognition to Vietnam had been an effort to assuage his guilt for what he did in the seventies.

"No!" Grady said out loud. The word reverberated in the empty family quarters.

Dale was accommodating, not tough enough by her standards. But he would never sell out American prisoners, no matter how much pressure he was under from the Nixon people.

The Hammonds had been principled Connecticut Yankees for nearly three centuries, following a stringent code of honorable conduct, performing selfless service in public office, fighting in their country's wars back to the Revolution. Dale had been a decorated Marine in Korea, a young captain leading his frightened and freezing company through a gauntlet of Chinese attackers in the retreat from the Yalu River.

No. He could not have written such a memo. It must have been Novasky or one of the other eight. If there had been any memo at all. Grady moved the mouse to clear the fish aquarium screen saver.

She studied the list that reappeared on the screen. Aside from Dale and Novasky, she recognized most of the other names. She'd met some of them. But she had no idea whether any of them had written a memo that McLean was investigating when he was poisoned.

She had to find out if such a memo was in the government's databases. If she found it, she would know for certain who wrote it. And who might have arranged Dan McLean's death in order to keep it from being revealed.

She padded silently to the kitchen and returned to her computer cubicle with another beer.

For a half-hour, Grady clicked and scrolled through menus and databases. At last, she arrived at the place where she was sure the memo was stored. The screen spelled out *National Security Archives, Special Files Section, Limited Access, Password Required, Key Code Certified Only*.

She clicked to open.

A box appeared on the screen. It read:

ACCESS DENIED
Not Key Code Certified

"Damn," the First Lady said aloud.

She tried again. Same response.

Grady retrieved from her wallet a laminated card the President's military aide had given her on Inauguration Day. It contained a list of code words and passwords, along with instructions on where she would be taken in the event of a nuclear attack, terrorist act, or other emergency. The card did not contain a "Key Code."

She tried some of the other codes on the card, but they didn't work. The computer refused to grant her access to the National Security Archives.

A skilled hacker, Grady considered trying some of the tricks she knew to tease the key code out of the machine. But she suspected the system was programmed to alert a security officer when someone tried to break in. In a few minutes, the Secret Service or FBI or one of those agencies would be banging on her door.

She didn't want that hassle.

In fact, within moments after Grady started her computer search, an Army private in a cubicle at the unmarked offices of the Magnum Project in Crystal City, Virginia, was monitoring her every keystroke and mouse click.

Grady's other choice to gain access to the National Security Archives was to try to sweet-talk Dale's military aide into giving her the key code. She was sure she could do it. She'd caught him eyeing her a couple of times.

But he might report her to Dale. Or the Secretary of Defense. It would leak to the press and they'd have a field day.

She'd better try to figure it out herself without risking a security alarm or a media frenzy.

She recalled the ten names to the screen, nine men and one woman who'd been relatively junior officials at the end of the Vietnam War in 1973 and were now senior officials in Dale's administration.

According to Jerry Knight, Dan McLean may have been about to reveal that one of them wrote a memo at the end of the war falsely reporting that all the American prisoners had been released. And that person may have hired a Vietnamese waiter to poison McLean at the correspondents dinner to keep him from revealing that secret.

The First Lady looked down the list of names again.

Dale?

If he wrote the memo, exposure would mean impeachment, the destruction of his presidency, unbearable shame. For what? For being a junior State Department officer who wasn't strong enough to resist the pressure from Kissinger and the thugs around Nixon? Not many people were able to resist that bunch in those days.

Why hadn't Dale told her what he'd done? It was such an awful burden to keep locked inside all those years, fearing exposure and ruin at any moment. And if he'd shared his secret with her, what would she have done? She would have helped him carry the burden. Made sure the episode stayed covered up. Maybe used her computer skills to erase any trace of the memo from government files. Killed anyone who threatened exposure.

My God! What was she thinking?

Could the President have arranged McLean's murder to

prevent the correspondent from broadcasting his terrible secret?

"No!" she protested aloud. "One of the others wrote that memo!"

Grady printed out the list of ten names and shut down the computer.

She retrieved a third beer from the refrigerator. She took it to bed with her, still dressed in the green warm-up pants and T-shirt.

CHAPTER TWENTY-EIGHT

FBI SPECIAL AGENT Michael Tagliaferro headed out Colesville Road toward Kavanaugh's Tavern at Four Corners in the Maryland suburbs in response to a phone call from Del Bloch requesting a meeting. The car salesman, a freelance FBI informant, had sounded nervous.

Something unusual had come up, Tagliaferro guessed, steering into a parking space in the old Woodmoor Shopping Center. Second meeting in less than a month. Normally, Bloch had information to pass on only a couple of times a year.

The FBI agent sat at their usual booth in the back, facing the door. They arranged their meetings for midafternoon, when the place was nearly empty. The lunch crowd had gone back to their jobs. The after-work drinkers hadn't arrived yet.

The ancient waitress in the Pepto-Bismol-colored nylon uniform appeared.

"Iced tea," he ordered.

A half-hour passed. The iced tea was gone. No Bloch. Tagliaferro wondered if he had the right day. He was sure he did.

He ordered another iced tea. Another twenty minutes passed. Still no Bloch. The after-work drinkers started to drift in.

"Dock of the Bay" played from the jukebox.

Bloch had never been late for their meetings. In fact, he usually arrived early. Tagliaferro was trained to be alert for changes in people's normal patterns of behavior. This was definitely a change in Bloch's pattern.

The agent had just about decided to drive to the Lincoln-Mercury dealership in the Montgomery Auto Park, where the informant worked, when Bloch sidled into the bar. He looked scared.

He hurried over and squeezed his bulk into the booth.

The skinny waitress came to take his order. Bloch waved her away.

"So, what's up?" Tagliaferro prompted.

The informant leaned across the Formica table. His chins quivered. "Saturday. Hammond's going to make a speech at the Vietnam Wall. Something's going down."

Bloch spoke so fast and in such a low whisper, the agent wasn't sure he'd heard correctly.

"Whoa. Slow it down, Del. What's going to happen Saturday?"

"I don't know exactly, Tag. Something. That's all I know."

Bloch looked around the tavern furtively. Sweat glistened among the gray strands plastered to his scalp.

He was definitely scared.

"Does it involve the President?"

The question made Bloch more agitated. "Tag, I told you everything I know. Something's going down Saturday at the Wall. That's all I know. Don't ask me no more."

"Are your friends in the Survivors of Cam Hoa involved?" Tagliaferro needed to keep Bloch talking, to milk every drop of information he had.

"Why do you ask me that?" the fat man sputtered. "Who said anything about the Survivors of Cam Hoa? Who said they were involved?"

"Well, who is involved?" Tagliaferro affected a relaxed, nonchalant tone. He hoped it would calm down Bloch, keep him talking.

But it didn't work.

"Tag, I gotta go. I told you everything I know. You gotta protect me on this. Totally. Okay? Promise you'll protect me?"

"Of course I'll protect you," the agent reassured him. "I always protect you. Come on, relax. I'll buy you a beer."

But Bloch hauled himself out of the booth and scurried for the door.

Now, that's definitely one frightened informant, Tagliaferro concluded. He didn't even wait to be paid.

The agent needed to get back downtown and report the conversation. Nebulous as it was, Bloch's tip required higher-level attention than his usual information about drug dealers paying cash for Lincoln Town Cars.

Tagliaferro paid for his iced tea and left.

Aretha was crying "Respect" from the jukebox.

The next morning, while President Dale Hammond was shaving, the telephone rang in his bathroom. It was Secret Service Director Colbert Clawson requesting a meeting as soon as possible.

"Well, come on over now, Colbert," the President suggested. "We'll have breakfast together in the family quarters."

When Dale told Grady Hammond about the call, she notified her office she'd be late and invited herself to the meeting. She didn't trust Clawson. And she didn't trust Dale to stand up to the Secret Service chief.

Clawson, back to black suit and gray tie, was surprised to find Grady at the round mahogany table set for three in the family dining room overlooking Pennsylvania Avenue.

He affected a chilly courtesy toward her. *Don't piss off First Ladies* was one of Clawson's rules for bureaucratic survival. They always won.

The three made small talk while the white-jacketed butlers poured coffee into the china cups and fresh-squeezed orange juice into the crystal goblets, and delivered their food—grapefruit slices for Grady, two bran muffins for Dale, scrambled eggs, bacon, and toast for Clawson.

As soon as the butlers withdrew, Grady asked Clawson, "So, why the hurry-up meeting?"

She was eager to hear what prompted the Secret Service chief's early-morning call. And she knew Dale would tell interminable anecdotes from his recent trip to Louisville if she didn't move things along.

Clawson put down his fork. *No one conveyed authority with a mouth full of food.* Another of the director's rules.

"We've received intelligence, which we deem reliable, that there's going to be an incident at the Vietnam Wall during the memorial ceremony on Saturday," Clawson explained. "In light of that warning, I'm recommending that you cancel your appearance there, Mr. President."

As he spoke, Clawson turned his pasty face back and forth between the President and the First Lady. Clawson never knew which one to look at. He had the title. But she had the influence.

"What kind of incident?" Grady challenged him before Dale could speak.

"We don't know for sure," the director replied. "The warning was not specific."

"Is it supposed to be directed at Dale?" she pressed.

"That's not clear."

"Is it some kind of demonstration? Or disrupting the ceremony? Or what?"

"We just don't know."

"You don't know?" Grady placed her coffee cup on the saucer with a disapproving clang. "If you don't know how serious the 'incident' is supposed to be, or *what* it's supposed to be, how can you recommend that Dale cancel a very important speech?"

"We have reason to believe the incident will be serious." Clawson addressed his response to Dale, hoping the President would take control of the conversation.

But Grady persisted.

"You have 'reason to believe' it will be a serious incident. What's the source of your information?"

"An informant."

"Who?"

"I can't tell you."

Clawson knew he'd said the wrong thing to the wrong person as soon as the words were out of his mouth.

"Can't tell me?" The First Lady jumped up and started pacing angrily. "This is the President of the United States. And I'm his wife. And you can't tell us your source?"

"Mrs. Hammond—*Ms.* Hammond, of course I can tell you. But the name wouldn't mean anything to you. The information comes from a freelance FBI informant who has provided reliable intelligence in the past. He's believed to have contacts with veterans groups which are unhappy about the discovery of the grave site of American prisoners in North Vietnam."

"So, based on a *vague* tip from a *freelance* informant—whatever that means—Dale is supposed to cancel his speech at the beginning of the Memorial Day weekend and cower inside the White House?"

Grady stood directly behind the Secret Service director so he had to twist around awkwardly to look at her. It was a tactic she often used to seize the advantage at corporate meetings.

"Is that your case?"

"Now, hon," the President spoke for the first time. "If Colbert didn't have what he considered good reasons to be concerned about my safety, he wouldn't recommend that I skip the Vietnam speech, would he?"

"Did your informant tell you the 'incident' will endanger the President's safety, Mr. Clawson?" Grady inquired.

"No," the Secret Service director conceded. "The informant warned only that an incident, a serious incident, may occur at the memorial ceremony."

"I don't get it, Mr. Clawson," Grady said. "A couple of weeks ago, a TV correspondent was murdered ten feet from where Dale was sitting and you couldn't wait to tell the world it had nothing to do with the President. Now you get an ambiguous tip from a third-string informant about an 'incident,' nothing specific, and you rush over here to tell Dale he should cancel his speech. Why the sudden excess of caution?"

"I get paid to be excessively cautious," the Secret Service director replied pompously. "On occasion, some of my predecessors did not exercise excessive caution in performing their duties, with tragic consequences. The day I fail to conduct my office with excessive caution is the day I should be fired."

"And I'm personally grateful you *do* exercise excessive caution." Dale Hammond chuckled, trying to lighten the mood in the dining room. He didn't like conflict.

Grady resumed her seat and addressed the President. "You can't cancel out of the Vietnam ceremony because of a vague tip from a part-time FBI informant," she lectured. "If the Secret Service had its way, you'd *never* leave the safety of the White House. Or, if you did, you'd go in a tank."

Clawson bristled, but did not contradict her.

"The wounds of the Vietnam War are still festering in this country, Dale," the First Lady said. "The people who served there, and the families of the ones who died there, feel their sacrifices aren't appreciated. The ones who avoided serving are feeling guilty that they stuck others, mostly the lower classes, with the burden of fighting and dying. Some think it's time to forget the whole thing so American companies can go after that market. A lot of wives and parents and buddies want to know what happened to their loved ones and friends who never came back. They want to know if the prisoners buried in that grave in Hanoi died *after* the war. There's no closure to their grief. A lot of veterans are wrestling with what that war did to them, not just physically but mentally, too. You've *got* to give that speech Saturday, Dale. That speech is going to be the start of the healing."

The dining room was still. The only sound was the muffled noise of a power mower on the North Lawn.

Dale Hammond stirred his coffee slowly with a silver spoon. He hadn't made a joke and he hadn't said "Now, hon," so Grady knew he was considering her words carefully.

"Everywhere you go, you encounter angry demonstrators demanding that you make Vietnam explain that grave and account for the missing," the First Lady reminded him, adding one more argument to her case. "Mr. Clawson says the disruption planned for Saturday may involve disgruntled veterans groups. Doesn't all that tell you a lot of people are still walking around in a lot of pain from the war? Doesn't that tell you this country is still deeply divided over Vietnam? History has given you the mission to reconcile those divisions once and for all. You can't let him scare you away from giving that speech Saturday."

Dale Hammond continued to stir his coffee in slow circles.

"Grady's right," the President said at last. "Unless you turn up more conclusive evidence of a serious threat to my safety, Colbert, I don't think I should cancel my speech. I assume the Secret Service and the police can cope with whatever demonstration or 'incident' your informant says is planned. Am I correct?"

"As always, my people will do whatever is required to protect the President," the Secret Service director replied stiffly. "We have three days, and we will be ready."

"Good, good," the President said, rising from his chair. "There are some things I need to say about Vietnam, Colbert, and Saturday at the Wall, on Memorial Day weekend, is the right time and the right place to say them."

"Yes, sir." Clawson scrambled to his feet. "Mr. President." They shook hands.

"Ms. Hammond." He shook her hand with cool civility.

The First Lady had won. As always.

That evening, being driven in her white Mercedes on the Dulles toll road from her office at H-Drive Computer Services to the White House, Grady Hammond called Jerry Knight at his apartment on her car phone.

Jerry, just getting up from his day's sleep, sounded flustered, as he usually did when she called.

The First Lady invited him to attend the ceremony at the Vietnam Wall on Saturday.

"Dale's giving a major speech," Grady told him. "Major. About how the nation should think about Vietnam, and what course we should follow now. I know you were a correspondent there, Jerry, and you talk about it a lot on your show. I think you'll want to attend the speech. Come as my guest. I'll make sure you have a seat."

He accepted immediately, of course.

Egotist that he was, Jerry was likely to blab endlessly on the *Night Talker* show about Dale's forthcoming major speech, Grady knew, telling listeners how he had been invited personally by the First Lady to attend as her guest.

Men! She smiled to herself. The invitation was part of her plan to generate public interest in the Vietnam speech.

Jerry asked the First Lady about her computer search for the alleged Vietnam memo McLean was investigating.

"I didn't find it," she told him. Her tone of finality told him not to pursue it further.

Before the uniformed guards waved the Mercedes through the black iron gate at the Southwest Entrance to the White House grounds, Grady called another half-dozen media celebrities and encouraged them to spread the word that Dale's speech Saturday would be a blockbuster.

As soon as he hung up from the First Lady, Jerry dialed Jane Day's extension in the *Post's* cubicle at the White House.

When she heard his voice, she gave an exaggerated moan of disapproval. Jane had given up trying to dissuade him from calling her at work.

"What's up, Jerry?" she asked impatiently. "I've got five hundred words to write and I'm getting tight for deadline."

"I just got off the phone with Grady Hammond."

"I'm so happy for both of you," Jane responded sarcastically.

"She did the computer search for that memo about the American prisoners in Vietnam at the end of the war."

"Yeah?" Jane's interest perked up.

"She couldn't find it."

Jane was crushed. It had been her best chance to learn the identity of the memo's author. If the President's wife couldn't ferret out the name, Jane couldn't think of anyone else who could. She'd hit a dead end in unraveling Dan McLean's murder.

"I'm sorry," Jerry said. He sounded like he meant it. "But listen, I have some news that will cheer you up."

"Yeah?"

"Dale Hammond is giving a big Vietnam speech at the Wall Saturday—"

"I know that."

"—and Grady's invited me to attend as her guest."

"Wow! That *does* cheer me up." Jane's voice oozed sarcasm.

"And I'm inviting you to be *my* guest."

"You're *her* guest and I'm *your* guest? Can you do that?"

"I don't know. If I ask her, I'm sure she'll get you a seat."

"I get *paid* to cover Hammond's speeches," Jane reminded him. "Why should I go to one on my own time?"

"You got something better to do Saturday?"

"Uh, let's see. Clean out the refrigerator. Root canal work. Getting mugged. You want some more?"

"It's supposed to be a nice day. We'll go to the speech, then drive out to Angler's and have lunch on the terrace. Remember when we ate there last year?"

"I remember."

"How about it? Say yes."

"I don't know, Jerry. I may have to work Saturday. I'll probably end up covering the speech for the Sunday paper."

"You cover the speech, I'll go as Grady's guest, and afterward we'll have lunch at Angler's. Okay?"

"I don't know. Maybe. I've got to hang up. I'm on deadline."

CHAPTER TWENTY-NINE

WHEN A. L. JONES arrived at Homicide's offices on the third floor of the Municipal Center, he found a note taped over his computer screen: "Captain Wheeler wants to see you, honey. Jonetta."

Just what he needed to start the day.

Actually, A.L. wasn't starting his day. The dispatcher had phoned him at three A.M. and directed him to the scene of a multiple murder in an apartment off Bladensburg Road near the Maryland line. A man and woman and a one-year-old baby. The uniformed cops found the baby cradled in the woman's arms, like she'd been trying to shield him. The victims and the apartment had been sprayed with more than twenty shots.

None of the neighbors had seen or heard anything.

A.L. needed coffee before he faced Captain Wheeler.

It was thick as sludge. And tepid.

"How you doing on the McLean case?" Wheeler asked when Jones was standing in front of his desk.

"Okay."

"Yeah? You got any leads?"

Wheeler, a light-skinned black man with close-cropped sandy hair and a pencil-thin mustache, was fashionably dressed, as always. He wore a tight-fitting bright blue suit tailored in a shiny silk fabric, a dark blue shirt with white collar and cuffs, clunky gold cuff links, and a blue tie patterned with gold saxophones.

"Looking to make the boy whacked that waiter, the one served McLean the poison. That might lead somewhere. Also, McLean was a stud. Fucked anything with tits. Lot of activity not involving Mrs. McLean. I'm checking out some angles there. You know, might of been a domestic thing."

"How soon you going to break something? Uncle don't want no part of it. So it's all you, A.L. That dude was high-profile, you know. I'm getting heat on this one. CNN is putting on a special program every day, something like, 'The Dan McLean Murder, Unsolved—Day Twenty.' Mayor ain't happy, A.L."

Oh, yeah. The mayor. Wheeler's benefactor. The word was out that Wheeler was on his way up, maybe to chief, if he didn't screw up. Screw up on a CNN news dude, the captain might be on his way back to riding patrol.

"So, A.L., we need a break here," Wheeler said. "By next Monday? No, Monday's a holiday. I'll be at the mayor's Memorial Day barbecue. By Tuesday?"

"By Tuesday," A.L. promised halfheartedly. "No sweat."

Jones sat at his cluttered desk, covering his face with his pudgy hands, trying to shut out the cacophony of the Homicide offices. He needed to put the jigsaw pieces of the McLean case together. But nothing fit.

"Hey, Jonetta," he shouted. "Go to the deli and get me some coffee I can drink."

"You buy me one?" she shouted back.

"Yeah."

"You got it, honey."

Jones reviewed three different piles of puzzle pieces.

There was the dead gook waiter pile. The waiter definitely put the poison in McLean's soup. The video showed that. But who cracked the waiter? And why? A.L. had no witnesses, or at least none who would talk. No fingerprints. And no clues.

The shooter might have been a neighborhood pipehead the waiter caught robbing his apartment. Jones decided to squeeze his snitches in the Columbia Heights neighborhood.

Then there were the McLean-the-swordsman puzzle pieces. The guy couldn't keep his dick in his pants. Senator Thatcher had been convincing when he claimed he was too busy with his official duties to care that his wife was banging McLean. But how many other husbands of the correspondent's conquests were that understanding? Jealousy was a powerful emotion.

When he was new on Homicide, before the drug thing hit D.C., jealousy had been one of the main reasons people busted each other. Hell, A.L. still felt pangs of jealousy when he thought about his ex-wife married to that doctor up in New Jersey. And Jones had been divorced—what? Eight years?

And there was McLean's widow. A big puzzle piece. In A.L.'s experience, the wives of cheating husbands were a lot more dangerous than the husbands of cheating wives. Willie Wu had reported that McLean was killed by a rare poison found in tropical climates like Africa. Patricia McLean taught tropical medicine at Georgetown University, and she had served in the Peace Corps in Africa. That could be Jones's hottest lead. The poison acted too fast for her to have fed it to him before he left for the dinner. But she could have paid the waiter to slip it into his soup.

He looked through his old notebooks until he found her phone number.

After three rings, a recorded message came on the line.

Hi. This is Pat McLean. The kids and I are going to be at our place in Rehobeth Beach until after Memorial Day. In an emergency, you can reach me there. Otherwise, leave a message when you hear the beep and I'll call you back.

He could drive to Rehobeth in three hours. It was Delaware, and he didn't have any jurisdiction there. But he might be able to bluff her into answering his questions. A day at the beach didn't sound too bad.

Nah. Patricia McLean's kids would be freaked if Jones showed up unannounced to question their mother about their father's murder. He'd visit her next week, when she got back.

If she'd hired the waiter to kill her husband because he was cheating on her, and she was still around, doing the grieving widow number, she wasn't likely to flee now, Jones concluded, unless she thought he was on to her. Another reason not to track her to the beach.

That left one more pile of puzzle pieces. Vietnam. It kept coming up.

The waiter was Vietnamese. Willie Wu said the poison that killed McLean could have come from Southeast Asia. That newsie from the *Post* thought McLean was working on some kind of exposé about Vietnam when he was chopped. When A.L. met her and Jerry Knight at the Vietnamese restaurant in Arlington, the owner acted like he knew something. He said, *"We'll take care of it, we don't need any cops."* Like he knew who chopped McLean, and the gooks were going to settle it themselves.

And then there was that thing came up at a meeting Jones attended in the Secret Service director's office. A warning of some kind from a bunch of former Green Berets, came in on the computer. Couldn't be traced. Something about the President better do something about making Vietnam account for the prisoners. Well, if they were ex–Green Berets, A.L. could believe just about anything. Some of those motherfuckers were crazy.

Once again a long-ago scene from Vietnam invaded the detective's mind.

His platoon was moving down a road, careful to stay in the brush on either side, so if Charlie was waiting for them, he wouldn't catch them in the open.

They came to a cement bridge over a stream. The platoon commander, a young lieutenant who'd been in-country a month, ordered his men to cross the bridge in two columns. Some of the seasoned soldiers protested, warning the lieutenant that he was inviting an ambush. They suggested that the platoon spread out along the stream and cross above and below the bridge.

The lieutenant was lazy, arrogant, and stupid—a bad combination in a combat commander. It had been a hot and unproductive day of patrolling. He was anxious to get back to their base, shower, and have a beer. He ordered the platoon to march across the bridge.

The point man, Scialino, was about five feet from the far end when Charlie opened up on them from the jungle on both sides. A.L. recognized the distinctive chatter of AK-47s and the flat explosion of grenades.

He jammed himself as close as he could against the cement sides of the bridge. They were low, less than two feet high. Chunky even then, A.L. tried to flatten himself, to burrow into the roadbed of the bridge. He felt the shock of VC bullets slamming into the outer side of his scanty shelter. Chips of cement pinged on his steel pot. He was so scared. So fucking scared. He never lifted his head or fired a shot.

It took thirty minutes for air cover to arrive. And another hour for evacuation choppers to land. Out of fifteen guys in the platoon, Scialino and three others were killed, six were wounded, including A.L. A hot shard from a VC grenade nicked his left shoulder. But it wasn't serious enough to get him shipped back to the World.

The lieutenant was one of the dead. Jones suspected he was shot with an M16 by one of his own men.

The detective shook off the memory.

It wouldn't surprise him if McLean's murder had something to do with Vietnam. Anybody who'd been there never got over it. The motive could have been anything. Some of the vets were crazy sons of bitches.

Which made A.L. think of Stump.

Yeah, Stump.

He was fucking crazy, all right.

And if any of the crazy vets had something to do with cracking McLean, Stump might have heard about it.

The legless Stump hung different places in his chrome-and-black wheelchair.

Sometimes A.L. found him with other messed-up vets around the Vietnam Wall, handing out pamphlets about the MIAs and POWs to the tourists.

Other times, Jones encountered Stump in the entranceway of the Farragut West Metro station, shaking a Styrofoam cup, intimidating and shaming the passengers into giving him money.

He had lettered I NEED MONEY FOR FOOD on a piece of cardboard box and propped it on his lap.

Touching. But bullshit. What he needed the money for, A.L. knew, was not food, but malt liquor.

Since it was raining, Jones surmised that Stump was spending the day indoors.

The detective thought he knew where to find him.

On the south side of Massachusetts Avenue, about halfway between the Mount Vernon Square Library and Union Station, stood an abandoned firehouse. It has been closed during some earlier budget-cutting crisis, A.L. recalled, although someone continued to carefully paint the cast-iron fire department emblem—a fireman's helmet above a red, white, and blue shield—embedded high in the brick front wall, above the wide red doors, now nailed closed.

At the library end of this stretch of Massachusetts Avenue, the neighborhood was making a minor comeback, with construction of a convention center and the promised construction of a sports arena, the erection of a conventioneers hotel, and the transplantation of National Public Radio's headquarters.

And at the other end of this stretch of the avenue, the massive, Roman-style Union Station had been renovated—getting it right on the second try, Jones noted—into an appealing center for shopping and dining, as well as catching the train.

But in between, the area was deplorable. Boarded-up stores and town houses. Burned-out buildings. Vacant lots littered with trash and human debris. The abandoned firehouse stood in this stretch.

And Stump lived inside.

A.L. pulled his vanilla-colored detective's car into the alley behind the firehouse, crunching on broken glass.

He shouldered open a rear door. The lock had long since been ripped out.

Inside it was dark and damp. And it stank, of shit, urine, vomit, and unwashed bodies.

A.L. almost gagged. Even armed, A.L. didn't feel secure in there.

"Hey, Stump?" the detective called out. "You here? It's A.L."

Jones heard a scurrying noise. It could have been rats. It could have been winos or drugheads who didn't want to have anything to do with a cop.

"Hey, Stump? You here, man?"

"Yeah, I'm here."

It was a gravelly whisper.

A.L. followed the sound.

The firehouse had been stripped of everything that could be used or sold for cash: lights, wiring, plumbing, pipes, furniture, flooring, stairways. The plaster had been hacked from the interior walls to get at the wood lathing.

Jones found Stump in his wheelchair by the big doors at the front.

He looked worse than A.L. remembered, with filthy, matted dreadlocks, clothes that looked like they hadn't been washed for weeks or months, and an ugly rash on his cheeks and neck. He wore a ragged blanket around his shoulders like a shawl.

Stump's eyes glinted madly in the dark.

Next to the wheelchair, someone reclined motionless under a greasy brown tarp.

"How you making it, bro?" A.L. asked Stump, casually as if the two men had run into each other in a bar.

"How'm I making it? Can't you tell? Didn't you see my new Cadillac parked outside?" He laughed hoarsely.

"Yeah, well."

"So, what brings you around, A.L.? You just come to cheer up your old war buddy? Or you working a case? I'll bet that's it. And you think ole Stump can help you. Am I right?"

"Sort of."

"Yeah, I figured that's it. Ole Stump sees a lot of shit going on as I make my rounds. A *lot* of shit. But A.L., can't you hear my throat? I'm dry, man. My throat's dry as a virgin's pussy. How'm I gonna tell you what I see when my throat's so dry I can't barely talk?"

A.L. walked through the drizzle to a barricaded liquor store on the corner, bought a six-pack of Schlitz malt liquor, with the blue bull on the cans, and carried it back to the fire-house.

Stump downed the first one in a gulp. He consumed the other five methodically while A.L. pumped him for information.

The detective wanted to know if he'd heard anything about McLean's murder through the Vietnam vets grapevine. Had he picked up any rumblings about the gook community in Arlington "taking care" of a problem that might be connected to McLean's murder? Had his vet buddies mentioned anything about an exposé concerning the war that the correspondent was working on?

The more malt liquor Stump drank, the more disjointed his responses were. Sometimes he rambled hoarsely about unrelated matters. Sometimes he didn't say anything for minutes, as if he were searching his memory. If he had any memory left, A.L. thought.

The detective stood the whole time. There was nothing to sit on.

Stump was on the streets, all day, every day, talking to people, listening, watching, seeing things, hearing things. He befriended dozens of other Vietnam veterans, broken in mind or body, who lived on the streets.

Slowly, painfully, over two hours, Jones extracted from the amputee some puzzle pieces that fit together. They didn't make a complete picture. There were a lot of holes in the puzzle, a lot of pieces still missing. But as A.L. emerged from the stinking firehouse into the damp air, he had some ideas about how to complete the puzzle.

"Take care of yourself, Stump," the detective called into the darkness.

"You, too, man," the gravelly rasp came back. "Have a nice day."

On the way back to Homicide, Jones tuned in to WTOP, the all-news radio station. The announcer read a list of activities planned for the coming Memorial Day weekend.

When A.L. heard that President Hammond was making a speech at the Vietnam Wall on Saturday, he thought he knew where all the puzzle pieces would be put together.

CHAPTER THIRTY

SATURDAY CAME, DARK and chilly. Leaden clouds hung low, threatening rain.

Mournful weather. A mournful day for the memorial ceremony.

Walking through the gloomy dawn streets from the ATN studios to his Rosslyn apartment after the *Night Talker* show, puffing the one cigar a day his doctor allowed him, Jerry Knight was weighed down by an ineffable sadness, as he always was when he thought about the war.

At his apartment, Jerry downed his usual sleeping potion, two warm beers, and pulled the blackout drapes over the windows.

Before getting into bed, he rummaged in the bottom of the hall closet looking for an umbrella to place next to the front door so he wouldn't forget to take it to the Wall.

In the back of the closet he came across his Vietnam combat boots, cracked brown leather, olive canvas, lug soles, forgotten for so many years.

Recollections of his years in Vietnam flooded back. Painful scenes he'd kept repressed returned. A sense of loss gripped his heart.

Jerry stared at the dusty boots for a long time. He was transported back to Vietnam. He'd never left it.

After discovering the boots, there was no sleep. Memories of the war wouldn't let him.

He flipped through the Saturday *Post* without really taking in the words.

He put on a CD of old Sinatra ballads. That didn't bring sleep, either.

Finally, Jerry decided to get up, shower, dress, and go to the Vietnam Wall early.

Initially, the wide V of black marble, sunken below ground level and engraved with the names of more than fifty thousand Americans killed in the war, was denounced as a black gash of shame.

The young Chinese-American architectural student at Yale who designed it explained that she intended the memorial to symbolize regeneration. Slash open the earth and, in time, the grass will heal it, she had said.

Indeed, the grass had grown up around the sunken tablets of marble. And people came every day by the thousands, seeking regeneration and healing. From loss, guilt, anger, pain, confusion.

Jerry arrived just before the Park Police closed the memorial to tourists to make ready for the presidential visit.

For the twentieth time, Jerry walked slowly down the sloping path beside the polished black walls, deeper and deeper into the trench, into the earth. The slabs bearing the thousands upon thousands of names of the dead towered higher and higher above him. He was overwhelmed, suffocating, drowning in grief. He'd been a correspondent in Vietnam, not a soldier. But he'd seen more fighting than many soldiers. And more death.

Jerry stopped at the bottom of the V, looking at his sorrowing face mirrored in the marble, merging with the names.

As always, he wept. Without trying to hide it. For all those boys, dying in pain and terror, most of them before they'd lived twenty-five years. For his guilt at coming back alive. For America, which had been unwilling or unable to save the Vietnamese people from subjugation.

Jerry uttered a high, involuntary moan.

"Tran," he sobbed.

And then he climbed up the slope on the other side of the V. The black tablets of names receded. He came out of the symbolic grave, out of the earth, back to the living.

He wiped away the tears.

Jerry bought a Styrofoam cup of coffee and a cellophane-wrapped donut from an Asian vendor in a white truck parked near the State Department. He carried them back to the memorial and sat in the last row of empty folding chairs set up for the ceremony.

Even with the preparations going on around him, the setting was placid.

To the left, the classically columned marble temple to Abraham Lincoln, enclosing the mournful seated statue of the Civil War President. Lincoln was the greatest of all the Presidents, Jerry believed, for leading the nation through that other divisive war.

He noticed a TV camera crew stationed on the long, wide marble staircase leading up to the Lincoln Memorial, panning back and forth between the statue and the Vietnam Wall. No doubt recording video to illustrate some politically correct put-down by a blow-dried anchor too young to remember Vietnam.

Jerry sometimes wondered whether Lincoln would have been able to withstand news-media demands to end the killing if there had been TV cameras at Antietam or Gettysburg. Would Lincoln have been accused of ordering atrocities against women and children if Peter Arnett had been reporting from Atlanta when Sherman burned it?

Through the trees in the other direction, the simple white marble obelisk honoring George Washington, towering over all other structures in the capital. The first President was derided these days as a slave-owning, woman-chasing, fatuous colonial dandy. But, Jerry thought, he had started the new nation down the right path, mostly reflecting his personal commitment to democracy and rectitude. Washington could have been crowned king, but he rejected it. Too bad some of his successors didn't feel the same.

Security for the Memorial Day ceremony seemed heavier than usual. Jerry counted twenty Secret Service agents in suits and sunglasses, talking into wrist microphones, scanning the trees and the growing crowd of tourists held behind orange ropes. Uniformed Executive Protective Service guards set up portable metal detectors through which the invited guests had to pass.

Dozens of Park Police and Metropolitan Police disembarked from blue buses and took up positions encircling the ceremonial area. When the side door of an official van parked on Constitution Avenue slid open for a moment, Jerry glimpsed what looked like a black-clad SWAT team inside.

Among the law-enforcement officers milling around the fringes of the ceremonial area was Detective A. L. Jones. But Jerry didn't see him.

The heavy security was probably in anticipation of demonstrations, Jerry assumed. Vietnam still generated strong emotions, even more than two decades after the end of the war and more than three years after Clinton officially ended hostilities by extending diplomatic recognition to the Vietnamese government. The old wounds had been reopened by the recent discovery of a mass grave of American prisoners near Hanoi. Dale Hammond was under pressure to react strongly to the grisly finding.

Jerry wondered what the President would say at the Wall. Grady had told him it would be "major." Jerry hoped the President would put the generation of smug yuppies in their place, so pleased with themselves for dodging the draft. So wrongheaded, in his view.

Jerry looked at his watch. Still an hour before noon.

A Secret Service agent approached and asked his name. The agent found the name on a list attached to his clipboard and placed a checkmark next to it. He directed Jerry to pass through the metal detector.

The other invited guests began to arrive. Jerry recognized the famous faces. Senator John McCain, who'd been held prisoner by the North Vietnamese but had favored Clinton's recognition. Robert McNamara, ghostly, every agony he'd felt and caused etched into his stony face. Henry Kissinger, fat in a dark gray tailored suit, grinning, slapping backs, making self-aggrandizing jokes. Legless Max Cleland, rolling majestically in his wheelchair. Bob Hope, ancient and rheumy-eyed. Neil Sheehan and David Halberstam, two of the first war correspondents in Vietnam. Senator Bob Kerrey, who'd lost part of his leg in the war. General Norman Schwartzkopf, who won his war, chatting with General William Westmoreland, who lost his.

But most of the guests passing through the metal detectors and taking their places on the folding chairs were not famous faces. They looked proud but solemn, a little dazed. Jerry guessed they were the parents, widows, and children of men who died or disappeared in the war.

The guests were escorted to their seats by members of veterans organizations acting as marshals. They wore black REMEMBER THE MIAS/POWS T-shirts, camouflage fatigue jackets and pants, and combat boots. Once trim young troopers, they were middle-aged now, with beer bellies and gray beards.

A military band unloaded from its bus and arrayed itself in a reserved area to the left of the podium.

Jerry heard a commotion from the short street that connected the road encircling the Lincoln Memorial to Constitution Avenue. The noise came from hordes of people pouring out of a bus and two black vans. They came running toward the Vietnam Wall. When they got closer, Jerry recognized them as the White House press corps—TV cameramen, photographers, and reporters, in full gallop.

Secret Service agents herded them into a roped-off pen behind the invited guests. The TV technicians jostled for tripod space on the raised camera platforms. The reporters shouted questions at members of the White House press office staff.

Jerry spotted Jane Day in the pack. He waved at her. But she either didn't see him or pretended not to see him lest her colleagues rib her about her friendship with such a Neanderthal. He imagined that Jane was not happy to be cooped up in a press pen on a drizzly Saturday covering a President she disapproved of. But, as the junior member of the *Post*'s White House team, she got stuck with the assignments the more senior reporters ducked.

Jerry tried waving at her again. Still no response. She'd never given him an answer to his invitation for lunch at Angler's after the President's speech. Well, it was too wet to eat on the terrace anyhow.

As soon as the TV cameras were spotted, chanting erupted from behind the seating area. Demonstrators, Jerry surmised. The security forces had kept the protesters away from the ceremony, back along the Reflecting Pool. A platoon of policemen quickstepped toward the noise. The Secret Service agents looked edgy.

Jerry picked up two competing chants. One was the now-famous *"Hanoi, Hanoi, hey, hey, hey. How many Americans did you bury today?"* The other was a ragged version of the old Beatles song, "Give Peace a Chance."

The TV cameramen snatched their cameras off the tripods, hoisted them onto their shoulders, and headed toward the demonstrators. The chanting got louder and angrier. Another platoon of policemen took off for the demonstration area.

The marshals escorted participants in the program and administration officials to their seats. Billy Graham, who would deliver the invocation. Placido Domingo, director of the Washington Opera, who would sing the "Star-Spangled Banner." The secretaries of Defense and State. Gregor Novasky, the President's national security adviser. The chairman of the Joint Chiefs of Staff, dazzling in full-dress military regalia. The secretary of the Department of Veterans Affairs, beaming on his one annual moment in the limelight.

The heavy presidential podium was set up in an isolated position on the grass so the inescapable shot for the TV cameras would be President Hammond standing all alone against the backdrop of the Wall. Nice photo op, Jerry thought. Of course, the TV crews would be looking for some way to portray the President in an unflattering way, an unplanned slipup, some embarrassing angle.

Suddenly there was a flurry of movement, the roar of motorcycle engines and limousines on Constitution Avenue. The band struck up "Hail to the Chief." Dale and Grady Hammond appeared, smiling, waving, almost hidden in a circle of Secret Service agents. The volume of the rival demonstrations rose.

The First Lady wore a khaki-colored suit tailored to look like a uniform, complete with epaulets and a hat that was loosely patterned after a Vietnam bush cap.

Her detractors were going to have a field day with that outfit, Jerry thought. Dale better give a strong speech, otherwise the reporters were likely to lead their stories with Grady's "affront" to the nation's military tradition.

After the prayers, the anthem, and the warm-up speeches, Dale Hammond waited a dramatic moment, then walked slowly and alone to the podium.

Colbert Clawson had wanted to post agents on each side of the rostrum, and one behind the President. But the press secretary, Garvin Dillon, vetoed that idea because the security guards would detract from the photo op of the solitary President in front of the Wall.

The President pulled his speech text out of his breast pocket and flattened it open. It was full of cross-outs and scribbled additions in red ink. Grady's last-minute edits.

Dale preferred to read his speeches from typewritten sheets, the old-fashioned way, rather than from glass TelePrompTers favored by his recent predecessors. Dillon told him that looking down at the text made him appear scripted and presented the top of his head to the TV cameras. But the President was afraid the TelePrompTer operator would scroll the words too fast or too slow and cause him to lose his place. Anyhow, Dale believed the words were what mattered, not a slick presentation.

He began.

Half a generation ago, this memorial was dedicated. What we say here today in its hallowed shadow will not be long remembered. What the men and women whose names are inscribed on the marble did for the cause of freedom will never be forgotten. They will live forever in the halls of the righteous, and in our memories. How can we, the living, honor the ultimate sacrifice they made? By ending the war that still divides us. We must march forward from those trampled and bloody battlegrounds of yesterday. It is time to make peace, within ourselves, and among ourselves. Let us, a wise people and a proud nation, turn our faces to the tasks ahead, for the sake of those gone, and those yet to come. The warriors we honor today gave their lives in a battle that was lost. But it was only one battle in a war that never ends, the struggle of freedom against tyranny, the struggle of liberty against oppression. From their sacrifice we gain a new measure of devotion to that struggle, and a new resolve that these honored dead shall not have died in vain.

Dale Hammond folded his script, replaced it in his breast pocket, and returned to his seat.

For a moment the only sound in the misty air was sobbing. Even the demonstrators were silent.

He delivered the goddamn Gettysburg address, Jerry marveled.

Grady Hammond leaned over and hugged the President, weeping on his shoulder.

Then the applause began. Hard, approving, sincere applause. It went on for many minutes.

Jerry looked over at the press pen to catch Jane's reaction. He couldn't find her. But he noticed some of the TV correspondents on the camera platform looked panicked. Apparently expecting a standard twenty-minute presidential speech and waiting for a passage that was controversial or made the President sound foolish, they hadn't turned on their cameras yet when Hammond's ninety-second speech ended.

Whatever was going to happen was going to happen soon, A. L. Jones sensed. He waited and watched from behind the band.

A little girl in a purple velvet pinafore, whose grandfather's name was carved on the Wall, left her seat in the family section and toddled to the President. She kissed him on the cheek.

More people started crying.

The applause swelled.

Even the security agents were affected by the emotion.

That's why they were slow reacting when one of the marshals, in black T-shirt and fatigues, slipped up behind Gregor Novasky, the President's national security adviser. The veteran flipped a thin plastic noose around Novasky's neck and yanked, severing his windpipe.

"Man down!" Colbert Clawson yelled when he grasped what had happened. "Move Teddybear! Now! Move! Move!"

Bedlam erupted.

Dale and Grady Hammond were rushed to the presidential limousine by a phalanx of Secret Service agents. The black armor-clad car sped down Constitution Avenue toward the White House and safety.

Other Secret Service agents, Metropolitan Police, Park Police, and bystanders swarmed on the veteran who had garroted Novasky, pinning him on the grass.

The veteran yelled "The prisoners are avenged! The prisoners are avenged!" over and over.

A. L. Jones contemplated jumping into the melee of bodies trying to subdue the man. But he saw that a dozen other law-enforcement officers had him under control. A.L. was too old for that shit.

At Colbert Clawson's first shouted alarm, Secret Service agents throughout the ceremonial area drew their weapons from holsters and canvas bags. At the sight of the guns, many in the crowd screamed in fear and ran.

The fleeing spectators collided with the White House press corps, which stampeded out of its pen and headed for the podium, yelling at anyone who looked official, "What happened? What happened?"

Some of the agents formed a protective ring around the VIP seats, scanning the chaotic scene anxiously.

Novasky lay on his back on the grass behind his overturned chair. A blue-uniformed D.C. Emergency Medical Services team and two Navy medical corpsmen ministered to him. But A.L. knew from the waxy blue-gray color of his face that he was dead.

Jerry Knight stood at the rear of the now-abandoned guest section, following the tumult. He wasn't sure what had happened and he didn't know what he should do.

He spotted Jane Day squatting under a tree, talking rapidly and loudly into her cellular telephone, apparently dictating a narrative of events at the ceremony to the *Post*. Her green eyes had a wild look. With one hand she repeatedly twisted and untwisted a curl of orange hair.

Jerry started toward the reporter. But before he reached her, he was grabbed by Bernard Shaw for a live interview on CNN.

Shaw's first question was, "Mr. Knight, do you think the extreme right-wing rhetoric spewed over the airways by you and the other ultraconservative radio talk-show hosts is responsible for encouraging the kind of violence we saw here today?"

"No," Jerry replied.

He waited serenely while the disconcerted Shaw fumbled for another line of questions.

CHAPTER THIRTY-ONE

Four o'clock. The afternoon had grown darker. A drizzle fell.

The scene at the Wall reminded Jerry of the disorder on a battlefield after the battle.

Park Service workers in green slickers folded and stacked the chairs, then loaded them onto a truck.

The area where Novasky had been killed was roped off with yellow police tape and guarded by a couple of policemen in shiny black raincoats.

TV correspondents jockeyed for position so the yellow tape would show in the background of their standuppers. Stoic producers held umbrellas over the heads of the stars.

Tourists snapped photos.

The emergency NO PARKING signs had been removed from Constitution Avenue, and the white vendor trucks were back, peddling T-shirts, snacks, and soft drinks.

On a knoll overlooking the Wall, aging Vietnam veterans in their fatigues and beards huddled around the card tables where they handed out literature. Some had known the man who strangled Novasky. One had been in his unit in the war.

They speculated among themselves about the aftermath of the killing.

"The goddamn news media will make all vets the villains," predicted a man who ran a dog-tag concession.

"Yeah, I can see the headlines now, 'Vietnam Psycho Killers,'" imagined another veteran, whose black T-shirt sleeve was pinned over the stump of his right arm.

Jerry stayed through the afternoon, mesmerized by the activity. He hadn't slept after his show. But he wasn't tired. Too much adrenaline. Too many questions.

Why Novasky? Did his murder have anything to do with the poisoning of Dan McLean? It must have. A Vietnamese waiter. A Vietnam veteran. McLean working on some kind of Vietnam exposé. Mr. Cao's comments. The scene of the killing, at the Vietnam Memorial.

But how did it all fit together?

Jerry wanted to talk to Jane, find out what she knew. But she was constantly busy, on her phone dictating, conducting interviews, scribbling in her notebook. At one point he handed her a Coke from one of the vendor trucks. She took it, giving him a grateful look, without breaking her dictation.

A. L. Jones nosed his dirty vanilla Ford to the curb on the north side of Constitution Avenue next to the enormous impressionistic statue of Albert Einstein on the lawn of the National Academy of Sciences. He walked across the street to the Wall.

He'd spent almost three hours in the Federal Courthouse at the foot of Capitol Hill participating in the interrogation of the veteran who took down Novasky. It was a federal case, no question, since the victim was a White House official. But Lawrence Frieze of the Secret Service had invited A.L. to sit in, since there was an immediate suspicion that Novasky's death was related to McLean's murder.

After the interrogation, A.L. returned to the Wall to see if any more evidence had been found.

Jerry Knight noticed that Jane seemed to have concluded her reporting duties. She dropped her phone and her notepad into her giant shoulder bag and drank what was left of the Coke Jerry had brought her.

He ducked under the limbs of the tree where she was

standing. The drizzle had turned her normally unruly hair into a bedraggled orange mess. Jerry guessed he didn't look so great himself, damp, wrinkled, and weary.

"Unbelievable," he commented on what had happened.

"Really," she agreed, still sounding wired. "Thanks for the Coke."

"I didn't think you noticed."

"I noticed."

She sagged against his shoulder for a moment.

"My story's leading the Sunday paper," she boasted. "Five-column head. You think it could be Pulitzer material? Breaking news written under deadline pressure?"

Jerry shrugged. He didn't understand the self-absorption of the news media. A man was dead and she was thinking Pulitzer.

A. L. Jones saw them under the tree branches and came over.

"Detective Jones," Jerry greeted him disparagingly. "This is one murder case even the D.C. police can't screw up, huh? Right in front of a couple of hundred cops. Think you can figure out who did it?"

"And a good afternoon to you, too, Mr. Night Talker," the stubby detective replied in a deep rumble.

Jane instantly resumed her reporter mode. She retrieved her notebook from her bag and started firing questions at Jones.

"Are you working on the case, Detective Jones?"

"Sort of."

"What's 'sort of'?"

"It's a federal case, but I attended the interrogation of the perp. D.C. Homicide is working on a few angles."

Jane scribbled faster and faster, not taking her eyes off A.L.'s face.

"Who's the perp?"

"The FBI released it, right?" Jones asked cautiously. "So I ain't giving away any secrets?"

Jane nodded affirmatively. She didn't know if the FBI had released the name. But she didn't want to discourage A.L. from spilling what he knew.

"Guy named Eldon Krohl," the detective intoned. "Vietnam vet. First Air Cav. Went through the Ia Drang Valley deal. He's dying of cancer. From breathing Agent Orange, he says, so he don't give a shit."

"What was his motive?" Jerry interjected.

"Didn't have no motive. He was recruited to do the job."

"By whom?" Jane asked.

She had run out of space in her notebook. She flipped over the pad and started scribbling on the back of her earlier notes.

"Group he belongs to called the Survivors of Cam Hoa. Bad dudes. Green Berets. Rangers. LERPs. And they're pissed because they think the government ain't doing enough to find out what happened to their buddies didn't come home."

"So am I," Jerry said. "So are a lot of people. But they don't kill the President's national security adviser because they're pissed off at the government."

"Well, the discovery of that grave of American prisoners kind of pushed the Survivors of Cam Hoa over the edge. And they're *especially* pissed at Nasky—whatever his name is—because he wrote a paper or a memo, some shit like that, back in the seventies, saying there was no more American prisoners left in Vietnam when he knew there was."

"That was the story Dan told Kristi he was working on when he was killed," Jane said.

"Who's Christy?" Jerry asked.

"Nobody," Jane answered dismissively. She continued her intense interrogation of Jones.

"So Novasky arranged to have Dan poisoned, to keep him from breaking the story, right?" Jane asked.

"Nope," the detective replied. "Nobody arranged McLean's murder."

"What do you mean? He's dead, isn't he?"

"He's dead, all right. But it was a mistake."

Jane's pen was a blur now.

"Mistake?" Jerry cut in, incredulous at what he was hearing. "So Dale Hammond *was* the intended target of the poison? I was right all along?"

"Nope, Mr. Night Talker, you was *wrong* all along. That waiter, Duc Phu something, was hired by the Survivors of

Cam Hoa to kill Nov . . . Novasky at that big dinner because they were so pissed at him about that memo thing. They knew Duc from Vietnam. He'd been a scout for the Green Berets and they helped him get to the States. They showed him a picture of Novasky. But he got Novasky and McLean mixed up. They looked a lot alike, you know . . ."

"Yeah. Yeah," Jane was writing furiously.

". . . and the waiter dropped the poison on the wrong guy."

"And then Krohl volunteered to kill the *right* guy," Jane filled in the rest. "He didn't care if he got caught because he was dying of cancer anyhow. So he strangled Novasky in plain view of thousands of people, in revenge for the memo."

"Hey, Miss *Washington Post,* you ain't a bad lady detective," A.L. said. "But, technically, he didn't *strangle* Novasky. He snapped the guy's windpipe with a cord. Learned it in Nam. Used plastic fishing line so the metal detectors wouldn't pick it up."

Jane shuddered at the vivid explanation.

"Who killed the waiter?" Jerry asked.

"Don't know yet. It's one angle I'm working on. Might of been some street boy he caught ripping off his stuff. But it was probably the Survivors of Cam Hoa, to make sure he didn't talk."

"Who took Dan's notebooks from his house?" Jane asked, cleaning up loose ends now. "Patricia McLean gave them to somebody who said he was from CNN, but he wasn't."

A.L. shrugged. "Dunno. Didn't even know somebody took McLean's notebooks. I'll look into it."

The detective made a note in his own bent pad.

"Maybe the widow didn't really give the notebooks to nobody," Jones suggested. "Maybe she just told you that to get you to stop bugging her."

And maybe the government's computer surveillance program tipped off Novasky that Dan was on to his memo, Jane speculated to herself, and the national security adviser sent somebody to trick Patricia McLean into giving up the incriminating notebooks.

"What about your theory that Dan was killed because he . . . played around?" Jane asked Jones.

"He left one widow and a bunch of husbands who ain't too happy with him," A.L. replied. "But they didn't get a chance to do anything about it."

"If rumors were circulating in the Vietnamese community about Dan McLean working on a story that could stir up old animosities, how come the FBI or the Secret Service didn't hear about it?" Jane asked.

"How do you know they didn't?" A.L. replied guardedly, recalling the mention of the Survivors of Cam Hoa at the early-morning meeting in the Secret Service director's office. Shit, even Stump heard something was going down.

"Did they?" Jane pressed.

"Ask 'em."

"I will."

"Don't be surprised if they play cover your ass," the detective advised.

"Who are the Survivors of Cam Hoa?" Jerry inquired. "Is it a big organization?"

A.L. shrugged. He didn't know.

"Probably a bunch of fat, middle-aged gun nuts who work at the gas station or raise pigs," Jane sneered, "and like to dress up like soldiers because they never got over the war."

"Yeah?" A. L. Jones said in an ominous growl. "A lot of us never got over the war, Miss *Washington Post.* We sure is fat and middle-aged. But we ain't no gun nuts. We went to Nam because we was told to go. And some of us is still trying to figure out what the fuck it was all about. You're so smart, maybe you can enlighten us."

"Amen," Jerry added.

Jane knew better than to taunt them further.

"Dale Hammond could be hurt by this," Jerry suggested, "for not knowing about the memo when he named Novasky to the NSC."

"I wish that was true," Jane replied. "But Novasky's been in and out of government for almost thirty years. He's been appointed by Republican presidents and Democratic presidents. And when he wasn't in the government, he was working as a newspaper and TV pundit. Nobody's going to hold Hammond responsible. Unfortunately."

"Hard as you try to suppress it, your objectivity just keeps breaking through," Jerry gibed.

"I've got to file," she said, punching buttons on her cellular phone. She walked away from the shelter of the tree. The drizzle had stopped.

Jerry and A.L. stood under the branches, not saying anything.

The detective's radio crackled.

"Say again?" He held it to his ear and listened.

"Oh, shit! Oh, shit! Those motherfuckers!" Jones appeared to stagger. He looked like he was going to sag down on the grass.

"How is he?" Jones spoke into the radio. His dark face contorted into an angry scowl as he listened to the reply.

"What's the matter?" Jerry asked.

"LaTroy . . . a boy . . . I been trying to keep him straight. Somebody just shot him. They found him out on Sixtieth Street with two bullets in him. But he's still alive, thank you sweet Jesus. He's still alive."

"What's wrong with this goddamn city?" Jerry asked. "Why can't somebody stop the shootings?"

"Yeah," A.L. said in a whisper. "Why can't somebody stop 'em? Why can't somebody stop 'em?"

"America lost the war in Vietnam and now we're losing the war on our own streets for the same reasons," Jerry lectured the detective. "We lack the will. We're reluctant to use the weapons necessary to win. And we are too soft-headed to recognize the viciousness of the enemy."

A.L. didn't seem to hear him. The detective trudged past the black memorial, crossed Constitution Avenue, and got into his car. He made a U-turn and headed for the Washington Hospital Center, feeling old and useless.

CHAPTER THIRTY-TWO

Having updated her story with the additional details from A.L. in time for the early edition of the Sunday *Post,* Jane searched in the gloom for Jerry.

She was still high from the excitement of the day. She wanted to rehash it with someone. She needed company, somebody to talk to. Her cat Bloomsbury wouldn't be enough.

Jane found Jerry at the Wall, in the deepest part of the trench. His head was pressed against the black marble, his fingers touching a name.

"Did you know him?" Jane asked.

"I was covering his unit," Jerry replied. "He tripped a claymore. It cut him in half. I held him while he bled to death."

Jerry started to cry.

Jane put her arm around his shoulders. She kissed him on the cheek, tasting salt from his tears.

"So many lives gone," he wept. "So many young lives gone."

"I don't understand how you can support the idea that America should have continued the war when you feel this way about so many men dying," she said. "If we'd continued the war, how many more names of dead young men would be on this wall?"

"How many more dead Vietnamese are there—their names aren't listed on a wall anywhere—most of them don't even have tombstones—because we cut and ran on them. This country used to believe there were things worth fighting and dying for. Like other people's freedom. Not anymore."

Jane had never heard him speak so bitterly.

"Wasn't Tran's freedom worth fighting and dying for?" he whispered.

"Who's Tran?"

Jerry turned back to the Wall, leaned his head against the marble again, and cried uncontrollably.

Jane could think of nothing to do but stand beside him, patting his shoulder.

In a few minutes, he took a deep, shuddering breath and turned to face her. His eyes glistened with tears.

"Tran Minh. She was a Vietnamese woman. Owned a restaurant on a boat on the Saigon River. She was so beautiful. Black hair down to her waist. Big black eyes. And smart. Her family sent her to be educated in France. She was . . . I loved Tran. We lived together for almost two years."

"What happened to her?"

"When it became obvious that Saigon was about to fall, the American networks chartered jetliners to fly their correspondents and camera crews out. ABC agreed to let Tran go on the plane with me."

Jane looked puzzled. Was this Vietnamese woman in the United States now, perhaps in Little Saigon?

"But she wouldn't go," he continued. "She refused to leave her family behind, and ABC said there wasn't room for her family on the plane. When I boarded the bus that was taking the network crews to our evacuation flight, Tran stood on the sidewalk in front of the Caravelle Hotel and glared at me through the bus window. To the day I die, I will never forget those two huge dark eyes blazing with hatred."

"Is she still alive?"

"Over the years I've pieced together the story from scraps of information. When the Communists took over Saigon, they sent Tran to a reeducation camp for Vietnamese who were friendly to Americans. They kept her there ten years and then sent her into the countryside to work in the rice fields. In 1988, she and the surviving members of her family some-how scraped together enough money to bribe a fisherman to take them to Thailand. They were never seen again. Maybe the boat sank. Maybe the fisherman took their money and threw them overboard. Maybe they were killed by pirates. Nobody knows."

He paused. "Now you know why I feel the way I do about bugging out of Vietnam."

Jane took his hand. She kissed away his tears. Then she kissed him on the lips.

"Come on," she urged gently.

"Where?"

"I don't know. Somewhere. Dinner, I guess."

"You're not ashamed anymore to be seen with a right-wing kook?"

"No."

"How come? What's changed?"

"You let me see you cry."

"You like me better now because you saw me crying?"

"I *know* you better because you let me see you cry. You let me see that you're more than a celebrity spouting conserva-tive slogans. You are so much more than your politics. You let me see your loss and your anguish, your ability to love, your tenderness. It takes a strong man to let a woman see him cry. And it means you trust me."

She took him in her arms and rocked him like a little boy.

"I have some *other* qualities I hope you'll find appealing, other than the ability to cry in front of you."

"I'll certainly be on the lookout for them."

They walked up out of the trench and left the Wall behind them.

Available by mail from

WINDY CITY • Hugh Holton
Twelve and a half weeks on the *Chicago Tribune* bestseller list! Commander Larry Cole is on the trail of a homicidal couple.

KILLER.APP • Barbara D'Amato
"Dazzling in its complexity and chilling in its exposure of how little privacy anyone has...totally mesmerizing."—*Cleveland Plain Dealer*

CAT IN A DIAMOND DAZZLE • Carole Nelson Douglas
The fifth title in Carole Nelson Douglas's Midnight Louie series—"All ailurphiles addicted to Lilian Jackson Braun's "The Cat Who..." mysteries...can latch onto a new *pur*rivate eye: Midnight Louie—slinking and sleuthing on his own, a la Mike Hammer."—*Fort Worth Star Telegram*

THE WANDERING ARM • Sharan Newman
Sharan Newman brings us a powerful novel of murder and religious persecution, filled with stolen saints, and family feuds, greedy nobles...and bloody murder.

PLAY IT AGAIN • Stephen Humphrey Bogart
In the classic style of a Bogart and Bacall movie, Stephen Humphrey Bogart delivers a gripping, fast-paced mystery."—*Baltimore Sun*

SECOND SHADOW • Aimee and David Thurlo
"[Thurlo is] a master of desert country as well as fast-moving adventure."
—Tony Hillerman